WHERE ARE THE CHILDREN NOW?

WHERE ARE THE CHILDREN NOW?

MARY HIGGINS CLARK AND ALAFAIR BURKE

THORNDIKE PRESS
A part of Gale, a Cengage Company

GALE
A Cengage Company

Copyright © 2023 by Nora Durkin Enterprises, Inc.
Thorndike Press, a part of Gale, a Cengage Company.

Thorndike Press® Large Print Basic.
The text of this Large Print edition is unabridged.
Other aspects of the book may vary from the original edition.
Set in 16 pt. Plantin.

LIBRARY OF CONGRESS CIP DATA ON FILE.
CATALOGUING IN PUBLICATION FOR THIS BOOK
IS AVAILABLE FROM THE LIBRARY OF CONGRESS.

ISBN-13: 978-1-4328-9481-8 (hardcover alk. paper).

Published in 2023 by arrangement with Simon & Schuster, Inc.

Printed in Mexico
Print Number: 1   Print Year: 2023

For William, Louis, Frederick, Emma, Katherine, Alexander, and Stella, the beloved great-grandchildren of the Queen of Suspense.

PROLOGUE

She could feel the damp evening winds coming in through the cracks around the windowpanes. Only a few years earlier, an incoming draft in this room — her childhood bedroom — would have been unthinkable. Her mother had a discerning eye for detail that would have twitched at the slightest imperfection in a home, especially if it affected the comfort of someone sleeping under her roof. And her father had been the best realtor on the Cape, the kind who had become an expert handyman over the years as an added service to his clients. But it wasn't only the seams around the windowsills that had cracked lately in the Eldredge family.

Eager to find sleep, Melissa stepped from the bed into her slippers and scuttled over to the window, not wanting to wake the rest of the house. After pulling the drapes closed, she took an extra blanket from the top of the closet, spread it over the bed, and then entered a reminder in her cell phone to have a handyman give the entire house a once-over before she returned to New York, just in case she could ever convince her mother to sell it.

She was returning her phone to the night-stand when she got a new text message. *Are you still awake?*

She smiled to herself, appreciating the fact that Charlie had stayed in constant contact with her in the four days she had been here. *Barely,* she replied.

As much as they both traveled for work, he always checked in with her when he awoke in the morning and before going to bed at night. *Any other ruffled feathers today?*

He was referring to the previous day's "silly sibling dustup," as her mother had called it dismissively. Given the seasonal nature of her brother Mike's work, this was the first time he had been able to come back to the States since the funeral, and Melissa had driven up to the Cape to make it a family homecoming. *All smiles and good behavior today. We visited the grave together.*

The historic cemetery down the road from Our Lady of the Cape Church was the setting of the country graveyard scene in the painting that hung over the piano in the living room, one of the numerous works of art that covered the home's mellow, creamy walls. When her mother had painted that haunting row of headstones more than forty years earlier, the idea of someday burying her husband there must have seemed un-imaginable.

She paused, recalling Mike holding first their mother's hand and then hers, as they stood at the foot of their father's grave that afternoon. They were still family, no matter what. *Family is family,* Melissa added. She never used to utter a negative word about them until she started grief counseling. Every time the subject matter of the El-dredges arose — and what had happened in their past — she found herself growing quiet, but she was told that talking about your childhood was an essential part of therapy. Nevertheless, she felt guilty some-times, wondering if she spoke too frequently during counseling about the small hiccups in the family to the exclusion of everything else that had been good. Today, at the grave, she had forgotten all about the occasional tensions and had been grateful once again for the wonderful life her parents had made possible for her.

She saw dots on the screen, indicating that Charlie was typing a new text. *Speaking of family, have I told you lately I can't wait for you to be my wife? Only two more months.*

He had proposed to Melissa only two weeks ago, and she had immediately said yes. It had been her mother's idea for them to get married on the one-year anniversary of her father's passing, even though it meant a very short engagement. The ceremony would be smaller than small — just the bride and groom, immediate family, and a few friends.

She found herself smiling as she typed a reply, as she always did when she thought about her future with him. *I was going to wait until tomorrow to tell you, but I passed the cutest little winery today. I know we said the courthouse, but maybe . . . ?* She hit Send and then attached the photographs she had taken when they stopped on the way home from the cemetery to share a toast to her father.

Only seconds later, her phone rang in her hand. An incoming FaceTime call from Charlie. "Well, hello there!" she chirped as his face appeared on the screen. He had close-cropped dark hair and clear blue eyes. And today, he sported a few days of facial hair across his square jaw.

"Too much texting," he said. "If we're talking wedding details, I at least want to see my fiancée."

"You got the pictures I sent of the winery?"

"I did, and it's absolutely perfect. That view is unbelievable!"

"But we already said we'd keep things simple and go to the courthouse."

"*You* were the one who was adamant about that."

Not long ago, Melissa had believed that she would have a big, formal wedding with a reception at an iconic New York City venue — perhaps the Loeb Boathouse in Central Park or the Rainbow Room overlooking Rockefeller Center. But when she had those dreams, she had imagined her father walking her down the aisle — and a man other than Charlie waiting for her at the altar. It didn't seem right to transfer her previous bridal fantasies onto a different relationship. Still, though, there might be something in between a fairy-tale wedding and the city courthouse. A small outdoor event at the winery on the Cape felt like a good match for Charlie and her.

"But we already gave everyone the date. And told them it would be in the city."

He flashed that perfect smile of his. "*Everyone?* Everyone in this case is like . . . six people — all of whom adore you and would

11

go to the moon if necessary to be there on your special day. *Our* special day."

At the mention of six guests, Melissa hoped that perhaps he was counting his sister, but Rachel Miller most definitely did not count as someone who "adored" Melissa. She had grudgingly agreed to meet Melissa, but only twice, and was reportedly furious when Charlie told her about his proposal, insisting that her brother was jumping into a new relationship too quickly. "Maybe Rachel will come around by then," Melissa said.

"Maybe so, or maybe not. We are getting married either way, and we are going to do it at this beautiful place you found for us. Consider it done. Let's book it."

"Really?"

"Promise. Text me the name of the place, and I'll call them first thing tomorrow for the details." And she knew immediately that the decision was, in fact, made. One of the thousands of things she adored about Charlie was the way he kept the trains running, always willing to take jobs off her plate so she could move on to other tasks. "Oh, someone wants to say hi."

The camera on Charlie's phone shifted lower until she saw a chubby-cheeked face gazing up toward her. Riley's fine blonde hair was tousled in every direction in a look that could only be described as bedhead. In the background, Melissa could see cardboard boxes stacked on the kitchen floor. They had just begun the process of slowly packing up his Upper West Side apartment since he and Riley would be moving in with Melissa.

"HI, MISSA!" It sounded almost like *Missy,* her nickname until she suddenly announced in the first grade that she wanted to be called Melissa. Riley was smiling so hard, her eyes were nearly closed. "We miss you!!!" Behind the phone camera and out of view, Charlie told Riley to blow a kiss. Her pudgy hand found her pink heart-shaped lips and pressed. Pretty close for a not-quite-three-year-old.

"I miss you, too, sweetie. I'll be coming back to New York in two days."

Her future stepdaughter held her fingers up in a vee. "Two! Like me!"

"Except only two days, not two years."

"I know." She turned away from the camera and began toddling away.

"Tough crowd," Melissa said once Charlie returned to the screen.

"It's almost as if she has the attention span of a two-year-old," he said, shaking his head and chuckling. "Not to mention you're

13

competing with the new Peppa Pig playhouse."

"How did she con you into letting her stay up this late?"

"She went to bed right after dinner but trotted out a while ago saying she heard noises. Figured I'd let her play while I finished up some work."

"Talk to you tomorrow?"

"Always," he said. "And all the other tomorrows after that."

After they ended the FaceTime call, she forced herself to respond to three emails from a persistent attorney who didn't seem to understand the meaning of an out-of-office message before she finally turned off the nightstand lamp. When she closed her eyes, she pictured herself standing next to Charlie. She's wearing the white ankle-length silk halter dress she selected from Bloomingdale's last week for the occasion. He's wearing the tan linen suit she already told him would be perfect for a summer wedding, even at the courthouse. They're sharing the I-now-pronounce-you-husband-and-wife kiss under a teak pergola wrapped in sparkling white lights. Riley runs toward them, roses braided in her hair, layers of pink tulle bouncing with every step.

She finds a swing set on the winery lawn

and climbs into the seat, careful not to let her dress get caught in the chains. "Push me high!" She's giggling and squealing, her nose wrinkling from her toothy grin. "Higher, Missa, higher!" She swings so high that she might fly right into the sky, where she'd blend in with the pink-white clouds. Her cries of joy subside as the swing's pace begins to slow. "Please, Missa — don't stop pushing." But three more futile kicks and the swing is nearly still. As she turns her head to search for another boost, a sharp pinch seems to sting the back of little Riley's hand. She looks down toward the pain and sees a red mitten holding the chain of the swing, the image of a smiling kitten face sewn on the back. Why is she wearing mittens in summer? Her weight slumps forward before she can answer her own question, her body — so small, but suddenly so heavy — caught by someone. Someone.

In her dream, she wakes to the sound of a zipper. It's her own jacket being unzipped. Her nostrils are filled with the stench of baby powder and sweat. She feels the uncomfortable tug of her turtleneck being pulled clumsily over her neck, her undershirt moving with it. She stirs and starts to blink her eyes. "Mommy, Mommy . . ."

When Melissa finally roused, she was in

her high school bed, uncertain whether the scream she felt lingering in her throat and echoing in her ears was real or just another part of the nightmare. The house was silent except for the sound of the crash of ocean waves in the distance. Her neck was damp from perspiration, and, for just one second, she thought she detected the faint smell of talcum.

The girl on the swing wasn't Riley. It had been three-year-old Missy, and this was the most vivid dream yet. After forty years, after all of her efforts, all of her progress toward having a happy, future-focused life, Melissa was finally starting to remember. *No,* she prayed silently to herself. *Make it stop. I don't want to know. I don't want that to be me.*

She jolted upright in a cold sweat. The bedside clock told her it was 2:30 in the morning. It was happening again. The dreams. They were getting worse.

1

Two months later

Nancy came down the stairs, securing the back of the gold-and-pearl drop earrings she'd selected as the final touch to her ensemble. Her dress was a modest, but not matronly, silk shift. The bright royal blue was what Ray had always called her "signature color," bringing out the blue in her eyes. The subtle shimmer from the metallic embroidery around the neckline made it a bit more celebratory than her usual understated fare.

On the first floor, Melissa sat at the kitchen table in a fluffy white robe, sipping coffee, Velcro rollers the size of soda cans in her hair with a still-sleepy Riley on her lap. She was in the chair closest to the window, the same spot she had inexplicably declared to be her "favorite" once she outgrew eating in a high chair. She put down her mug and sucked in an exaggerated gasp of approval.

"Look at you! I don't know how I feel about this. The mother of the bride is not supposed to be the hottest woman in the room."

Nancy wrinkled her nose and shook her head. "Stop teasing me. And you shouldn't talk that way in front of this little angel anyway." Nancy leaned over and dropped a kiss on Riley's head, which she found warm and smelling of baby shampoo.

Riley looked up at her with sleepy eyes and grinned. "Hi, Grand-Nan. You look pretty." Nancy hoped that Riley's name for her — Grand-Nan — would never change.

She means you're hot, Melissa mouthed silently while Riley wasn't looking.

Nancy noticed that Melissa was also looking especially beautiful today, and it wasn't only because of the full face of makeup she had already expertly applied. She was almost glowing with happiness. "You were able to sleep last night?" When she'd noticed how tired Melissa had seemed during both of her last visits to the Cape, her daughter had explained she'd been having trouble sleeping. Sometimes she worried that her ambitious little girl simply worked too hard for one person to handle.

"Like a baby. Thanks."

After all these years, Nancy was finally able to confine most of her thoughts to the here and now. Forty years ago, she would still lose herself in remembering. But she had tried so hard to live each day in the present . . . not look back or try to predict the future. And eventually it worked, at least for the most part. She was seventy-two years old, and more than half of her lifetime had been as fortunate and blessed as any person could dare to hope for. When dark memories from the past did resurface, they tended to hit her either completely randomly, or — like today — at moments that paralleled her own life.

A wedding. Her daughter's wedding. A new son-in-law who adored Melissa, and an adorable little girl for Melissa to love and help raise. It was a time to celebrate. And yet . . .

The past never leaves. A wedding. Her mind fell not to Melissa's big day, nor even to her own marriage to her beloved Ray, but to that other wedding that altered her life forever. Nancy rarely felt like an elderly woman, and yet the fact that she had a first marriage that began at the age of eighteen, when she was a college freshman, seemed nearly impossible now — not to mention the nightmare that followed. She had been determined to wear white for that wedding, so rushed after she lost her cherished mother. Nancy had owned only one white dress — a wool knit. It would do given the simplicity of their wedding plans, but then she saw the unexplained grease stain on the sleeve. If only she had connected the dots right then and there to her mother's car accident, there would have been no wedding to Carl Harmon and therefore no Peter and Lisa for her to mourn, even now, after all these years.

Her thoughts were broken by the sound of footsteps thundering down the stairs. She turned to see her son, Mike, in a perfectly tailored navy suit, his silk tie spotted with sailboats, looking proud of his athletic sprint downstairs. "Like riding a bike!" he declared, holding up both arms like a gymnast who had stuck the perfect landing.

This house was an authentic old Cape with steps so steep they were nearly vertical. Ray used to say that the old settlers must have descended from mountain goats the way they built their staircases.

"Whoa, Mom, you look like a million bucks."

"You aren't too shabby yourself."

"You do look spiffy," Melissa chimed in. "But really, you didn't need to splurge on a new suit. Weddings shouldn't be work for other people."

"I own a suit, little sis. Two of them, in fact. I'm a boat captain, not a cretin."

Forty years ago, she had been so certain that she already knew her children to their core. Michael, always so organized, was the boy who not only followed instructions to the tee within seconds, but also told other children that they should fall in line as well. His baby sister, Missy, was the one who always managed to come home with a tear in her pants, bemoaning the loss of whichever treasured stuffed animal she had carried off on her latest pursuit of adventure.

In retrospect, Nancy could not believe how wrong she had been. Her rebellious little ragamuffin Missy was now Melissa, a star law student who became a prosecutor and was now an outspoken advocate for what she called a common-sense criminal justice system. Just the previous night, they had made a toast not only to the happy couple, but also to the news that Melissa's podcast had hit the top 100 list on iTunes. Meanwhile, the previously earnest and somber Michael had lasted only three semesters in college before heading to the Caribbean for a "couple of years off." Now he was a boat captain on St. Maarten, where everyone called him either Mike or Mikey.

Mike and Melissa even looked different

now. Mike was tanned and sinewy compared to his sister with her alabaster skin and dimpled cheeks. While Mike's formerly blond hair became darker as he entered his tweens, Melissa still maintained the same strawberry blonde curls she'd had as a child — a reflection of Nancy's hair color until she relocated to the Cape and changed both her name and appearance. These days, Nancy was neither a redhead nor a brunette. Her perfectly groomed silver bob looked "regal," according to her hairdresser.

Mike pulled a phone from his front pants pocket and snapped a photo as Melissa held up a protective hand as if warding off the paparazzi.

"Nooo. I look ridiculous!"

"The last photo of you as a single lady. And the curlers are cute," he said, turning the screen so she could see the picture. "You should post this for your thousands of fawning social media followers. They'll love it."

Nancy braced herself for another round of sibling bickering. Would Melissa construe her brother's comment as backhanded criticism of her increasingly prominent public profile? Was that in fact Mike's intent? Nancy didn't want to take sides and wished they would just adore each other the way they had as children.

"You know what?" Melissa said, slipping Riley off her lap. "I just might do that! Thanks. But first, I've got a dress I need to get into. Someone's getting married today!"

"You and Daddy," Riley added with a giggle. "He's in the bucky-ord. Can I go?" In the language they affectionately called Ril-ese, she added an extra syllable to the word — not backyard, but *bucky-ord.* Charlie had spent the previous two nights not literally in the backyard, but in the guest house so as not to see the bride right before the wedding. Ray and Nancy had built the addition to the property when Melissa was in college. They imagined they would need the extra room once the kids got married and began to have their own children. Now that was finally happening — at least for Melissa.

"Of course," Melissa said. She stood up and gave her soon-to-be stepdaughter a quick hug before pushing open the back door for her. "Let your dad know I'm counting down the minutes."

"I wish Mommy was here. I miss her."

Nancy could see her daughter's face briefly fall, the way it always did whenever Riley mentioned her mother. Charlie's first wife, Linda, had died in a fatal drowning accident in Europe while they were on their

23

first and only vacation after the baby was born. Riley was simply too young to understand the connection between her mother's death and the new role that Melissa now played in her life.

She watched as Melissa placed a gentle hand on top of Riley's head. "I know, sweetie. We all wish she was here with you."

"I asked, but she can't."

Once Riley slipped outside, Melissa explained, "Neil assures us it's completely normal for children to imagine communicating with their parents who have passed. It might even be in her dreams. It's a way to keep remembering them."

Neil Keeney was one of the neighborhood kids Mike and Melissa had stayed close friends with over the years. He was now a highly regarded psychiatrist in New York City. If he said there was nothing to worry about, Nancy believed him. Still, she could see how much Melissa wished she could take some of the child's pain away.

"Well, the person who *should* be here today for your husband is his sister," Nancy said pointedly. Melissa had reached out to Rachel personally, pleading with her to be here to support her brother and niece, if not to bless their marriage.

Melissa waved a hand in the air as she

walked toward the staircase. "Don't get me started on that one. I'm going to be a part of her family for a very long time, and she'll come around eventually. We're determined not to let her decision ruin the day."

Nancy's eyes remained glued on Riley until she reached the sliding glass door of the guest house. She suspected that as long as she lived, she would never be able to be in the presence of children without watching them as vigilantly as a member of the Secret Service. She smiled to herself as Charlie, in the middle of knotting his tie, slid open the door to greet his daughter. He threw a wave in Nancy's direction before scooping Riley up to his hip. He was a good man — kind, understanding, loyal. Like her husband, Ray.

As Melissa padded up the stairs and Mike flipped on ESPN in the living room, Nancy took a moment to breathe in the feeling of having her entire family — including two new additions — in this house. She could still remember the feeling of peace and welcome this place had given her when she'd first seen it, only in her mid-twenties, searching for a place to start over again. Ray had been the realtor to help her find a rental. "The Cape is a good place to come when you want to be by yourself," he had said. "You can't be lonesome walking on the beach or watching the sunset or just looking out the window in the morning."

The moment Ray had brought her to this house, she knew that she would stay. The combination family and dining room had been fashioned from the old keeping room that had once been the heart of the house. She loved the rocking chair in front of the fireplace and the way the table was in front of the windows so that it was possible to eat and look down over the harbor and the bay. And then after they had married, Ray arranged for them to purchase the house, because he knew that she loved everything about it.

It had now been a year to the day since she had woken up to find him cold beside her. Their physician said that Ray probably didn't feel a thing. His last words to her had been "I love you so much" as he'd crawled into bed with her on what they had no way of knowing would be their last night together. The memories they had made in this house belonged to both of them.

By the time she spoke aloud to her beloved home, there was no one around to hear her. "Oh, how I'm going to miss you, old girl."

Maybe Riley wasn't the only one who spoke to ghosts.

2

Some mornings Jayden Kennedy pedaled on his bike through the town's covered bridge, then along the Housatonic River into town to the only coffee shop in his small corner of Connecticut that sold all of his morning papers. Other days he hopped into his zippy electric sedan to head for the diner in Sharon, where he'd pore over the newsprint pages as he enjoyed a plate of the best blueberry pancakes he'd ever tasted. The *New York Times, Wall Street Journal,* and *New York Post* were his media trifecta. His consumption of TV news and pop culture was similarly diverse. He sincerely believed that the closest one could come to objective truth was reading and listening and trying to understand as many viewpoints as possible.

This particular morning was a pancake kind of day — no Zoom calls overseas and no ups and downs of the market to try to time with the precision of a luxury quartz watch. Plus, he'd completed a double session of yoga the day before, so had no need to knock himself out with another workout today. Sundays were a time for indulgences.

To some people — the kind of people Jayden had moved to West Cornwall to avoid — "indulgences" meant something entirely different: high-rise condos, private jets, and custom-cut designer suits. Jayden had left all that behind when he quit his Wall Street job two years earlier and moved to the country. He was almost entirely self-sufficient, with solar panels to generate enough electricity for both his home and his car charger. One medium-sized propane tank provided backup in case the solar-powered baseboard heating and wood-burning stove fell short.

These days, Jayden's splurges were simple: time away from his screens, the true crime podcasts that had become his addiction, a well-prepared meal, and good old-fashioned newspapers made from actual paper. He took in a deep breath as he tried to find the merit in an op-ed that struck him as absurd. The smell of the newsprint was slightly dusty with just a hint of bitterness. As he flipped to the next page, the paper left behind a chalky feeling on his fingertips.

Jayden understood that from some angles, he fit the stereotype of a certain kind of man of his generation. He shunned cash for Apple Pay. He lived in front of a computer. The solar panels and the e-car. The yoga. He'd even been known to pull his hair into what some would call a man-bun when he got too busy for a trip to the barber. And, more than anything — as his parents liked to remind him — there was his decision to walk away from a six-figure entry-level job after incurring a quarter-million dollars of tuition debt at an Ivy League college, all because that lifestyle didn't feel "right" to him.

But his current life in Connecticut, with simple pleasures like pancakes, bacon, and newspapers, felt absolutely perfect to Jayden. His girlfriend, Julie, had also moved from the city, exchanging her job as a personal assistant to one of television's "real housewives" for a position managing a quirky little antique store in Millerton. Julie earned a modest but reliable salary, with a lovely setup residing in the guest house of an older couple who asked little of her other than token rent and some manageable care of the property during the many weeks and months when they were traveling elsewhere.

Jayden's own life away from the beaten

path was turning out to be a bit rockier. He'd used most of his savings for the down payment on the house, and then signed on the dotted line for the maximum mortgage he could obtain while interest rates were low and he still had his Wall Street salary to qualify for the loan. Plus there was the car lease. And of course his school loans. His income day-trading the stock market and providing "social responsibility consulting" to a growing number of corporate clients was respectable, but not quite enough to check all the boxes.

His ever-present anxiety was beginning to outweigh the bliss of newspapers and pancakes when his phone buzzed with a new alert. According to the screen, the message was from the app Domiluxe. The dot-com's founder had been a year behind Jayden at Yale. According to the propaganda that accompanied the organization's highly anticipated IPO, Domiluxe was for the "most discerning providers and consumers within the online marketplace for high-end temporary vacation rentals — coupling five-star luxury and security-clearance-level anonymity." Despite all the fancy phrases, it was exactly like all the other rent-your-own-home websites but with three additional features: an "aesthetic consultant" who must approve detailed photographs of a property; much higher costs in terms of both deposits and fees; and, most importantly, a promise of complete anonymity. Both renters and home owners had the option of withholding their actual names, and — the real "game changer," as the market was calling it — Domiluxe was accepting Bitcoin and similar digital currencies as payment. As fluently as Jayden could recite the many legitimate reasons why customers might want a service like Domiluxe, he was certain that some would use it to avoid taxes and other financial reporting obligations. He also suspected that more than a few customers would be hiding the expenses of a luxury vacation rental from someone a bit closer to home — such as a spouse who wasn't invited.

He tapped the screen to pull up the new message. It was from "Helen," a name that may or may not be authentic. They'd already exchanged an initial round of messages where he'd learned that Helen wasn't certain of her exact arrival and departure dates but wanted a "relaxing, scenic, EXTREMELY PRIVATE retreat away from the hustle and bustle." It was the all-caps on privacy that had led Jayden to suspect that Helen was most likely a man sneaking off to enjoy the company of someone with whom he could not be seen in public. Jayden didn't approve of infidelity, but he also needed to pay his bills, and the mainstream vacation-rental websites hadn't brought in enough income to cover his shortfall.

This latest message from Helen confirmed that she was still interested in the house but wanted the precise address so she could inspect it on a satellite map before committing.

Jayden was tempted to text his college friend to tell him he'd already spotted an obvious hole in the company's promise of "security-clearance-level anonymity," but instead typed in his address. Once the message was sent, he asked for his check from his favorite waitress Clarissa, and then texted Julie to see if she wanted to watch another episode of their latest binge show tonight and if she was "absolutely sure" she wanted him to stay with her while he rented out his house.

She texted back immediately. *100 percent. It will be like camping.* She added a tent emoji followed by three hearts. He didn't want her to think he would need to lean on her forever, but the "maybe a full month" that Helen had floated in her initial message could earn him enough money to cover his mortgage for almost a year.

He was walking to his car, his stack of newspapers folded beneath one arm, when his phone buzzed again. It was Helen. *Just pulled up the property on satellite. What's that metal-looking structure in the backyard?*

Oh boy, he thought. *I'm going to lose this golden goose over that rickety old swing set in the woods that I never bothered to pull down.* The "aesthetic consultant" from the website had not requested photographs beyond the house and immediate surroundings before approving the property.

He tossed his papers onto the passenger seat and typed in a reply. *It's probably fifty yards from the main house. I can remove it if it's an eyesore. It's a swing set. And not for adults either . . . I tried it - LOL. It's only for children.*

He was pulling away from the curb, wondering if his tone had been too breezy, when he heard from Helen again.

That's perfect.

He didn't understand the reply and was about to ask for clarification when another message arrived. *I meant there's no reason to change anything at all. Your house is perfect for my needs. Be in touch soon with a start date.*

Jayden had learned by now to trust his instincts, and his gut was telling him that Helen was going to come through. It was just a matter of time.

3

Mike Eldredge pushed open the driver's side door of his mother's SUV, unable to shake the nagging sensation of worry that was throbbing somewhere inside him like a toothache. What was the matter? It was more than just his usual discomfort around his sister, who was still in complete denial about what they'd gone through as children and the ways it had affected them both.

He had been pleasantly surprised when Melissa took her friend Katie's advice and started seeing a counselor last year to help her cope with her grief after their father had died. A good counselor would force Melissa to talk about her childhood. And how could she talk about her childhood without eventually confronting the truth about Carl Harmon, a name she still refused to utter and that would cause her to leave a room if Mike dared to say it in her presence? But when Mike made the mistake of mentioning Melissa's therapy to her, she had replied, "I really wish Mom hadn't told you that." Mike took it as a sign that Melissa wasn't fully committed. She had probably planned to go to a few sessions until she convinced herself she was completely okay again and didn't want Mike to know when she eventually quit without doing the real work.

Three months later, Mike got another report from his mother: Melissa was still in therapy all right, but instead of finding her true emotions buried beneath her increasingly perfect surface, she had found a boyfriend. He was a widower and a single father — a geologist, apparently. And they were already talking about getting married.

And that's what explained today's nagging sensation of something throbbing inside of him. It was a feeling of foreboding. *Happiness is a choice,* his sister always liked to say. He had suspected she'd gone to therapy for all the wrong reasons. Instead of truly grieving their father, she was treating her grief as one more thing she could control. If she could just find the right program, or complete the necessary steps, she could go back to being "happy" again — carefree, untroubled.

To Mike, that wasn't happiness. Happiness, he believed, required honesty. Happi-

36

ness could be messy and even painful. If you never feel pain, how do you appreciate its absence? If you're never afraid, how do you know comfort? But Melissa wanted to live in her perfectly controlled Melissa bubble, brushing off any unwanted emotions as "drama." Was that why she was marrying a man she'd only known for ten months — to convince herself that she was still happy?

"Earth to Michael." Mike looked up, startled. His mother had already exited the car and was waiting for him to do the same.

As he stepped from the car, he could see Melissa making her way across the grass lawn toward two figures in the distance. He recognized them as Neil Keeney and his wife, Amanda. He could hear Amanda cooing over Melissa's dress.

"Looks like we're going to have a Mik-eil reunion!" his mother declared. "I'm going to go inside and make sure they've got everything ready for the ceremony, but you go and see your friends."

Growing up, Neil Keeney had paid little attention to young Missy. Mike had been the member of the Eldredge family who had become Neil's best friend. The two of them were so inseparable that Neil's mother, Ellen, had taken the first three letters of

Mike's name and the last three of Neil's to label them collectively as "Mik-eil."

When Melissa moved to New York City to attend Columbia University, Neil was living nearby, attending the Albert Einstein College of Medicine to become a psychiatrist. Fast-forward to today: now Neil and his wife were two of Melissa's closest friends and had never once taken Mike up on his invitations to visit the slice of paradise he now called home in the Caribbean.

His sister's words rang in his ears from the argument they'd had the previous day when he asked her if she was really sure about this marriage: *You know, sometimes I think you're just jealous, Mike. Focus more on your own life and leave mine alone.* Maybe there was some truth there.

As he joined his sister, Neil, and Amanda, he wondered if he was imagining the brief moment of awkward silence that seemed to fall over the trio.

"Hey, good to see you, man. Looking sharp." Neil raised a fist for a quick tap, while Amanda leaned forward and kissed Mike's cheek.

Amanda looked like she could be on the cover of a beauty magazine, but was actually a detective with the NYPD. "Always so tan," she said. "I'm jealous."

In her high heels, Amanda towered a good five inches over Neil. Mike could still remember Neil hanging slack on the pull-up bars at the park, hoping to get taller. His mother would tell him to remember that his father and brothers and uncle were all tall. *Just give it time.*

"You're always welcome to join me down on the island," Mike said. "I'm captaining a forty-four-foot catamaran now. She cuts through the water like butter."

"Sounds like heaven," Amanda said. "Maybe this winter, babe? I do have a lot of vacation time with the department."

Neil nodded and then gave a "Maybe" that sounded more like, *Yeah, we're definitely not coming.* Changing the subject, Neil said, "Little Missy's getting married. Can you believe it?"

"Um . . ." Mike found himself struggling to find the right words. He wasn't about to lie, but he also didn't want to cause a scene at his sister's wedding — which apparently no one but him thought was a mistake. "Yeah, my baby sister is tying the knot. Guess in a way she wouldn't even be here without you, Neil. If you hadn't recognized Carl . . ."

He felt the judgment of three disapproving sets of eyes as Melissa let out a loud scoff next to him. "Seriously, Mike? You had to go there right now?"

But it's true, Mike wanted to explain. It had been Neil, only seven years old at the time, who had recognized Carl Harmon's face from a photograph on the local news while Mike and Melissa were still missing. Even though Harmon was presumed to be dead, Neil had insisted that he was the man who had paid him a dollar to pick up his mail from the post office. That piece of information had led police to the house where Harmon had taken Melissa and him after the kidnapping — the house where Harmon had wrapped Mike's head in plastic and left him on a bed to suffocate as he carried Melissa away to the attic.

"Dude," Neil said, shaking his head. "Not today of all days. You got to just leave that stuff in the past, man."

Mike forced himself to apologize as he made a mental note that apparently Neil was on Melissa's side when it came to ignoring the past, even though the man was a psychiatrist.

Mike might not have the fancy degrees they had hanging on their office walls, but he'd been around the sun enough times to believe that it was not for mere mortals to decide where the past lives. The past has its

own plans. And more often than not, the
past finds a way into the here and now.

4

It was timing. The whole universe existed because of split-second timing. That's what Melissa's best friend, Katie, had said when Melissa told her that Charlie had proposed and she had accepted. When Melissa was in the throes of what she now realized was low-grade depression after her father's passing, Neil suggested therapy, and then Katie followed up by researching therapists who specialized in grief counseling. That was where Melissa and Charlie met. At least the loss of a parent was expected in the natural cycle of life. Charlie had been left as a single father. But now here they were.

Melissa found Katie in a small alcove off the winery's kitchen, leaning over a white double-tiered cake topped with a cascade of summer flowers. Squinting with the concentration of a surgeon, she used her thumb and index finger to adjust the position of one of the shimmering pearls forming a circle at the cake's base. Melissa knew well enough to wait until the master's work was complete before startling her. Once Katie stood erect and looked pleased with her handiwork, Melissa finally let her presence be known.

"That is the most beautiful cake I have ever seen. Too pretty to eat."

Katie turned toward her, her face breaking out into a broad smile.

"But you, however, do look pretty enough to eat!" she declared, leaning forward to greet Melissa with a quick kiss on the cheek, holding her hands back to protect their dresses from any lingering frosting.

"I can't believe you did all that. You promised me you'd keep it simple!"

Katie Palmer, in addition to being Melissa's best friend, was also a talented pastry chef and owner of Katie Cakes, a small but popular bakery on the Upper East Side. When they met each other a dozen years earlier, they were both "baby ADAs" — junior assistant district attorneys in the Manhattan DA's Office. Though Katie stayed at the office longer than Melissa did, she eventually left for a stint at a family law practice before deciding that the law might not be for her after all. After going to Paris to check a pastry-making class off her bucket list, she returned to New York determined to leave the practice of law behind and open her own bakery. Katie was initially worried that Melissa would be disappointed in her, but Melissa had assured her that she'd support Katie wherever her dreams led. Besides, she had added, "I have a feeling I'll be benefiting from your newfound expertise more than your brilliant legal mind." And now Katie had made her this fairy-tale wedding cake. The whole universe existed because of split-second timing, indeed.

"How'd you find me back here?" Katie asked.

"When you weren't outside with Neil and Amanda, I had a feeling. I asked one of the staff if he'd seen a gorgeous brunette fussing over a cake nearby. According to him, you wouldn't let anyone help you carry in the box."

"For all I know, someone could be a huge klutz. I don't want anyone ruining Rosie."

"Rosie?" Melissa asked with an arched brow. She knew that Katie had a tendency to name the cakes she worked on personally.

She shrugged. "The roses in the mix of flowers on top. Not the most original name, I suppose, but it also sort of reminded me

44

of Riley. So this is the big day: you're going to be a 'Sadie, Sadie, married lady' — and a mom to boot."

Technically, Melissa was going to be a stepmother, but Riley had no other mother in her life.

"I'm just so deliriously happy, Katie. Is that cheesy?"

"Of course not," she said, giggling as she gave her hands a quick wash in the nearby sink. "You're *supposed* to be happy. *Happiness is a choice,* remember?"

It had been Melissa's mantra ever since she had spotted a book with that title in the public library when she was in the eighth grade. As her friends went through teen-aged angst from boys who wouldn't be boyfriends, or being too short or tall or chubby or thin, or wondering whether they were popular enough, Melissa was the one who kept her eye on the prize. Be a loyal friend. Be a kind person. Work hard. And choose to be happy.

"I know, I know. But I've got to say, when Patrick called things off —" She felt a tinge of disloyalty for even mentioning her ex-fiancé's name on her wedding day. A year and a half ago, the idea that she'd be in this beautiful place, surrounded by her family and closest friends, committing her future to a kind man who truly understood and loved her, would have been unthinkable. Because eighteen months ago, the man she thought she would spend the rest of her life with had suddenly left her. "I was really thrown for a loop. I needed the whole *choose-happiness* thing. Fake it till you make it, you know? Because I was hurt. And mostly, I was convinced that the only way to keep from getting crushed like that again was to never let anyone else in. It's not like I don't have everything else in the world going for me."

"So humble," Katie teased.

"You know what I mean. I figured I have my work, my friends, my life." Melissa's career had taken off in directions she never would have dreamed of. She remembered how her friends had encouraged her to *get back out there,* going so far as to sign her up for the usual internet dating websites. But being single again wasn't the thing that broke her spirit. In some ways, that horrible call from her mother felt years in the past, but part of her still couldn't believe that her father was really gone. "But then Dad died, and I go for counseling, and there's this caring, amazing man in the group, and the pieces just fell into place. I never thought I'd have . . . Charlie and Riley, and even a

Rosie," she said, gesturing toward the cake Katie had made for them. "The happiness found me." Feeling her eyes begin to water, she waved her palms at her face. "Aagh, look what I've done. The one day I manage to get my makeup just right."

"Stop it. Don't you know that tears are contagious? We're not going to let anything ruin your perfect day." Katie pulled her phone from her apron pocket and snapped a few photos of her masterpiece. "Want me to tag you?"

Melissa's first instinct was always toward privacy, but her agent had been hounding her about being more personal on her social media, and she knew that a mention of her name on Katie's account might be a boost for her bakery, which was still struggling to find solid footing, despite Katie's dream of growing it into a national chain. "Sure," she said.

She watched as Katie's thumbs flew across her screen at lightning speed. "Voilà," she declared, holding up the photograph. Katie smiled at her screen as Rosie the cake began to rack up heart signs, but then her brow furrowed.

"What is it?"

Katie shook her head. "It can wait. We've got a wedding to get to."

"Will you stop? I want to know. You're clearly upset."

Katie extended her phone toward Melissa. "It's that account you told me about last week."

Rosie the cake had garnered 52 likes already and a short list of comments primarily filled with heart, cake, and fork emojis until Melissa's eyes stopped on the last post:

Pretty cake, but give it to someone who actually deserves it. Melissa Eldredge is a phony and a fraud. I know the truth. Is that a wedding cake? May God have mercy on whatever idiot she duped into marrying her.

The user's name, ironically, was Truth-Teller. Melissa recognized TruthTeller's profile picture from the first nasty post that had appeared on her page. It was a Chinese symbol that she had since learned meant "truth." TruthTeller's page had no posts, and, as far as Melissa could tell, the account existed for no reason other than to troll one specific user — Melissa.

"She seems nice, right?" Melissa asked dryly. *He? She? More than one person?* Thanks to the anonymity of the internet, she had no way to know, but she had her suspicions. After all, she only had one former client who had ever spoken to her that way before.

"The so-called TruthTeller just earned an instant block from me," Katie said, tapping her phone with a satisfied smirk. "Sorry you can't do the same."

She shrugged. Melissa's agent insisted that blocking online trolls only served to attract more of them. "You can't let them know they got under your skin."

Katie shook her head and tucked her phone away again. "You've got a lot thicker skin than I do. I'd be running to the courthouse for a restraining order."

"Against an anonymous internet account? The account won't even get suspended unless they're actually threatening me or posting my address or something."

Katie feigned a shudder. "Just the idea of it gives me the willies."

"That's why it's best not to read the comments."

"To quote a wise woman, *happiness is a choice,* right?" Katie held out an arm, and Melissa quickly linked hers to Katie's.

"Exactly."

As they made their way through the tasting room toward the front lawn, Katie asked quietly, "Not to raise another touchy subject, but has your brother been on good behavior?" Melissa had mentioned that Mike left the distinct impression that he did not approve of this marriage — or anything else about her life, for that matter.

"He made some ridiculous comment earlier that Neil's responsible for my happy day because he was the one who . . . well, you know the whole story," she said, waving a hand. "If anything, you deserve the credit, you accidental matchmaker — not that group therapy is the most romantic meet-cute in the world, but you were the one who suggested that particular counselor."

As they stepped into the bright light of the sun gleaming over the bay, Melissa heard her mother call out from the lawn, "There you are! Riley's so excited, she's jumping out of her sandals."

Melissa paid little heed to the traditional wedding rituals, but her mother had told Riley so many stories about how weddings worked that somehow Riley's young mind had clung to the idea that everything would be ruined if the groom saw the bride before the march down the aisle. Even though their proverbial aisle was a makeshift lane of grass marked with tea candles outside of a winery, they were playing by this one traditional rule.

Riley came bounding toward her, nearly tripping in her excitement. "I want Daddy to come out. It's wedding time. Uncle Mike's here."

Her brother, in one of the two suits she had no idea he owned, was making his way toward her. Despite her frustrations with him, he was here, while Charlie's sister was not. He had even offered to walk her down the aisle in their father's absence. He bent down toward Riley, pressing his palms against his thighs, and eagerly leaned his face toward hers. "Is it go time?"

She flashed a giant grin, bobbing her head up and down with an enthusiastic nod. "I'm going to have a second mommy!"

Melissa felt her eyes begin to well up again as they turned toward the patio where they would wait until Charlie was in place. She was surprised when her brother gently took her hand in his. They walked and waited in silence.

A spark of energy shot from her fingertips to her heart as she and Charlie joined hands. This was it.

An added perk of moving their wedding plans here from the courthouse in Manhattan was having one of her closest friends preside over the ceremony. Neil had gotten

51

a license to officiate at the wedding of one of his brothers on the Cape three years earlier.

"Charlie and Melissa will now declare their consent to be married by stating their own vows."

Melissa did everything in her power to freeze time for the next few minutes. She wanted to remember these words, this moment, this feeling forever. She and Charlie had met when they were both suffering through extraordinary pain, and somehow they had worked through it, individually but also together. They had known each other less than a year, and yet she could not imagine a life without him.

"I now pronounce you husband and wife." She immediately heard the sound of a cork popping. Their small group of family and friends began to cheer, and a wave of applause rippled across the winery lawn as strangers joined in the celebration.

Melissa was halfway through a flute of champagne when her mother wrapped an arm around her shoulder and said she had news to share. "This is such a special day."

She didn't need to explain further. When her mother suggested scheduling the wedding on this one-year anniversary of their family's greatest loss, she had said, "We'll pack away our sorrow in the morning and have a brand-new reason to celebrate this date."

"I hope it hasn't been too rough for you," Melissa said. She had to assume that her mother would be remembering her own wedding day with bittersweetness. And she had wondered whether wedding ceremonies might also remind her mother of the first wedding, when she had married . . . Melissa forced the thought from her mind, as she always did when that man's existence crept into her consciousness. *Not today, not today.*

Her mother, however, appeared untroubled. "No, this was just what we all needed — a focus on the future. That's what your daddy would have wanted. So, on that note, I have something to tell you that I truly hope you'll welcome as good news. I'm putting the house on the market. The broker should have the listing online now, in fact, with a sign out front and all."

"Mom, are you sure? I know we talked about it, but today of all days — don't make any rash decisions."

She gave a head shake that was Nancy Eldredge's way of saying there was no room for discussion. "I think of it as bookends. I came to the Cape to have a shot at a second phase of life in a new place. I met your father when he showed me that house, and I was luckier than I could have ever hoped. I fell in love, first with the property and then with him, and then with you and your brother. But Mike is in St. Maarten now. You're in New York. I'm ready to say good-bye. You're about to enter a second phase in your life, and if it's okay with you, I'd like to be there for it."

"Are you kidding? Of course. I'd love it. I can start looking for apartments near us."

Her mother let out an uncharacteristically loud hoot. "Oh, me — in the city? Absolutely not. I've done my research. I'd like to move to Long Island, on the east end. I'm thinking Southampton. That way, I can still live near the water but also be close to you. Especially now that I'm going to be Grand-Nan to your adorable stepdaughter. What do you think?"

The move would put her mother within a two-hour train ride instead of a six-hour drive. "I absolutely love it. But are you sure?"

"Indeed I am. I'm a very, very grown woman and know what I want for myself. Now, let me get you back to your husband."

As Charlie pulled her into a tight embrace, Melissa was so filled with joy that she did not notice someone nearby focused only on

Riley, counting down the days when the two of them could be alone together, away from all these people. It was just a matter of time.

5

Patrick Higgins stood at the windows of his office overlooking Rockefeller Plaza. The national morning show filmed in the studio on the ground-floor level had kicked off its summer concert series with one of his favorite bands. Even from the seventeenth floor, he could hear the one-name-only lead singer's voice clearly. *Touch me . . . take me to that other place.* The crowd that had lined up early to fill the audience swayed in time with the rhythm. It was, indeed, a beautiful day, but the song that used to fill his heart with hope now pulled him into a state of remorse.

It had been a year and a half, but reminders of her were still everywhere, from the potted succulent that for some reason she had named Nigel on the windowsill, to this song — the one she had wanted to play as she walked down the aisle. He suspected that no matter how much time passed, he would never stop thinking about Melissa Eldredge. He had even splurged on a Tesla as a distraction, but it only reminded him of the way she would tease him for the hours he spent researching the potential purchase. "Some men dream about other women, but my competition is a computerized car."

Of course, he might stand a semblance of a chance of getting over her if he made the slightest effort to erase the traces of her from his life, but as much as he had tried, he couldn't bring himself to toss Nigel in the garbage. The photograph of them that had rested next to his computer remained in his top drawer. He also subscribed to her podcast, listening to her voice before falling asleep. And now, as he did at least once a week — promising himself this time would be the last — he found himself pulling up her social media accounts for updates.

He recognized the expression on her face — a mix of surprise and amusement with a dash of annoyance. Whoever took the shot caught her off guard. She wore a halo of giant hair curlers. She was gorgeous and radiant and absolutely adorable.

The photo was cropped but he could make out wisps of someone's blonde hair at the bottom edge. Was she holding a child?

The picture's caption felt like a punch to the stomach: *Taking the leap. Let's do this.*

His thoughts raced, searching for any other interpretation. If his suspicions were right, Katie certainly would have been there. He pulled up the account for Katie Cakes. The most recent post was of a giant table covered with cupcakes decorated alternatively with the Yankees or Red Sox logos. *The sweetest rivalry,* read the caption.

The fourth picture in the bakery's photo stream looked like a wedding cake. White with two flower-draped tiers. A winery in Cape Cod had been tagged in the post. So had Melissa. *Had to keep tears from falling on the cake for my BFF the bride.*

He closed the website on his browser and pulled up his current coding job instead. The new app he was creating for a banking client was almost ready for beta testing. As he forced himself to focus on the strings of letters and numbers on his screen, a new song broke out from the plaza below his office. He pictured Melissa holding his hand and dancing the last time they had seen that band together at Madison Square Garden.

He opened his internet browser again and searched for the courthouse closest to Nancy Eldredge's house. He needed to know.

6

Three weeks later

Melissa carefully washed and rinsed their lunch dishes, scoured the grill pan, and gave the kitchen floor a quick sweep. She had always been naturally and effortlessly tidy, finding comfort in the rituals of neatness. She cleaned up immediately after meals, unloaded the dishwasher every morning, and returned anything she used back to its designated spot. Katie had teased her relentlessly when she learned that Melissa emptied her medicine cabinet twice a month to wipe down the shelves for dust.

An amused chuckle pulled her out of her trancelike state.

The chuckle came from Grant "Mac" Macintosh. He was on the other side of her kitchen island, at the dining room table, his headset already on. Mac, in addition to being her friend and former coworker, was now her most frequent guest cohost on *The*

Justice Club, the true crime podcast Melissa had launched six months earlier. Each episode of *The Justice Club* featured a criminal investigation where arguably justice had been denied.

"As much as I'm oddly mesmerized by watching you clean, are we about ready?" Mac asked. "I'm on the clock today."

"I'm so sorry, but looking at all that mess was going to destroy my concentration."

"I have to say, I can't remember a time I came here to find dirty dishes on your countertops."

"Turns out that keeping an apartment spotless is a little tougher with a three-year-old Tasmanian devil around."

"Speaking of which, where is that precious little peanut?"

"Charlie's in meetings with a new client, so his sister picked up Riley to spend the day with her in Brooklyn."

"Nice to have an auntie nearby who's also willing to babysit," he said.

Melissa suppressed the involuntary eye roll that had nearly revealed itself. In addition to boycotting their wedding ceremony, Rachel was continuing her refusal to visit her niece in Melissa's presence. She had even declined the invitation to the small party they had over the weekend for Riley's third birthday, insisting on seeing her separately the next day. She pushed off the thought and pulled on her headset, settling in beside Mac at the table. "So . . . are we ready to do some justice for Evan?"

The Evan in question was Evan Moore, a boy who had vanished from the suburbs of Seattle nearly eight years earlier when he was six years old. Evan's father remained convinced to this day that the boy's step-mother, Judith, murdered him and hid the body somewhere it might never be found because she felt trapped raising another woman's child after a prolonged custody battle was decided in the father's favor. Evan's disappearance would be the basis for the next four episodes of *The Justice Club*. She and Mac had decided to pre-record them all at once, giving her time over the next few weeks to pull together the research for her next case.

Four hours later, Melissa gave a nod to Mac and flashed five fingers as a sign that they could begin to wrap up the final episode.

"Okay, Melissa. I know this is probably a lost cause, but just tell me: Do you think Judith Moore is guilty or not?"

"You're asking the wrong question, Mac. Everyone is innocent until they receive due process in a court of law and either plead guilty or are found to be guilty beyond a reasonable doubt. As a criminal defense lawyer, you of all people should know that."

"But I'm also fun!" Mac replied. "Do you see any courtroom around here? Is there a judge hiding under this table? I swear sometimes I don't even understand how you have a hit pod."

"Because I'm smart enough to invite mesmerizing friends like you on the air."

Melissa had always been obsessed with true crime stories, especially unsolved mysteries. She knew she had a good eye for a gripping story, and trying cases in court had turned her into a natural storyteller. When Melissa first left the prosecutor's office, she started her own practice, marketing herself as a "justice lawyer," specializing in private lawsuits on behalf of victims of abuse, crimes, and other injustices. Though she handled some criminal defense cases, she only accepted defendants whom she believed were either wrongly accused or otherwise treated unfairly. Then, two years ago, she won a wrongful conviction case for Jennifer Duncan, a battered woman who had killed her husband in self-defense. She had been convicted of murder at her trial, but Melissa had convinced a court to vacate it. The exoneration was as high profile as the original murder trial had been — she was a former model, and her husband was a wealthy and well-known real estate developer. But in an added twist, Melissa herself had worked as part of the prosecution team during the original trial and used what she knew about the case to reverse Jennifer's conviction.

She suddenly found herself on the cable news circuit, which led to a two-page feature in *New York* magazine, which led to an appearance for her and Jennifer on *The View*. Melissa wasn't surprised that producers and publishers were interested in hearing more from Jennifer, but ten minutes after their joint television appearance aired, an agent named Annabel Marino had called Melissa to ask how she planned to use her newfound "platform." Melissa's plan, she had explained, was to go right back to her law office and keep doing the work.

Annabel warned that a moment like Melissa's came only once in a lifetime — or never at all. She could leverage the case into a movie deal, a series of mystery novels based on herself, or maybe even a gig as the next cohost of a program like *The View*. The promises all sounded like hot air, but Annabel eventually convinced Melissa that she could have more impact as a public policy advocate than as yet another trial lawyer — and if a little bit of celebrity would help the cause, Melissa was willing to go along for the ride. Now, two years later, she was a bestselling author, sought-after speaker on the lecture circuit, and star of her own podcast. Despite the toxic way her relationship with Jennifer Duncan had ended, she owed her current career to Jennifer's case.

Mac tried one more time to get Melissa to share her own theory of the case.

"Why don't I end on a personal note?" she replied. "Some listeners may not know this, but I recently became a stepmother myself, and I'm so in love with this little toddler that I could tell you the plot of every single episode of *Peppa Pig*. I can see why Judith's behavior after Evan went missing was a red flag. She couldn't even remember what her stepson was wearing when she supposedly dropped him off for school, or what his school science project was, even though it was due that day. I can tell you every last detail about my stepdaughter. And if something ever happened to her, God forbid, I wouldn't be able to think straight. I certainly wouldn't go to the gym and post workout selfies."

"Aha," Mac gloated, "you *do* think she did it."

"Presumption of innocence, my friend."

"Well, I'm not her lawyer, and we're not in a courtroom," Mac said. "In my humble opinion, Judith Moore did it."

They exchanged a glance that confirmed they were done. "And that, dear listeners, is another episode of *The Justice Club*." She hit the Stop button on the recorder and pulled off her headphones.

"You're such a pro," she said. "All the online reviews say you're the best cohost."

"That's because I'm the one writing them," he joked. "My way of auditioning for a permanent gig."

"Now that would be the dream. It doesn't even feel like work when we do this together. Just two friends talking about juicy cases." She could tell from his arched brow that he was surprised by her response. "Wait. Weren't you kidding about the permanent gig?"

"I mean . . . I guess I was. But I would absolutely do it."

"Do you have enough time?" Melissa had largely wound down her legal practice, but Mac was in hot demand as a criminal defense lawyer.

Mac mulled the question over for a few

seconds. "I could do it as long as I wasn't in the middle of a long trial. But we could always pre-record a couple of episodes to roll out in a pinch. And you could still bring in other cohosts whenever you wanted."

Melissa was thrilled at the thought of being coworkers with Mac again. She noticed a new text message on her phone. It was from Katie. *I'm in your lobby. You done recording? Didn't want your doorman to interrupt by calling.*

She typed a reply and hit Send. *Perfect timing. We just finished. Come on up.*

"Katie's coming up for a drink. She wants to hear all about the honeymoon."

Another arched brow from Mac.

"Stop it," she said. "Not like that."

"Uh-huh."

"You want to stick around? The Three Musketeers, back together again."

"And in much nicer digs than the DA's office."

"Better beverages, too," she said, sliding a bottle of Billecart-Salmon champagne from the wine refrigerator beneath the kitchen island and displaying it for his approval.

"Ooh la la. I'd love to, but I'm on the clock. I'm meeting my sister —" He glanced at his watch. "Oops, in three minutes."

As she walked Mac out, she heard the

ding of an arriving elevator down the hall. Katie stepped out. She and Mac greeted each other with a quick hug before Mac explained why he had to run. Once Melissa and Katie were alone, Katie asked if Mac was still dating "what's her name."

"Sarah. And yes."

Katie shook her head in disappointment. Katie's last serious relationship had ended nearly six years earlier when she was still working at the district attorney's office. She liked to joke that she could also be a best-selling author if she wrote about her nightmarish online dating experiences: "Talk about a horror story."

Spotting the champagne waiting on the counter, Katie said, "Wow. What are we celebrating? I know you're living your best life right now, but if it gets any better, I might officially be jealous."

"Nothing specific," Melissa said. She knew her friend was only joking. Despite the different paths they had taken since their early days in the DA's office, Katie always seemed to celebrate each of Melissa's successes as if it belonged to her as well. "We haven't seen each other for a while, and I know this is your favorite." She tipped the bottle over two flutes, which they clinked before getting settled on the living room sofa. "So . . . you will never guess who called me yesterday."

Katie's eyes flashed with the thrill of juicy incoming gossip. "Um . . . Brad Pitt saying he wants to be my new boyfriend?"

"Cute, but no. Patrick."

Katie's jaw dropped with exaggerated surprise. "As in Patrick Higgins, *your* Patrick?"

"*Formerly* mine." Melissa hadn't realized she had never changed his nickname in her phone — Future Husband — until the words popped up on her screen when he called. After he suddenly broke off their engagement, there had been no messy on-and-off phase, not even a single follow-up conversation — until yesterday.

"So what happened?"

"I was so stunned, I decided not to pick up."

"Okay, so why did he call?"

"I have no idea. He didn't leave a message."

"Oh my God, why didn't you pick up? Now you'll never know."

"It was probably just a butt-dial," Melissa said, even as she imagined Patrick holding his phone, waiting to see if she would answer.

"So, are you going to call him back?"

"And say what? You called me but didn't leave a message? And by the way, I'm married now?" She held up her ringed left hand for emphasis. "Calling an ex-fiancé is just asking for trouble."

Melissa had never been so happy. She had no room in her life for the man who broke her heart so badly she thought she'd never be willing to share it again.

They were on their second glass of bubbles when she finally finished showing Katie all of the photographs from the honeymoon — two weeks in Italy, zigzagging from Milan to Genoa to Florence to Rome. "You should have posted those to your Instagram account," Katie said. "My travel pictures always boost engagement."

She shook her head. "It's too personal." Melissa was still getting used to the jargon of social media, which she saw as a necessary evil of her unexpected career path. "That time together was just for us. I didn't think it was possible, but I fell more in love with him every day. Obviously I love Riley, but Charlie and I have never been alone that long, just the two of us."

Katie grimaced slightly, and Melissa wondered if her schmaltzy comments were insensitive given Katie's own situation. Katie didn't linger on the moment, however.

"Speaking of social media," she said, "any more posts from your stalker?"

"More of the same." The user who identified as TruthTeller seemed to have nothing but time to chime in — often repeatedly — on every post Melissa created. "It stings, but Annabel insists it's actually good for my profile. The more they attack me, the more my supporters engage."

"Well, Annabel's your agent, and I'm your best friend. That person's posts are deranged, Melissa — clearly obsessed with you." This morning's comments had been especially pointed. In response to a post teasing her upcoming podcast episodes, TruthTeller replied: *The Evan Moore case is perfect for you. Spoiler alert: The stepmother's evil.* An hour later: *I still can't believe you tricked some poor sucker into marrying you, but I feel worse for his daughter. If she's lucky, you'll have the decency to dump her on the nannies.* Forty minutes later: *Maybe when he finds out what I know about you, he'll dump you.* "And what is it with all these vague references to having some kind of deep, dark secret that's going to bring you down?"

Not for the first time, Melissa's thoughts went from the TruthTeller account to Jennifer Duncan. When Jennifer's conviction was first set aside, it seemed only natural that the two women would remain connected. They had formed a bond during the wrongful conviction proceedings, and they both believed that sharing Jennifer's story with the public could help other survivors.

But then Jennifer also wanted Melissa's help in probate court, where her husband's estate was still pending. Under the law, Jennifer's criminal conviction prevented her from inheriting what she otherwise would have received under their will — which was the entire estate. Once her conviction was set aside, Jennifer claimed she was entitled to inherit everything after all. According to her, Doug's now-adult children were practically strangers — the products of a brief and early marriage before he stopped drinking, went to business school, and started the real estate business that would make him a millionaire many times over. Melissa tried to explain that she wasn't an estate lawyer and wanted to focus her attention on criminal justice and not a probate battle with Doug's children, but Jennifer lashed out at her in a fierce rage.

But the TruthTeller could be anyone, so Melissa had never shared her lingering suspicions. "Who knows what they're talking about. To be honest, it was actually the comment about the nannies that stung the worst."

Melissa and her brother had rarely been left even with a babysitter, but Charlie was currently ramping up his business after scaling back when Linda died, and he was insistent that Melissa continue to aggressively pursue her own career. The plan was to hire a nanny at least part-time once Riley adjusted to the changes they had already imposed upon her young world.

Katie waved away the concern. "That poor little girl already lost a parent. The more people she has in her life to love her, the better. Sometimes you have to find your own family."

Melissa gave Katie's hand a quick squeeze. She could always count on her to understand. "Speaking of family, Mike's coming back up for the big move." Melissa's mother had accepted an offer on the house. "Instead of just hiring a mover, we are going to sort through everything together. That way, we can all keep some memories from the old house, and Mom can store anything that won't fit in the new place. Oh, and get this: Mike and I are renting a U-Haul and taking a road trip together. This is his off-season, so he had time to come up again."

"And whose brilliant idea was that?"

"Mom's, if I had to guess. I think since Dad passed away, she really wants the two of us to be closer."

Katie stroked her chin as if deep in thought. "Well, maybe if he dated your best friend, that would help."

"Don't even joke," Melissa scolded.

"You sure you don't need an assistant for the move? He looked pretty good in that suit at your wedding."

"That would be like my sister dating my brother or something. You really need to stop."

"Fine, I was only kidding anyway. *Mostly.* You sure you don't need a buffer? I know it drives you crazy the way he's always trying to talk about . . . well, you know."

Melissa shrugged. "No, I need to do this on my own. It's important to Mom, and it's what Dad would want, too."

Melissa had no idea that three weeks later, she would desperately regret not taking Katie up on her offer to make the trip with them.

7

Three weeks later

It was so cold. *Mommy, Mommy . . . I don't want in the bath.* There was a gritty taste in her mouth. Sand — why? Where was she? Had she spoken those words, or only imagined them?

Melissa's eyelids fluttered as the summer sun moved into position above the whitecaps churning in the water. Even though it was summer, the beach winds had her arms covered in goose bumps. She was still processing the feeling of the cool sand against her bare legs when she heard a high, quiet voice beside her.

"Missa, you miss Mommy?"

At the sound of her stepdaughter's voice, Melissa turned her head to find Riley standing over her. In the distance, she could see her childhood home, on the last day she'd ever be here.

"I miss Mommy. Grand-Nan was looking

for you."

Melissa couldn't imagine how panicked her mother must have been to wake up to find Melissa's room empty. She pressed her palms against her face, trying to bring herself back to reality. To the present. She'd had another nightmare. They were getting worse. Charlie had heard her cry out before in her sleep. She had even sleepwalked once, despite taking one of the sleeping pills she'd gotten from her doctor to see if they might help. Charlie had found her in the bathroom, wrapped in a towel, staring at the tub while the water ran with no explanation. But now she had apparently managed to crawl her way out to the beach in the middle of the night.

She gave Riley a good-morning hug and told her not to worry. "I was excited about today and came outside early to watch the sunrise. I think I must have turned into a sleepyhead again and was saying crazy words in my dreams." Riley matched the giggle Melissa dropped at the end of her own sentence. Melissa held Riley's hand as they made their way back to the house, where her brother and mother were watching them. Melissa could see the relief in her mother's face.

"Is everything okay, sweetie? We all assumed you were still in your room until Riley noticed the back door was open."

She forced a reassuring smile. "Just saying goodbye to that special view."

Mike let out a frustrated sigh. "Thanks for the scare."

They had spent the past two days helping their mother finalize the process of sorting everything in the house as either donate, store, or move to her much-smaller cottage on Long Island. Melissa allowed herself a silent moment of gratitude that she had opted to bring Riley instead of leaving her with her aunt Rachel after Charlie needed to go on a last-minute work trip. Toddlers couldn't ride in U-Hauls, which meant that she and Riley would take Melissa's car while Mike drove the moving truck. Their mother would remain in Cape Cod to handle the real estate closing on Monday and meet them in Southampton afterward. Melissa was determined to use their head start to make the new house as comfortable as possible before their mother's arrival.

Later that morning, she found herself lingering, finding last-minute tasks to complete. Checking the various Post-it notes left behind on the items being donated or stored. Another walk-through of the guest house to be sure nothing had been left behind. One more sweep of her childhood bedroom, where a tippy-toed graze of her fingertips along the top shelf of her closet pulled down a tiny pink plush bear with a rainbow on its belly and a heart for a nose. "Pookie Bear," she whispered. He smelled like the closet's cedar walls.

When she returned downstairs, Riley jumped up from her spot beside Grand-Nan on the sofa, her eyes lighting up at the sight of the stuffed toy. "Who's that?"

"You still have that thing?" Mike said, looking up as he laced his sneakers near the front door.

"How dare you?" she said with feigned outrage. "Pookie's not a *thing*. Pookie's family. Riley, this is Pookie. She was the very first Christmas present your uncle Mike ever gave me. I think I was four at the time. Until then, all the surprises under the tree had always been from Grand-Nan, or our daddy, or Santa Claus. But then Mike declared that he was old enough to give me a present, too." Melissa learned later that her brother had paid for the stuffed bear with money he made raking leaves in the neighborhood. "Pookie's what's called a Care Bear. When I was your age, they had their own television show and movies. I loved Care Bears the way you love Peppa Pig."

Riley chuckled, placing her hands on her cheeks. "That's a *lot.*"

"Exactly. And the Care Bears were guardian angels who were supposed to be able to protect you from the boogeyman. Pookie here is called the Cheer Bear, the happiest of all the bears who always tries to brighten other people's days." She hadn't thought about Pookie since whenever she had apparently decided to place her on the top shelf of her closet. Had six-year-old Mike been trying to protect his little sister with a stuffed animal, or just buy her a favorite toy?

"You're leaving Pookie?" Riley asked, her voice strained with concern.

"Absolutely not. Pookie and I are for life," she said. She gave a small smile to her brother, who winked in return.

"I think the two of you have been running out the clock long enough," her mother said. "Did you say your final goodbyes to this old girl, because it's time."

They both nodded. Mike even cried up to the ceiling, "Goodbye, house! We're going to miss you."

"And you're sure you've got the keys to the new cottage?" Nancy asked.

"Sure do." Melissa gave her key ring a jingle to confirm. Rather than mail the cottage keys to the Cape, her mother's broker had left them at her real estate office in the city for Melissa to pick up.

Her mother gave them each a long hug, making them promise to drive safe and to call when they got to the cottage.

Melissa pulled up the GPS directions to her mother's new address and then reminded Mike to change the settings on his phone to share his location with her.

"We're going to the same place," he said.

"Just humor me, okay? I want to make sure we can find each other if we get separated."

He muttered "Control freak" under his breath, but complied with the request.

After Melissa strapped Riley into her car seat, Mike was waiting for her on the driver's side of the SUV. "So what was that out on the beach?" he asked in a low voice.

"I already told you. I couldn't sleep."

"That's bull. You were calling out for your mommy, saying you didn't want a bath."

Her lips parted, but no words came out. He glanced toward Riley in the back seat. Obviously, she had told her uncle Mike whatever she had overheard when she found Melissa on the beach.

"She's barely three years old. And confused."

"Come on. Don't gaslight your own stepdaughter. She told me what you were saying, and I immediately knew what it referred to. You remember what he did to us, don't you? After all these years of insisting you didn't."

"It was just a stupid dream. I've told you a million times, I was too young back then. I'm sorry you remember every awful bit of it, but I don't. And, more importantly, I don't want to."

"You were four years old when I gave you Pookie. You remembered that, no problem."

"That was like a year and a half after the abduction."

"I've learned a lot about this. Back when we were little, the experts thought kids were protected if they couldn't access their most damaging memories. But now they know suppressed memories can cause all kinds of problems as an adult — anxiety, depression, PTSD, amnesia . . ."

"Mike," she said dryly, "I can literally remember what I ate for dinner three weeks ago. I'm not getting amnesia."

"And you also remember what he did to us. I know you do."

He held her gaze until she climbed behind

the wheel of her car. "Let's go. We've got a long drive."

She closed the door before he could say anything further. Happiness was a choice, she reminded herself. Pookie the Cheer Bear would definitely agree.

8

Jayden Kennedy felt as if he and Julie had spent the entire day scurrying around like ants — attending to every last detail before he had to turn his house over to the Domi-luxe renter.

Julie gave the empty refrigerator a final wipe-down with a soapy paper towel. "I think we are officially done," she pronounced. "Move-in ready." Her berry-glossed lips spread into a bright smile as she tucked a stray lock of strawberry blonde hair back into the loose ponytail at the nape of her neck.

The Domiluxe standards required him to deliver the rental in five-star condition, which meant storing all of his clothing, photographs, toiletries, and personal effects in one guest room that would remain locked off. He would not have agreed to what amounted to a miniature move except that the person who called herself Helen confirmed that she would take the property for four full weeks.

Even though the Domiluxe app promised "security-clearance-level anonymity" for "discerning providers and consumers," he had learned quite a bit about his tenant during their online correspondence. She was an author completing her second novel, the first time she had ever written under a deadline. According to her, it was harder than expected to write a book in one year while also being a mother to two teenagers. Her husband was the one to suggest the idea of a writing retreat — an escape from both the Atlanta summer heat and the daily intrusions upon her writing schedule. She decided that the so-called greenest town in Connecticut, only a two-hour drive from LaGuardia Airport, might be the perfect getaway.

After he finished locking off his belongings in the guest room, he found Julie standing before the floor-to-ceiling windows of the living room. "I can see why this would be a perfect house to write a book in," she said, looking out at his eight wooded acres. "You can't see another living soul from here. But I think I'd be afraid, all alone."

He wrapped an arm around her waist and gave her a tight squeeze. "That's because you read all those crime novels and let your imagination get away from you."

She wrinkled her freckled nose at the gibe. "Maybe just a teeny bit."

Oh, how he adored her. He was looking forward to the extra income he'd be earning from the rental, but sharing a roof with this amazing woman for nearly a month was even more exciting. He hoped it would pave the way toward a more permanent situation. "Are you saying you could never live here?" he asked.

"Hmmmm." She placed an index finger on her chin, feigning a long moment of deep reflection. "I assume I wouldn't be here alone, though. And that would be pretty lovely."

It was going to happen. Soon. He pulled her in closer and kissed the top of her head. "It's pretty cool someone's going to finish a book in my house. Maybe she'll even end up writing about it."

"Or 'Helen' " — she made air quotes with her fingers — "made up that whole story and is a lying scoundrel hiding out with his mistress for a few weeks."

"You really do have some kind of imagination. So . . . ready for your new roommate?" He eyed the two suitcases he had placed by the front door.

"Can't wait."

Julie's place was only eight miles away. As she buckled her seat belt in his passenger seat, she asked if they could resume the latest *Justice Club* episode. She had turned it off earlier because they'd been working too hard on the house to pay attention. Of all her true crime podcasts, this one was her favorite. She had even met the host, Melissa Eldredge, when she attended her book signing in the city.

He hit Play on his car's Bluetooth screen as he pulled onto the long dirt road that would bring them to Route 7. As Melissa and her cohost Mac continued their dive into the facts surrounding Evan Moore's disappearance and the evidence against his stepmother, he found himself thinking that the money from this rental would be more than enough to pay for an engagement ring.

"Why are you smiling over there?"

He turned to find Julie watching him.

"Just happy. That's all."

9

Oh, the activity.

Melissa had been up since five in the morning. The final episode covering the Evan Moore case had gone live this morning, and she always tried to stay at least a week ahead of schedule. She was able to finish her final edits of the next three episodes before Riley began stirring inside the Pack 'n Play positioned next to Melissa's bed in her mother's new guest room, automatically reaching for Pookie the Care Bear beside her.

Mike surprised her by having breakfast ready to go when she and Riley came downstairs. The cottage was less than half the size of their childhood home on the Cape, but she could see why her mother had fallen in love with it at first sight. Soaked in natural sunlight, the rooms were bright and airy with cream-colored walls and driftwood accents. She could almost taste the beach air from the bay at the end of the road. Melissa had always been uncomfortable in water, so much so that she could barely dog-paddle in a pool, and yet she loved the smell and the sound of the ocean.

Three hours later, they were nearly done unpacking the rest of the moving boxes. Mike opened the final one and pulled out a smaller rectangular box from the top. "Check this out!" He proudly displayed a beaten-up game of Operation.

"Talk about a blast from the past," she said. She recognized the game board — an "operation table" holding a cartoonlike patient with bowl-cut brown hair and a large red lightbulb for a nose. Players used the game's tweezers to extract various pieces from the patient, such as butterflies from his stomach or a funny bone from his elbow.

"Come on. Let's play!"

"Seriously, Mike? We have so much work to do."

"Not really. We've been cranking. We deserve a break, and it'll be fun to teach my niece a game we used to love."

Riley's eager eyes left Melissa no choice, and soon they were gathered around the breakfast table again, this time to operate on the patient she now remembered was named Cavity Sam. Riley's chubby fingers struggled with the tweezers at first, but instead of being frustrated, she giggled every time she accidentally touched the metal to the board, setting off Sam's red-light nose and the accompanying buzzer. On the second rematch, Melissa sensed that she and her brother had formed a silent conspiracy to let Riley win. When she successfully pulled out the wishbone and the bread basket, they gave a hearty round of applause to congratulate her.

As Melissa packed the game pieces back into their box, she mused, "Funny how the batteries worked after all these years."

Mike smiled but said nothing.

"I didn't think Mom would keep this old game."

"I might have found an old set on eBay," he said with a shrug.

She gave his shoulders a quick squeeze. "We can break these boxes down to recycle, and then get some lunch in town?"

"If you don't mind, I might skip lunch. I want to check out some of the boat charter operations. I was thinking I might be able to work up here during my hurricane season. Long Island summers, Caribbean winters . . . ?"

"Not a bad life, big brother."

"You're okay with that?" he asked. "For all of us to live a little closer to each other?"

"Of course I'm okay — *more* than okay," she quickly corrected.

He opened his mouth to say more, but then noticed Riley within earshot, standing over a *Peppa Pig* sticker book on the living room coffee table. Melissa used the pause to hop onto social media to see the early feedback coming in for the latest episode of *The Justice Club*.

OMG, what a cliffhanger! I'm so addicted. I need to know what happened.

Poor little Evan. It's obvious his stepmother did it! I hope Melissa can prove it.

I pray this podcast brings in new tips to the police. #BringEvanHome

But despite all of the positive comments, one post brought her scrolling to a halt. *The irony. You of all people know about lying stepmothers, don't you? You're a liar and a fraud. It's all going to come out.*

The moment was interrupted by the buzz of her phone in her hand. It was an incoming FaceTime call from Charlie. Without any hesitation, she deleted TruthTeller's comment and then blocked the account from seeing her posts. The move was long overdue, no matter what her agent thought. Between work, this move, her new family, and those horrible nightmares, anonymous heckling from an online troll was the last thing she needed.

Good riddance, she thought, clicking Accept on Charlie's call.

"Hi," she said, holding up the screen as she made her way over to Riley.

"How are my favorite girls?" In the background, she could see the unmade bed in his tropically decorated hotel room, a room-service tray resting on the ottoman of a chair in the corner.

"Hi Daddy!" Riley grinned up at the phone. "We played a game with Uncle Mike, and I won."

"How's the rough life in Antigua?" Melissa asked. Charlie had been retained by a major developer after recent earthquakes in Puerto Rico had affected several other Caribbean islands. The client had decided to bring in outside geological consultants to conduct a risk assessment before moving forward with a planned resort.

"Not to complain, but . . . hot. And sticky. I don't know how Mike can live down here all year."

"Well, as of today, he's talking about moving to Southampton for the summers." She flashed a smile to Mike, who was breaking down empty cardboard boxes. "Have you checked your flight?"

"On time for now. I should land at JFK at six thirty. With any luck, I'll be in Southampton by eight."

Riley would be in bed by then, but Melissa would wait to have a late dinner alone with him. As she nestled onto the floor to show Charlie the sticker book Riley was working on, she didn't think about her podcast or TruthTeller or the nightmares that had kept waking her every hour the previous night. She was choosing happiness. She was happy.

She found the perfect lunch spot in town, an old-fashioned soda fountain called Sip 'N Soda, with a Greek salad for her and a grilled cheese sandwich for Riley, followed up by an ice cream order from each of them.

As she rose from the table, she realized that her difficulty sleeping the previous night had taken its toll. Between sound editing, unpacking, entertaining Riley, and lunch, she had been on the go the entire day. Now she was on the verge of exhaustion. Spotting a Starbucks across the street, she decided she needed a giant container of caffeine. When they hit the sidewalk again, venti iced French roast in Melissa's hand, Riley began skipping toward the car, apparently all revved up after a long night's sleep and the sugar from her chocolate fudge sundae.

"Wait for me," Melissa called out, catching up to Riley and reminding her gently that she couldn't run off by herself.

Once they were in the car, Melissa Googled "parks near me." She was delighted to see they were only half a mile from a public park with a well-reviewed playground. Riley could work off some of her extra energy while Melissa caught up on emails.

After pushing Riley on the merry-go-round and the swing set, she found a bench near the park's tree line where she could sit in the shade and keep an eye on Riley while she continued to play with the other children. Riley was bouncing between a yellow plastic slide and a red horse-shaped spring rider, with accompanying sound effects. Each three-foot-long ride down the slide came with a long *woooo*, starting low and quiet, growing louder and higher pitched until she landed firmly on the child-safe rubber flooring. She giggled gleefully as she rocked back and forth on the bouncy horse, letting out an occasional, "Whoa, horsey, whoa."

A photo popped up on Melissa's phone. It was from Neil Keeney's mother, Ellen, and showed her and Melissa's mother, side by side at Melissa's favorite beach shack on the Cape, holding up raw oysters. After young Neil's recollection of a strange man at the post office had helped the police locate Mike and Melissa, Neil's parents had accepted the Eldredge family's invitation to join them at their house to celebrate the safe rescue of their children. The Eldredge and Keeney families had remained close ever since.

Melissa set down her coffee to text a response. *Yummy. She seems OK about the house?*

Better than OK, Ellen replied. *I'm going to miss my dear friend, but she's excited to move.*

Melissa typed three heart emojis and then hit Enter. When she looked up, a woman was next to Riley as she rocked on her bouncy horse. She hadn't noticed her before and didn't see any child she didn't recognize from a few minutes earlier.

She jumped up from her bench and ran toward the playground area. "Riley?"

Other parents' heads turned at the panicked sound of her voice. She noticed one mother in a Mets cap near the merry-go-round roll her eyes. Was she overreacting? Was she *that* parent, assuming that danger lurks behind every piece of playground equipment? That man . . . what he had done to her. Was she paranoid . . . because of him?

"Hello?" she said. Her voice had a slight quiver as she approached the stranger talking to Riley. The woman wore a black linen tank dress, tan cotton sneakers, and a floppy straw hat over a long blonde ponytail at the nape of her neck. Something about her appearance immediately put Melissa's fears at ease, but then she reminded herself how many dangerous people looked completely normal on the outside — people like Carl Harmon. His name. She hated that name and wished she could forget it forever.

The woman flashed a warm smile. "Hi there. Is this cute little one with you? She really takes after you."

Does she? Melissa wondered. Strawberry blonde versus blonde-blonde, but they were both fair-skinned with heart-shaped faces. "Oh, that's sweet. Actually, she's my stepdaughter."

"Is that why you were on your phone, drinking your coffee and ignoring her? Because she's only your stepdaughter?"

"What? No . . . I was sitting right —"

"Because you're never wrong, are you? I know all about you. You're a fraud. And a hypocrite."

Melissa stepped back, as if distance could keep the words from hurting her. The woman turned and began walking away.

"Who are you?" Melissa cried out desperately.

Riley continued rocking and giggling, unfazed by the exchange, if she had even heard it. The mom with the Mets cap near the merry-go-round was now approaching her, a genuine look of concern across her face. "Are you okay?"

"Do you know that woman? Did you see her here before? Is she one of the moms?"

"No, I didn't notice her until you rushed over. Did something happen?"

She shook her head, knowing there was no point in trying to explain. "Riley, I think your horsey friend is tired from all that springing back and forth. We should give him a rest."

"You're silly, Missa. He's not a real horse." Even so, she climbed off her ride. "You forgot your coffee, Missa." Riley pointed to the bench by the tree line on the opposite side of the playground.

"That's okay. I was almost done." That

wasn't true. Even after that strange interaction, she really wanted that coffee, but she also wanted to get out of this park and away from that horrible woman as quickly as possible.

"I'll get it!" Riley insisted.

She finally gave up and marched hand in hand with Riley to retrieve her coffee. When they got into the car, she found herself locking the doors on instinct.

When they returned to the cottage, the U-Haul was parked in the driveway, but she heard nothing when they walked inside. "Mike?" she yelled out. "Where do we think Uncle Mike went?"

"Who knows?" Riley said, holding up her palms for an exaggerated shrug. Melissa was starting to notice little mannerisms that Riley was picking up from her.

Despite finishing the giant cup of iced coffee, Melissa was still exhausted. They were on yet another round of Operation when she felt her eyelids begin to drop a third time, snapping herself back awake. She was so tired. She checked her watch. It was almost two o'clock, Riley's usual nap time. Close enough.

"I think it's about time to go upstairs and take a nap. I could use one, too."

"Can't we finish this game? Pl-eeease?"

"First thing when we wake up, it will be your turn. I bet the nap will help steady your operating hand."

Riley chuckled. Accepting the decision, she began walking up the stairs, using her hands on the higher steps to support herself.

Once Riley was tucked comfortably into her temporary Pack 'n Play bed, clinging to her little white blanket with pink and purple hearts, Melissa fell onto the bed, not even bothering to change her clothes or pull back the covers.

So, so tired. As she fell into a deep sleep, she remembered her mother's own words, which Melissa had read once she finally sought out the most authoritative true crime book written about her own abduction. It had taken a psychiatrist's hypnotism to open up her mother's memories of what had happened during her marriage to Carl Harmon, before their two children, Peter and Lisa, disappeared and were then found murdered. *But during those five years,* she had explained to the hypnotist, *I was so terribly tired so much . . . After Mother died . . . always so tired. Poor Carl . . . so patient. He did everything for me. He got up with the children at night — even when they were babies.*

Only after Carl had abducted Mike and

Melissa were officials able to piece together the full story of how Carl had drugged his young wife to keep her isolated, dependent, and unaware of what was happening in her own house. To conceal his pedophilia, he killed Peter and Lisa, framed Nancy, and faked his own suicide. She was found guilty, but the conviction was reversed for juror misconduct, and the district attorney was unable to retry her because a key witness was missing. She eventually moved across the country, where she started a new life with a local realtor and had two children, Mike and Melissa.

And then Carl Harmon found them all.

A yellow rubber ducky. That smell. Baby powder. Talc . . . and sweat. Melissa was tired then, too, from the drug he had injected into her hand. So, so tired, when Carl Harmon had lowered her body into the water. "Mommy, Mommy . . ."

She heard sounds beyond her weak, childish voice crying out for her mother. What was that noise? The ocean? No, the sound was the water rushing from the bathtub faucet. The yellow rubber ducky bobbled as the water level rose. The toy was for a child like her, but it wasn't playful. It wasn't fun. It was menacing — dangerous and predatory with black eyes and sharp teeth as it floated closer to her bare skin.

She felt a man's hand grip her wrist. She bolted upright in the bed, gasping for air as if she were drowning, even though the cotton coverlet was still neatly in place beneath her.

"Missy, can you hear me? Wake up. Wake up!" Mike stood over her, his fingers digging into her arm. Her neck was wet with perspiration. "Missy, you need to get up right now! Where's Riley?"

10

Melissa did not realize how much time was slipping by. She could hear the fear in Mike's voice as he cradled her against him. "Melissa, what's the matter? Melissa, where is Riley?"

She tried to raise her hand, but felt it fall loosely by her side. She tried to speak, but no words formed on her lips. The rest of the outside world existed, but she couldn't connect to it.

She heard her brother say, "Pick yourself up, Missy. We have to find Riley."

The child. Charlie's child. *Her* child now. They must find her. She felt her lips moving, but no sound escaped her throat. So, so tired.

"Oh my God!" She heard the desperation in her brother's voice. She wanted to say, "Don't worry about me. Find Riley." But she couldn't speak. She felt him pull her up to her feet, her weight falling against him.

"What is wrong?" he asked. "After everything I thought was wrong with you, this is too much. Riley is gone. Don't you get it?"

She finally found her words, which landed on her first instinct. "The police," Melissa said, "you must call the police."

Almost as if in the distance, she heard her brother's voice recite their mother's new address and the name of a missing girl, only three years old as of last month — Riley Miller.

Remotely she knew she was shivering. But that wasn't what she was thinking about. She thought about her abrupt decision to delete and block TruthTeller earlier that morning. She envisioned that horrible woman at the park. *Because you're never wrong, are you? I know all about you. You're a fraud. And a hypocrite.*

And now Riley was gone. Was there a connection?

"Did you call the police, Mike?" Somehow, she didn't know if it had been a minute or an hour since she first insisted on it. She grabbed frantically for the cell phone next to her on the bed and checked the time. After so many sleepless nights, how had she been down for so many hours?

"Yes, didn't you hear me? They're on their way," he assured her.

Melissa felt the darkness coming at her. She began sliding back and away . . . No . . . no . . . no. . . . She forced herself to stand up. She spotted the stuffed Pookie bear Riley had been clutching earlier. Now, it was tossed carelessly to the floor, looking sadder and more threadbare than she remembered. She struggled to rush down the stairs to search the rest of the house. On the floor beside the front door she spotted a pile of cotton. Recognizing the pink and purple hearts as Riley's blanket, she gasped loudly. As she started to reach down to pick it up, she stopped herself, realizing this house might now be a crime scene.

She stumbled out the door, her brother at her heels, asking her where she was going. Walking swiftly on the sidewalk outside of the cottage, her bare feet on the concrete and the evening wind beginning to chill her bare arms, she was wide awake now. What Mike had gone through . . . what *she* had suffered when she was abducted — no, no, she could not let that happen to Riley.

These memories from her past were making it clear they were not about to disappear. More clearly than in any of her earlier nightmares, Melissa heard her younger self crying in earnest as she squeezed her eyes shut. "Mommy . . .

Mommy." That's when Carl Harmon had unzipped her jacket. "There, there," he had said soothingly. "It's all right."

He had taken them to his creepy top-floor rental of the Lookout, a bleak and weather-beaten old waterfront mansion built high on a bluff over nine acres of land. She remembered Mike demanding to know who the man was and where they were. Harmon told them he was a friend of their mommy's and that he had planned a game for all of them on her birthday. Melissa could still feel the way the man patted her skin while he spoke until Mike had tried to push his hands away. His efforts did not last for long. Harmon had yanked Melissa back from her brother and then asked Mike, "Do you know what it's like to be dead?"

"It means to go to God," Mike had answered.

That's when Harmon told them that their mommy had gone to God that morning and their daddy had asked him to watch over them for a little while. Mike had cried, "If my mommy went to God, I want to go, too."

Running his fingers through Mike's hair, Harmon had rocked Missy on his lap, holding her against his chest. "You will," he said. "Tonight. I promise."

There was no denying it now. She remembered. She remembered all of it. And what was happening with Riley was like what happened back then. It was like last time. Last time, and would they find Riley the same way they'd found Mike and Melissa, abused by an equally depraved and soulless man? Carl Harmon had bound Mike's head in plastic wrap and left him to die while he fled with Melissa to the attic, planning to throw her from the roof or drown her in the ocean.

She needed to tell Charlie. Please, God, how was she going to tell Charlie?

He picked up on the second ring. "Hey, you. I'm making great time from the airport. Be there in about an hour."

She would never be able to remember the precise words she finally managed to speak between her tears, but the point was made: Riley was missing, and it was all Melissa's fault.

11

More than a hundred miles away, Jayden Kennedy felt an odd wave of paranoia fall over him as Julie took a left turn onto the unpaved road leading to his house.

"Babe, let's just turn around," he said. "You said you wanted to listen to the last episode of *The Justice Club*. Don't you want to find out what Evan's stepmother has been up to after all these years?"

"Best thing about a podcast is I can listen whenever. We can at least drive by your house. She might be totally friendly and tell you to come on in."

Julie had come up with this idea as they were leaving the new farm-to-table restaurant they had tried for dinner. After all the time they had spent preparing the house for "Helen" the renter, Jayden had neglected to pack proper business attire, something he had little use for since leaving Wall Street behind. But later that day, he got a nibble on a pitch he had made for a new consulting contract, and now the potential client wanted to meet him in the city tomorrow for lunch. Dropping money on a new suit would be a stretch, even assuming he could get it tailored in time. Now that they were approaching the house, it seemed a small price to pay to avoid a potential disaster.

"This is where I remind both of us that this rental website isn't exactly normal," he said. "Domiluxe is supposed to be completely anonymous."

"It's not exactly a spy operation," she said. "It's just more upscale, right?"

"And also super secretive. Showing up at the house when the renter's there is a major violation of the terms. She could freak out and cancel the contract or worse."

"Well . . . maybe she's not even there yet."

Jayden felt the pinch in the pit of his stomach deepen as Julie's Mini continued its slow crawl toward the house. He noticed that she turned off the headlights before coming to a stop about fifty yards from his driveway. She cracked her door ajar, and the interior dome light turned on.

"Where are you going?" His voice came out in a whisper, even though no one else was around.

"Let's just walk up far enough to see if

anyone's there," she replied, climbing out of the tiny car. He scurried to catch up. "If the house is dark, you can just run in, grab a suit, and dash right out. Think of it as an adventure. I'll time you."

"Or if the lights are out, it's because Helen's asleep and I scare the poor woman senseless. Or Helen's not a Helen working on her second book after all. She's a fugitive hiding out from the law and greets me at the bottom of the stairs with a sawed-off shotgun."

"Now who has the wild imagination?" she said with a sideways smile.

They were almost to the darkened house when Julie let out a small squeal at the sound of a car hitting the gravel of the driveway entrance. Jayden ducked behind a rhododendron and pulled Julie next to him. As they hid from the glare of the oncoming headlights, she looked up at him with wide eyes, clearly on the verge of one of those adorable fits of laughter she could suddenly fall into. "We're hiding in the bushes at your own house," she whispered once the car passed them.

He grabbed her hand and led the way back to her parked Mini. The entire drive home, they laughed at the absurdity of the situation. Jayden would remember later that the renter's car was a sedan, probably white, and that it struck him as a rental, which made sense since Helen said she was flying into LaGuardia from Atlanta.

He did not, however, see the car's driver or any other occupants, including the three-year-old girl in the back seat.

12

When Charlie walked through the front door of the cottage, Melissa rushed to him. She felt a wave of relief wash over her as he held her. Nothing about the horrible situation had changed, but somehow, now that they were together, she could believe that everything would be okay.

When he finally let go, she had a hard time meeting his eyes. "I'm so sorry."

The male detective — Marino was his name — stepped inside as well and seemed to be monitoring their interaction.

"Shh," Charlie whispered. "It's all going to be all right. We're going to find her. You're not to blame," he added, as if reading her mind.

She felt a pang of guilt that he was the one comforting her. Riley was his daughter, and she was the one who lost her.

The female detective offered Charlie a handshake as an introduction. "Mr. Miller,

I'm Detective Hall. You've already met my partner, Detective Marino."

Earlier, Marino had stepped outside to call Charlie on his cell phone while Detective Hall had continued to gather details from Melissa and Mike. They had explained it was in the interest of "efficiency" since Charlie was still making his way from the airport. Perhaps. But Melissa had been a prosecutor. She knew the reasons to interview spouses separately when family matters were involved.

"I was just talking to Detective Hall about putting out an Amber Alert as soon as possible," Melissa said. She noticed the two detectives exchange an annoyed look. She had already insisted that they bring a crime scene analyst to the scene to search for fingerprints or other possible physical evidence.

Melissa's cell phone buzzed on the sofa next to her. Another call from Katie, her second in the last few minutes. She declined the call.

"Do you need to get that?" Hall asked.

She shook her head. "My friend, Katie. My guess is our friends are calling each other about Riley." While they'd been waiting for the police to arrive, Melissa had contacted Neil and Amanda to see if

Amanda, as an NYPD officer, might be able to help.

Marino held up his palms. "Look, I know you're all worried. Of course you are. But Amber Alerts are a tightly controlled system. They won't let us put out an alert unless we're confident there's been an abduction. And luckily we're not there yet."

"With due respect," Mike said, "my niece just turned three. It's not like she climbed out a window and swiped the car keys for the night."

"My son can slip a Pack 'n Play like a miniature Houdini," Hall said with a sympathetic smile. "And Melissa, you said you were certain the doors were all locked, correct?"

She nodded eagerly, wanting desperately to believe that someday they'd tell the funny story about the time adventurous little Riley gave them all a scare by sneaking off from her travel bed and exploring Grand-Nan's new neighborhood by herself. The front doorknob was set to lock automatically when closed, and Mike had confirmed he had to use his key to enter when he got home. The back door was also locked. The sliding windows in the cottage were old and could possibly have given someone a way in, but they all appeared secured now. It was plausible Riley had walked out the front door and then couldn't get back inside. But then where was she now? Certainly, someone would have stopped to check on a toddler walking down the sidewalk alone, unless, she realized, someone stopped for reasons other than Riley's safety.

The thought of it made her nauseous.

Detective Hall continued her attempts to reassure them, emphasizing how rare it was for children to be abducted by a stranger.

Marino interrupted. "That does raise the question of whether we should be looking at someone who's not a stranger. Far and away, the most common explanation when a child goes missing is some kind of custody issue."

"That's not the case here," Charlie said. "As I already explained, my wife — my first wife, Linda — died when Riley was just a baby."

"What about other family?" Marino asked. "Your siblings? Parents? Any acrimony there we should know about?"

He shook his head. "My parents have both passed. My sister lives in Brooklyn. She's great. She's the one who helped me keep it together after Linda passed. She babysits for us all the time. Kept Riley so we could take a honeymoon. We're close."

"And you think she's okay with the two of you?" Marino asked. "No chance she feels threatened?"

Charlie's eyes widened in shock. "Of course not," he said testily. "She's my sister."

From his seat in the corner, Mike spoke quietly. "They're only asking questions, Charlie, and your sister didn't even go to the wedding. I managed, didn't I?"

A silence fell over the room. Charlie walked stiffly to the kitchen, scribbled a note, and tore it abruptly from the pad. "Rachel Miller. Here's her number. She's an esthetician. She performs facials and other kinds of spa treatments in clients' homes. I know for a fact she had stacked appointments all weekend. That's why Riley came out here instead of staying with her aunt."

"And if you don't mind," Hall said, "how did Riley's mother pass away?"

Melissa was about to ask why it even mattered when Charlie explained that Linda had slipped while trying to take a selfie above a waterfall when they were on vacation in Norway. Melissa reached for Charlie's hand and gave it a reassuring squeeze. She knew this was the explanation he had given to their family and friends after he witnessed Linda's fatal plunge to the rocks below. It was during her fourth session in the grief-counseling meetings where she had first met Charlie that he shared his suspicion that the deathly fall wasn't an accident at all.

The entire reason for taking the trip without Riley was because Linda had been struggling with the adjustment to parenthood and had asked for a vacation alone with Charlie as a chance to "find themselves" again. On the last full day of their trip, they took a long hike above the cascades, one that she had requested. Despite Charlie's pleas, Linda ventured off the main trail, eager to get a better look at the water crashing against the rocks a thousand feet below. When she reached the cliff's edge, she turned around. Assuming she was positioning herself to take a selfie, Charlie cried out over the sounds of the falls for her to be careful. Melissa would never forget how haunted he sounded in therapy as he described the scene: "She gave me this look that felt like a goodbye, and then she was just . . . gone."

Charlie had no way of knowing whether Linda's death was an accident or a suicide, but he had decided it would be better for everyone, especially Riley, if he kept his suspicions to himself.

"What about Linda's family?" Marino asked. "Any in-laws?"

"She was an only child."

"No parents?"

"Her parents are still alive," he said, "but they're in their seventies. And live in Oregon."

"Have you told them Riley's missing?"

Charlie shook his head, then ran his fingers across his face. "Wow, I don't think it really sank in until I heard you say that just now. She's missing. I have a missing daughter."

"If you give us their contact information, we can make the call for you," Hall offered. "Sometimes it's easier that way. We can break the news, and they can follow up with you."

"I'm going to need to think about that. It's complicated."

"If it's complicated, that might be exactly why we need to have a word with them," Hall said.

"Trust me, if there was any chance at all they were involved, I'd fly to Oregon right now and grill them myself. I just don't want to turn their lives upside down, okay?"

The two partners exchanged a skeptical look, but it was Mike who interrupted to change the subject. "What about that weird woman who accosted my sister in the park? Melissa gave you her description and said she'd definitely recognize her again. She left the park on foot, so she probably lives nearby. Can't you find her? Melissa's also been getting all these crazy stalker comments on social media. Maybe this woman's obsessed with her and decided to follow her home."

"We're going to look into that as well," Hall said. "Ms. Eldredge, do you have a theory about why this TruthTeller person is accusing you of being hypocritical or hiding the truth?"

The pause that followed felt long, even to Melissa. When she finally spoke, she didn't have a name to offer. While Jennifer Duncan might be resentful enough to lash out at her online, there was no way she would kidnap a child. "My agent tells me it's all part of the online landscape these days," she said. "You can say the sky is blue and someone will find a reason to attack you."

"Okay," Marino said, "but do let us know if something more specific comes to mind. Maybe a disgruntled client or whatnot. The most urgent thing right now is to find Riley. We've got officers on the street organizing a search. The department's putting out the press release and social media alerts as we speak. I know you're new to the area, moving your mom and all, but we're a real tight community here on the East End. Volunteers will be scouring the neighborhood into the night if that's what it takes."

Charlie choked back a sob. "I know you need to ask questions, Detectives, but all I want to do right now is jump back into my car and start looking for my daughter. I'll cover every square inch of Long Island if I have to. Do you need anything else from us here?"

"CSI's still doing their work," Hall said, "but by all means, of course you want to get out there and look for Riley."

"I'll go, too," Mike offered. "The more eyes, the better."

When Mike stood, Melissa gave him a hug and thanked him. From the second he had found Melissa asleep without Riley, he had been fighting for them — from rousing Melissa to calling the police to pushing the detectives to locate the woman from the park. And he had referred to Riley as his niece and was now going to search for her. Inside, he was still the same boy who had always looked out for Melissa, their whole lives.

She pressed her car keys into Mike's hand, thanked him again, and said she'd ride with

Charlie. The detectives assured them that uniformed officers would remain on site in case Riley returned.

"I'm positive there are private helicopter operations out here," Melissa said. "You could call them and see if any of the pilots will volunteer to help with the search."

"Appreciate the advice, counselor." The tone of Detective Hall's voice was professional, but Melissa noticed another loaded glance between the two partners.

They were walking out the front door when Detective Marino said, almost as an afterthought, "You know, Charlie, if we do our job getting the word out, your former in-laws could even hear the news about Riley in Oregon. You sure you don't want us to contact them?"

"That's not going to bring my daughter home."

13

Marino popped a Nicorette in his mouth as soon as he landed in the passenger seat of the department-issued Impala.

"So how's that quitting thing going, Guy?" Marino's first name was Gaetano, but everyone, including his partner, Heather Hall, called him Guy.

"I'm officially an addict. A nicotine junkie. Even with this gum, I give it another three days. Five, max, before I break. I'm a weak man, Hall."

Hall knew from experience that her partner was anything but weak. She would never agree to partner with someone who was weak.

"So what'd you get from the husband before he showed up at the house?"

"Nothing that didn't line up with everything the wife said. Recently married. Super happy. All rainbows and unicorns. I did ask whether it was normal for her to nap so long in the middle of the day, and he said she'd been having problems sleeping lately. Stress or something. I pushed him hard to see if there was a glimmer of doubt there about the wife, but he didn't give up a thing. I Googled her. She's got a big career. I hinted around that maybe she wasn't so happy about suddenly being saddled with a kid to babysit."

"Sounds real subtle," Hall said.

"Hey, I'm in withdrawal. What can I say? But I may have come on a little strong, because I got the impression if the guy could've thrown a punch over the phone, he might have taken his shot. That was not an idea he seemed willing to entertain."

"Same with the wife. The way she describes it, Charlie could be teaching classes on how to be a doting single father."

"*Widower* father," Marino added. "Look, I know nothing about in-laws or parenting or having a kid, but if your kid went missing, wouldn't you tell his grandparents?"

Hall made a point of moving into the right lane once the light changed and slowing her speed. "First of all, don't ever say anything about my sunshine Milo going missing, even as a hypothetical. And second? In my case, Frank's parents would be leading the charge of the search team, but that's just our family. They don't live all the way in Oregon. And plenty of in-laws have bad blood. Like the husband said, those things can be complicated."

They didn't need to spell out the possibilities they were entertaining. A dad or a stepmom had no motive to abduct a child who was already living at home with them. If Charlie Miller or Melissa Eldredge had anything to do with Riley's disappearance, it was to remove her from the picture entirely. Hall imagined her own son, Milo, the miniature Houdini in training. Even after everything she had seen in this job, she would never understand how someone could hurt a child.

"You still think we made the right move playing it low-key with the brother?" Guy asked. "He strikes me as the black sheep of the family, a beach bum type." They had already run Michael Eldredge in the system. His record was clean, but it wouldn't pull up any complaints that might have been filed against him in the Caribbean.

"You know how Melissa Eldredge made a name for herself, don't you?"

"Like I said, I Googled her. Some wrongful conviction case, right?"

"Wrongful in whose eyes?" Hall asked. "The defendant's name was Jennifer Duncan. She was a struggling fashion model who married up — way up — to a real estate developer named Doug Hanover, who was killed by his own handgun at their carriage house in the West Village. Jennifer called nine-one-one, but then wouldn't answer any questions at the scene, acting like she was in a state of shock. The investigation found proof that Jennifer had met with two different divorce lawyers in the previous month. If the couple got divorced, she'd be left with almost nothing under their prenuptial agreement. But under the current terms of the will? She got everything. The state built the case almost entirely around motive and the physical evidence at the scene, mostly the blood spatter. The jury agreed she was the one who pulled the trigger."

"You learned all that today?" He was continually impressed by Hall's photographic memory for case details.

"Nope. I got really into true crime stories while I was on maternity leave, which is when Melissa Eldredge swept in and claimed that Jennifer was actually a battered woman. By that time, she had been in prison for three years."

"So she didn't admit to shooting her husband, but when that didn't work, she claimed self-defense?"

"It's a long story, but basically, the prosecution messed up. Jennifer's defense lawyer asked the state for any evidence that the husband had used violence in prior relationships. Well, turns out the guy's ex had called the office years ago looking for help getting a restraining order. But when the prosecution team contacted the lady, she said it was all a misunderstanding and denied the abuse. The prosecution decided not to disclose any of this to the defense, and that's how Jennifer got her conviction tossed. The irony, though, is that Melissa Eldredge was a lawyer on the prosecution's side of the case during the original trial."

"So she used her own mistake to attack the conviction later?" Marino asked.

"Exactly. She said she was a junior assistant and assumed the head honchos knew better, but the decision always bothered her. After she was in private practice, she decided to represent Jennifer. And once the woman was out of prison, they ran around together on cable news and daytime talk shows. Jennifer inherited all of her dead husband's money. Even the guy's kids got nothing. And now Melissa's practically a celebrity — which brings me back to your original question. She was already ordering us around about Amber Alerts and helicopters. How do you think she would have responded if we started asking her brother hard questions?"

"But she has to realize the family needs to be eliminated as suspects," Guy said. "It's just part of the drill. Finding the girl's got to be the top priority."

"What did the scorpion say to the frog? *It's in his nature.* That woman's a lawyer, and, in my experience, they don't like it when their own are questioned."

"So, when do we have a go at him?"

Just as they didn't need to spell out why a parent might harm a child, they did not verbalize the dark motives a man of Mike Eldredge's age might have to find a way to be alone with his sister's young stepdaughter.

Hall shrugged. "For now, we're just keeping an eye on him."

"And how are we going to manage that?"

"See the gray Volvo SUV six cars up? That's Mike Eldredge in his sister's car. You didn't notice I've been following him since he left the house?"

It wasn't the first time Marino was certain his partner was good at her job.

14

Charlie's knuckles were wrapped around the steering wheel, white from the pressure of his grip. Even in the darkness, Melissa could see the agony in his eyes and the ashen pallor of his face. She struggled to sound reassuring. "At least the detectives meant it when they said they were searching for Riley."

As soon as they had stepped from the house, they saw uniformed officers swarming the blocks around the cottage, knocking on doors with photographs of Riley. At this point, it felt as if they were simply driving along random streets while Melissa called the few nearby hospitals to see if they had heard anything new.

The screen of her phone continued to glow with each new text message from Neil and Amanda on one thread, and Katie on another. They were all offering to drive east to help with the search, but Charlie insisted that it would only create more chaos. It was a reminder that even though she, Charlie, and Riley were now a family, he still did not view her friends as part of his inner circle.

The car's Bluetooth screen showed an incoming call from his sister, Rachel. He connected immediately. "Hey. Melissa and I are in the car. Just . . . looking. The police have got people out searching everywhere. We're not even sure what to do at this point."

"There's no other trains tonight, but I can rent a car. Or get a driver. Anything you need." Melissa could tell from the hoarseness of Rachel's voice that she had been crying. "I just feel so guilty. I should have canceled my weekend appointments. That way, Riley would have been here with me during your trip."

Melissa kept her gaze fixed on the sidewalks beyond the car window, feeling the burn of judgment. This was her fault. If she had listened to Mike, if she had talked to someone about those nightmares, maybe she wouldn't have fallen into such a deep sleep.

"No one is to blame for this," Charlie said. He placed a hand on Melissa's for emphasis. "You know Riley. She wants to explore everything. She probably found her way outside and got lost. She knows not to talk to strangers. She could have even fallen asleep somewhere by now."

It was the one hopeful scenario they kept returning to.

"Okay," Rachel said, "but I'm planning to take the first train out in the morning, and I'm going to tell myself my little niece will be there to meet me and we can make breakfast together. And Melissa? Are you there?"

"Right here, Rachel."

"I know I haven't been the best sister-in-law so far . . ."

"I totally understand it's been hard. I'm sure it all felt really fast. We don't need to talk about that now."

"Okay, but I want you to know I'm glad Charlie has you in his life. And you're so good for Riley, too. I'm going to do better from now on."

Melissa swallowed a lump in her throat, praying that there would be a "from now on" — a happily ever after, with Riley back home. "As will I. We're family."

Rachel was saying goodbye when Melissa's own phone rang. It was Mike. She didn't bother with a greeting. "Did you find her?" she said, holding in her breath with anticipation.

"No, sorry. But the police found me. We need to talk."

They returned to the house to find Mike in the corner chair in the living room, his head in his hands until he startled upward when they entered. The strain and fatigue in his face had aged him, or maybe she tended to still see him in his youth, the way he seemed to see her as his little sister, Missy. But in this moment, she couldn't believe how much he had grown to resemble their father.

"Can you give us a second, Charlie?" he asked wearily.

Charlie pressed his lips together, then shook his head, placing his hands on his hips. "Sorry, man. No. This is my daughter we're talking about. I need to hear every word."

Mike nodded his acceptance. "I went back to the park, figuring people who go there in the day might take an evening stroll, too. I saw one couple with a dog, but the description of the woman who harassed you didn't ring a bell to them. I was heading for my car to leave, figuring I'd take a drive around the neighborhood, but those detectives pulled up, saying they had more questions. I asked if they had followed me. They said they were checking on the park, but it didn't make sense. I pulled out from the house before they did. They had gone there to find me, not the park."

Charlie's breathing was growing more intense, and his hands were gripped into fists. "Why would they do that, Mike? Did you do something to my daughter?" Mike flinched as if he had been slapped, and Melissa let out a shocked gasp. Anger flared from Charlie's eyes as he turned to her. "How many times have you told me how messed up he is from what happened when you were children? I knew I should have been more careful letting him around Riley."

For the first time since they had buried their father, she could see tears forming in Mike's eyes. "That's really great," he said. "Both of you." The sarcasm was not enough to cover his pain.

"Please, Mike," she pleaded, "we can talk about us and everything else later, but right now, it's about Riley. What did the police want to know?"

"What Charlie apparently wants to know, too," Mike said. "Where I was all day. So, you'll both be happy to know that after Melissa left with Riley for lunch, I walked down to the bait and tackle shop in the village to get the lay of the land on the boating situation here. A couple buying a new reel overheard me talking to the shop owner. Turns out they're serious anglers who live out here but also spend time island-hopping in the Caribbean. We stopped for a beer at the tavern and they wound up taking me all the way to Montauk to introduce me to a few outfits who might need a captain in the summer. I was excited to tell you the news, but the house was dark when I got home. Their names are Christian and Lea. Didn't get the last name, but I kept Christian's number. They must be well known to the locals, because that male detective immediately knew who I meant and called them to confirm they were with me all day and dropped me back here. You can call them, too, if you want."

"Of course that's not necessary," Melissa said.

"Oh my God," Charlie said. "I'm so sorry, Mike. I'm not thinking rationally right now."

Mike waved off Charlie's apology. "I get it. We're good, man."

"So, is that it?" Melissa asked. "They checked your alibi, and you had one. But when you called, you sounded worried."

"They didn't only ask about me." His gaze shifted to his feet. "They were asking how long the two of you had known each other, how well I knew Charlie, how well *you* knew

130

Charlie — along those lines. They only got more specific with their questions."

He swallowed, continuing to avoid eye contact with Charlie. Melissa knew in her gut that whatever he was about to say was the reason he had asked to speak to her privately. His worries had never been for himself. They were about Charlie. She needed to know. "Specific about what?"

When Mike finally spoke, he looked directly at Charlie. "About your in-laws, the ones in Oregon. They asked if I knew their names or how to get in touch with them. They wanted to know whether you keep in contact and if they ever see Riley — that sort of thing."

"That doesn't make any sense," Melissa said. "If Charlie thought for one second they were involved, why wouldn't he just have the police check on them?"

"I said the same thing. And that's when they asked if Charlie ever seemed like he'd be happier without his daughter around. It got really dark."

Charlie's face was contorted with confusion and dismay. "So, they think . . . I sent her to live with Linda's parents? If I did that, I would just tell them. I wouldn't need to stage a kidnapping."

Mike said nothing, but Melissa knew her

brother. There was something he still wasn't saying. He needed a push. "Is that what they were suggesting, Mike?"

He shook his head slowly and muttered, "It was darker than that. Like maybe they think your in-laws will say you're the kind of person who might have done something really bad to Riley. So you wouldn't have to deal with her anymore."

15

Charlie's hands were clenching and un-clenching as he watched Mike walk upstairs, leaving them alone with the shrapnel of the bomb he had dropped. Melissa hated seeing him in pain. "Please, Charlie, I don't understand why you won't tell the police how to reach Linda's parents."

"You can't possibly be entertaining the idea that I would hurt my own daughter," he snapped.

Melissa reached for Charlie's hand, and was so relieved when he returned her grasp. "Of course not, just like I assume you didn't truly doubt Mike. But like the police said, most children who go missing end up with a family member. They're putting us to the test right now, if only to eliminate us as suspects."

"And until then, they don't care about finding Riley?"

"We know they have search teams looking

for her. We saw them." She wrapped an arm around his waist.

"I'm sorry I was rough on Mike," he said. "And I dragged you into it."

"My brother and I will work it out. We always do. But he called us back to the house for a reason. The police are obviously barking up the wrong tree. Just give them the phone number and get it over with." She decided to press further. "And it's not crazy to make absolutely sure Linda's parents aren't involved given the circumstances."

"Trust me. I know them. They did not fly all the way out here and steal Riley. It's ludicrous."

"Okay, so let the police call. Whatever suspicions the police have about them or you will be put to rest, and then the investigation will move on. If anything, it gives me confidence they're doing their jobs."

Charlie slammed his palms against the coffee table. "No one is calling Linda's parents!"

"You're scaring me, sweetie. What is going on?"

He raked his fingers through his hair and shook his head. "They hate me, okay?"

Melissa knew that Charlie's former in-laws had been upset when he decided to relocate from Oregon to New York, and it was clear to her that he had not stayed in close touch with them since the move. "*Hate you? I can't imagine that's true.*"

"So, I told you part of the reason I moved out here was so my sister could help me with Riley."

She nodded.

"That wasn't the only reason. After Linda died, I found out that she had a flirtation with a coworker at her office."

"You never mentioned —"

"That's not all. Let me finish. I don't think it ever became a full-blown affair, but apparently, she and this man even talked about being together if she left our marriage. I think maybe that's why she wanted to take that vacation — to decide whether to stay with me. When I found out about this other man, that's when I replayed the entire hiking accident in my mind. Maybe Riley and I weren't enough to make her happy, but the idea of leaving us was just too much. But when Linda's parents found out she may have been considering a divorce, they jumped to a different conclusion." He held her gaze.

Her eyes widened as she realized what he was saying. "Oh, Charlie, no —"

He wiped away a tear that was forming in

the corner of one eye. "They became convinced that she was going to leave me and I somehow found out. They actually accused me of pushing her. They even hired a lawyer to try to take Riley away from me. They never filed the papers because all they had was this crazy conspiracy theory, but after that, how was I supposed to stay part of their family? I couldn't have my daughter exposed to people who think I murdered her mother."

"Of course not. But it sounds to me like they should be the number one suspects. They might have convinced themselves they were justified in taking Riley from you."

He shook his head adamantly. "I've known them for twenty years. They're the types who call lawyers, not kidnappers. If they had really wanted to, they could have kept me from moving by bogging me down in family court for years. There's no way they would take matters into their own hands. But if the police call Oregon, God knows what they may say —"

"I understand," Melissa said quietly, even though she wasn't certain that she agreed.

"I'm sorry," he said, letting go of her hand and rising to his feet. "I can't just sit here any longer. I'm going back out to search for her. Why don't you go smooth things over with Mike?"

"No, I'll come with you."

"I just need to be alone for a few minutes." He walked out the door without another word.

16

"At least eat a few bites, Melissa. You're so exhausted. It will help you. You need your strength." Mike's voice was urgent. Melissa shook her head and pushed the plate away. He had hoped the aroma of the eggs and bacon he had cooked might tempt her.

"The bacon was supposed to be for breakfast tomorrow," Melissa said tonelessly, "with blueberry pancakes, her favorite. Riley must be so hungry. She hasn't eaten for hours and hours."

Outside, they heard the clatter of helicopters flying low. "Sounds like they at least took your suggestion," Mike said. "They have volunteers across the entire East End of Long Island. Everyone's helping. You must stop torturing yourself. You didn't do anything wrong, and we need you back into full-on Melissa-always-knows-what-to-do mode. You were the one who thought to call the private helicopter services in the area."

"I haven't told Mom yet," she said. "Have you?"

"I figured that was your call to make, but I'm worried the news could put her in the grave."

She was still grieving the death of her husband, and Riley's disappearance was likely to retrigger all the trauma their mother had experienced when her own children were taken from her.

The silence felt like an agreement to wait. "You know Charlie didn't really think you'd hurt Riley, don't you?"

He avoided her gaze. "Well, you obviously gave him the impression I'm seriously messed up."

She shrugged and gave him a sad smile. "We both are, aren't we? How could we *not* be? You and I dealt with the damage differently, that's all. You were always a constant reminder to me of the danger and agony we faced as children. Given what I went through, I thought I deserved the right to leave it in the past if I wanted."

"What *you* went through? It happened to both of us."

She couldn't believe he was bringing this up now, of all times. "But I was the girl, Charlie. I was the one he put in the bathtub. Why do you think I hate going into the water so much that I can't swim even though I grew up on the Cape? I was the one he carried away with him when he tried to escape."

"Wow, you really don't know, do you? I was just as much of a victim as you were." He spoke the words slowly, waiting for their full impact to land. "Everything he was planning to do to you? I was the one he got to first. That is the reason why he left me behind to die, Melissa, and tried to leave with you."

After all these years of Mike wanting to sort through the trauma they had experienced, he had never made clear the full extent of the abuse that man had inflicted on him. Their parents, convinced that Melissa was too young to remember, had decided it was better not to rehash the details of the case with her. She began to shake uncontrollably, picturing the two of them, so small, locked in the attic. Riley . . . Was Riley somewhere terrifying like that now? With a predator like Carl Harmon?

Her darkest thoughts were broken by the sound of her cell phone. It was Katie again.

"You should get that," Mike said. He was already upstairs by the time she picked up the call.

"You answered!" The sound of Katie's

voice was an immediate comfort. "Please tell me that means Riley's home."

"No, and we're absolutely terrified. I can't stop this nagging feeling that Riley's disappearance is related to those TruthTeller posts. The police said the messages weren't threatening enough to get a warrant for the user information, but now I'm wondering whether I should tell them about my falling-out with Jennifer."

"Wait. You think TruthTeller's Jennifer Duncan? Why didn't you ever say anything?"

"Because I didn't really believe it. I still don't. I'm sure it's some random loudmouth who doesn't even know me. I think Jennifer only came to mind because I've never really gotten over how suddenly everything came to an end between the two of us. She was more than a client, and you know how much I hate losing a friend."

Though she officially never got involved in the details of Jennifer's probate case, Melissa's understanding was that the lawyers for Doug Hanover's children were arguing that, despite Jennifer's conviction being set aside, she was still the person who had killed him and was therefore barred from inheriting a dime. When Melissa initially suggested that there should be more than enough money in the estate to reach a reasonable settlement, Jennifer made it clear she wanted everything. In her view, any dollar paid to Doug's children was the same as money to their mother. "That woman knew exactly what kind of man Doug could be behind closed doors, and when I was arrested, she did nothing to help me. She even lied to the DA's office and refused to confirm that Doug abused her. And do you know why? Because she wanted me to rot in that prison for life while she and her kids took all the money. So, no settlement. I deserve what I am owed."

Even though Melissa gave her multiple referrals to esteemed estate litigators, Jennifer continued to press her to take on the case. She remembered the burn of their final conversation, when Jennifer screamed, "You built a name for yourself on my misery, and now you're throwing me away like a used tissue." Having seen firsthand Jennifer's obsession with the inheritance, combined with a rage when she did not get her way, Melissa even found herself second-guessing Jennifer's innocence. They had never spoken since.

Several months later, Melissa read in the *New York Post* that Jennifer had gotten her way. The probate court enforced the original terms of the will, giving the entire estate to

Jennifer. The estate was estimated as being worth nearly forty million dollars.

"If you don't have any proof," Katie said, "I don't think you should tell the police about that. To explain your suspicions, you'd have to break attorney-client privilege. You could get disbarred." Melissa had only told Katie about the falling-out with Jennifer with the understanding that she was seeking ethical advice from a fellow attorney. "You'd be sacrificing your entire career."

"I'd give up everything if it could lead to finding Riley . . ."

"Of course," she said, "but it's one thing for Jennifer to be angry because you wouldn't take up her estate fight. Going after your stepdaughter? There's nothing for her to gain there, and she'd end up back in prison. If you're right that she's TruthTeller — and you may well be — then the posts aren't related to Riley being missing."

Katie was right. Jennifer Duncan might despise her now, but she had no reason to kidnap her stepdaughter. "I'll keep my suspicions to myself for now," she said. "But speaking of attorney-client privilege, I need your advice on something with Charlie and the police." After getting Katie's assurances that she would not share the information with anyone, she explained Charlie's reasons for not wanting Detectives Hall and Marino to contact his former in-laws.

When Melissa was finished, Katie did not mince words. "He needs a lawyer. Now. Two hours ago, in fact."

"I am a lawyer," Melissa said.

"Sorry, but a lawyer who's objective. Not his wife."

"You're acting like you think Charlie did something wrong. And the police will think we're guilty if we start calling defense lawyers. I think he should just call her grandparents himself. They should know she's missing. And then the police can dig into us as much as they need to. There's nothing to find."

"Are you listening to yourself? You know better than that. That's how innocent people end up arrested."

"Sorry, Katie, but I can't put on my lawyer hat right now, okay? I'm in momma-bear mode here. All that matters is finding Riley."

"Of course, but can I remind you that you literally wrote an entire book showing that when police scapegoat innocent people on a hunch, it lets the actual perpetrators get away? If Charlie's former in-laws have really convinced themselves that he killed their daughter, they'll go nuclear if they find out he's remarried and now can't find Riley. And then their wild theories will become the narrative. The police will assume Riley's disappearance is related to her mother's death, and it will affect the search. And you just said that's all that matters: bringing that sweet girl home. Charlie can blame you for bringing in a lawyer. The police probably expect it, in fact."

Melissa knew that Katie was right. "Can you do it?"

"I'm enough of a lawyer for this conversation to be confidential, but you guys need someone who doesn't bake cakes for a living. What about Mac? He's the best defense lawyer we know . . . other than you. And he's your friend, so he can just tell the police he's there to help out. Because, frankly, you guys can use all the help you can get."

17

Kevin Berry winced as he nestled his head into his pillow. Next to him, his wife, Cheryl, squinted at her laptop. She placed a sympathetic hand on his chest.

"The sunburn's bad, huh?"

"My penalty for not using all that lotion you buy me." He'd run a 10K with friends in Montauk midmorning, without sunscreen. Now he was paying the price. "Will it bug you if I watch the news? Or I can go downstairs."

He knew how much work she had put into the paper she was presenting at a global health initiative conference next month. Technically, the article was due to the conference organizers tomorrow, but the conference was in Paris, where it was already tomorrow.

She held up one finger, returned her gaze to her screen, and then hit the Enter key dramatically. "And . . . sent." She reached for the remote control on the nightstand and clicked on the local news, a usual bedtime ritual for them.

A child's smiling face filled half of the television screen. She had chubby cheeks and two tiny blonde pigtails high on her head. Streaming text announced SEARCH UNDERWAY FOR MISSING SUFFOLK COUNTY THREE-YEAR-OLD. There were bullet points next to her photograph:

- Riley Miller
- 35 inches tall
- 28 pounds
- Wearing blue "Frozen" pajamas. Princess Elsa top, snowflake bottoms
- May have Peppa Pig plush toy

Cheryl's hand was over her mouth as the story ended. "That's so horrifying. Those poor parents."

"Kids wander off. It could be a false alarm. The report said they've got search teams scouring the entire East End."

"But she's only three years old. And she's been missing for several hours. How far could she have possibly gotten on her own? That does not sound good."

It was a news story no one wanted to hear, but Cheryl didn't just watch the news. She felt it, personally. It was one of the many things he adored about her. She was, without question, the most compassionate person he had ever met. He had learned over the years that she was what experts called an empath, feeling and absorbing the emotions and experiences of others. It made her a wonderful partner in life and the best friend anyone could ask for, but it also meant that she carried the weight of other people's problems as if they were her own.

"You're actually thinking about getting out of bed and joining the search team, aren't you?" he asked.

"Of course. Maybe one person can't make a difference, but if everyone plays a small part? We're all connected."

It was the way she looked at the world in general. "And assuming you could even get to Southampton tonight, how do you plan to get back?"

They were two of roughly 3,200 residents on Shelter Island, tucked between the North and South Forks of the East End of the county. In his view, there was no prettier place on earth, and it didn't have the crowds or the price tags that came with the surrounding communities. It was, however, an island of twelve square miles that could only be reached — or departed from — by ferry. And even if Cheryl caught the final ferry of the night to join the search, there certainly would be no getting home.

"Good thing I happen to be married to the ferry captain," she said with arched brows.

In addition to being the local track and field coach, Kevin had also been the captain of the South Ferry for half his lifetime. "I've told you before, it's not our personal limousine. If word gets out that I did a run for the two of us, our friends will be calling me in the middle of the night like I'm a taxi driver."

He turned off the television and lights and pulled her closer to him. The sleep deprivation from the work on her conference submission kicked in, and soon her breath grew heavy and rhythmic. His eyes were closed, but he kept seeing that photograph of Riley Miller, missing in her pajamas with nothing but a favorite stuffed animal.

Maybe Cheryl wasn't the only empath in this house.

He decided he would find a way to play his small part in the morning, if they hadn't found her yet.

18

The following morning did not feel like a new day. How could time move forward when Riley was still missing? The only way Melissa knew she may have fallen asleep for a few minutes here and there were the nightmares, this time about Riley, not her own memories. Every time her eyes jolted open, Charlie was awake, too. Now he was moving at a frantic pace — freshly showered, searching for his keys — but his face was chalky and drawn. They were both forcing themselves to put one foot in front of the other.

His sister Rachel's train was ten minutes away.

"Are you sure I can't go with you?" she asked.

"That would be fine with me. Rachel, too, in fact. But Mac said you and Mike should stay home. Look, you're also a lawyer, and the one I'm in love with and married to. So,

I'll do whatever you want . . ."

She shook her head. "No, Mac knows what he's doing." When she'd called Mac last night, he had immediately agreed to act as Charlie's lawyer. He also arranged for the police to interview both Charlie and Rachel at the police station to eliminate them as suspects and convince them to treat the case as a likely abduction by a stranger, which would trigger an Amber Alert to the surrounding area. "The interview shouldn't take long. You were literally on a plane when Riley disappeared."

"And Rachel had four client appointments in the city. I still can't believe they're treating us like we're criminals," he said with disgust.

"I know, but it's what they're trained to do. Mac will get them refocused. I told him about that weird woman at the park."

"I was up all night thinking through every horrible possibility. But that nutty woman in the park is the kind of thing that comes with the territory of having a high profile these days. You said she left on foot, right? And then you and Riley left the park in another direction. How could she have followed you?"

"She may have been watching us earlier and already knew we'd be coming back

151

here." She immediately saw the problem with her theory. "But then why would she draw attention to herself at the park? And why would she target Riley?" She couldn't shake the feeling that the bizarre incident had to be related somehow, but she couldn't connect the dots.

"She was probably just a weirdo who recognized you from social media."

"That's what the police obviously think, too. Maybe Mac can at least get them to look into it. Speaking of which, you better go," she said, tapping her watch. She adjusted the collar of his shirt and gave him a quick kiss. "I'll set the sofa bed up in the den for Rachel. I'm really glad she's going to be here, by the way."

"Like you said about Mike, family's family. For what it's worth, Rachel told me last night she's sorry she didn't come to the wedding."

"None of that matters now. Only Riley."

"Are you going to be okay talking to your mother? Do you want me to wait here with you?"

She and Mike had decided that morning that Riley had been missing too long to keep their mother in the dark any longer. As traumatic as the news would be for her, it would be worse if she learned the truth from a news story instead of her family.

She shook her head. "This is going to dig up old memories. Mike and I should be the ones to tell her."

They used Mike's phone in case Melissa got a call about Riley. Their mother's voice was bright and cheerful. "The first person I hear from on a Monday morning is my handsome son. This bodes well for the week."

"Hey, Mom," Mike said warmly. "I've got you on speaker with Melissa."

"Oh, even better," she said. "Do you two still approve of the cottage? It's smaller than the house, I know, but there's still room for all of us — for now, at least. If necessary, the former owner assured me the property is approved for a small guest house in the back."

Mike's brow furrowed as he looked to Melissa to break the news.

"The cottage is great," Melissa said, "but there's something I need to tell you. Riley is missing. She and I both went down for a nap yesterday, and when I woke up, she was gone."

Even over the phone, Melissa could hear the air leave her mother's lungs.

"The police are searching for her," Melissa added.

"No, please. This can't be true."

Oh, how Melissa wished it were not.

Later, in the kitchen, Melissa could feel Mike watching her as she began to pick at a breakfast sandwich he had made for her using last night's eggs and bacon and other items he had pulled from the refrigerator.

"You really think Mom was okay?" she asked.

Once their mother realized that Riley truly was missing, there was no wallowing or talking about the past. She had a list of suggestions ready to go: flyers, search teams, contacting all the local schools and fire stations.

"Yeah. She's a lot tougher than we give her credit for. The way she said she was looking up flight times on her computer while promising to get on the next plane reminded me of you. Totally TCB."

Taking care of business, something Melissa always prided herself on. She took an eager bite of the sandwich she had expected only to nibble at. "This is really good." In addition to eggs, bacon, and cheese, he had thrown together some kind of sauce that pulled it all together.

"Amazing what you can learn to cook when you live on a boat half the time."

"Thank you again for trying to take care of me," she said.

"I'm glad you're eating. You really scared me yesterday. I thought you were unconscious. I've never seen you that way. It's like you were in a coma. Was that from the nightmares?"

There was no reason for her to deny the truth to him any longer. "I don't think so. They've been going on for a while now, but it's usually just insomnia."

"Which is basically the opposite of what you had yesterday. I tried everything, but I could not get you alert. I wanted to fill an IV with coffee."

As if she were watching herself in a movie, she pictured herself in the cottage guest room, heavy and vague. "My coffee," she suddenly muttered. "From Starbucks. I ordered a large iced coffee. I drank all of it." She had been sipping it, checking her phone, when she noticed the woman talking to Riley on the playground. She heard that woman's vile words in her ear: *Is that why you were on your phone, drinking your coffee and ignoring her?*

She grabbed her car keys from the kitchen counter and rushed outside. Mike followed, desperate to know where she was going. She pulled open the driver's side door of her car and leaned inside, running her left hand frantically beneath the car seats.

"What is going on?" Mike pleaded.

"My cup. There should be a plastic coffee cup here, with a straw and a lid. I'm sure of it. That woman. We have to find it. You drove my car last night. Did you throw it out?"

"No, I didn't see any kind of cup."

She imagined Riley's sweet voice as she tried to rush her away from the stranger in the park. *You forgot your coffee, Missa. I'll get it!* Melissa had picked up what remained of her coffee. She was certain of it. They went to the car, then drove straight home. Had they passed a trash can on their way to the car? She didn't think so, but couldn't be sure. She ran to the kitchen and began to toss trash onto the floor from the bin beneath the sink. "Did we take out the garbage? I can't remember. We have to find it. My cup. It's important."

"It definitely wasn't in your car when I drove it. I put my cell phone in the cup holder. There was nothing there."

"Are you sure you didn't throw it away?"

"Positive. I went directly to the park to look for Riley. The police stopped me and asked all those questions. I came right back without stopping."

"Oh my God." Why hadn't she realized it earlier? "It was that woman in the park. It's the only explanation. And how could Riley just disappear, and I'm still asleep? I would never sleep through something like that. It's the only explanation."

"You're losing me, Melissa. What are you talking about?"

"Someone planned this. That woman from the park. Somehow she drugged my coffee, and when I passed out, she came here and took Riley. If I can find the cup, they could check the lid for fingerprints."

She pulled her cell phone from her back packet and called Charlie. When it went straight to voicemail, she tried Mac, only to hear his outgoing message as well. She got the same result when she tried the cell phone numbers that Detectives Marino and Hall had scrawled on their business cards. She left a message for Detective Hall asking that she contact her as soon as possible, and then sent a text message to both Charlie and Mac about her theory.

She headed toward the front door again, her car keys still in hand.

"Where are you going?" Mike asked.

"To the park to find that woman. I'll knock on every door in the neighborhood if

I have to."

He had his shoes on before she reached the door.

19

From the sofa in the living room of their Upper East Side apartment, Neil Keeney pecked away at a text message. *Checking in again. Any news? Let us know how we can help. Amanda sends love too.*

He hit the Send button. He could not imagine what Melissa and Charlie were going through.

"Oh, there's Riley," Amanda called out from the kitchen, setting down the knife she was using to chop an onion. "Turn on the volume."

He reached for the remote control on the coffee table and unmuted the television. They had been monitoring NY1 for updates.

On the left side of the screen was a now-familiar photograph of Riley, smiling up at the camera, as the anchor somberly recited the disturbing facts, a missing toddler who had not been seen for more than twenty-four hours. The screen cut to a montage of footage of people wandering in groups, scouring the East End of the South Fork, as the anchor reported, "The search for little Riley Miller has become a united effort across all of Suffolk County. Here, you can see even residents of Shelter Island searching the Mashomack Preserve, all in an increasingly desperate hope of reaching a happy ending to this terrifying story."

When the coverage shifted to a spree of robberies in Brooklyn, Neil hit the Mute button on the remote control again. "Nancy's cottage is in Southhampton. I'm no expert on Long Island, but isn't Shelter Island quite a distance from there? I think it's literally a separate island."

"We were there once, remember? That dinner when your brother was dating . . . oh, what was her name? The publicist. The night ran late and we had to rush to make the last ferry. It's probably an hour away from Nancy's new place."

Her cell phone buzzed on the counter next to the chopping board. She answered right away, using what Neil called her "work voice." He joked that when she was in police officer mode, he felt like he was in grade school, waiting for his turn in the confessional.

He listened as she nodded and muttered words like *okay* and *I see* until he suddenly heard his own name. "Yes, I am aware of that. In fact, when they were missing, my husband, Neil, recognized the perpetrator's picture on television. It ultimately led the police to the house where they were being held. That's his original connection to the Eldredge family."

She extended the phone in his direction. "Detective Hall from Long Island. They're asking about what happened to Mike and Melissa when they were kids."

He changed the audio to speaker mode so Amanda could listen in. Neil knew the facts cold, of course. In addition to his personal connection, he'd written a paper about the case during graduate school, focusing on the ways Nancy Eldredge's first husband had slowly but certainly eroded her self-confidence to the point that she became completely dependent upon him. For his research, he had reached out to Lendon Miles, the psychiatrist whose unorthodox treatment of Nancy had enabled her to recall details of her first marriage that she had suppressed due to the trauma she had experienced in that relationship. The two men had remained in touch as friends and colleagues until his passing five years ago at the age of eighty-nine.

Neil was so familiar with the facts of Carl Harmon's case that he had been answering all of Detective Hall's questions with clinical expertise, until her curiosity suddenly took a personal turn. "And as a trained psychiatrist," Detective Hall asked, "how would you say Melissa and Mike have coped given the trauma they experienced?"

He wondered now why any of this ancient history was relevant to Riley's disappearance. "Better than anyone could have possibly expected under the circumstances," he replied. It was an honest answer.

"But is it fair to say the tolls of that kind of victimization linger in the psyche?" Detective Hall asked.

He looked to Amanda, searching for some kind of guidance, but she simply shook her head. She clearly didn't expect this avenue of questioning either. "Neither Mike nor Melissa has ever been a patient, so it really wouldn't be fair to speculate. What I can say is that I've watched them both with Riley. Melissa gives a hundred percent of herself to anything that matters to her, but I've never seen her as committed as she is to that little girl. And Mike is the perfect uncle. If there's something specific I can help you with —"

"We're just making sure we have the lay of the land, Dr. Keeney. Thank you for your time."

When the call ended, he passed Amanda's phone to her over the kitchen island. "Why are they asking about Carl Harmon?"

"I have no idea," she said. "At first, I thought it was a courtesy call since I've been reaching out to every cop I know in Suffolk County. But they did tell me that Melissa and Charlie hired a defense attorney, her friend Grant Macintosh — the one who's been helping with her podcast. I don't think they realize how bad that looks from the perspective of the police."

"But now the detectives are wasting precious time asking questions about a nightmare from forty years ago. Is there some way to explain that Melissa truly believes that an outside lawyer can actually help the police do their jobs better? That's been the point of her entire career."

Amanda stepped around the island, pressed her forehead against his, and gave him a kiss. "I love you for thinking that could work."

"I guess I sound naive, huh? Spell it out from their perspective."

"Honestly? If you gave me the raw facts and I didn't know the parties involved, my gut would tell me someone in the family knows more than they're saying."

"But we do know the people involved," he said. "Maybe not Charlie, but it's clear he adores his daughter, and you said yesterday the police already confirmed he was on a plane when Riley went missing."

She returned to the business of chopping the onion, even though it was already thoroughly minced.

"You can't possibly mean Mike and Melissa. I've known them as long as I can remember."

She set aside the knife, and he could tell that she was choosing her words carefully. "You haven't been close to Mike since he moved to the Caribbean. You told me yourself you thought he distanced himself from others because of what happened to him as a child. And how many times have you said you worry Melissa puts too much pressure on herself to be perfect to prove that she wasn't damaged by whatever abuse she suffered?"

"That doesn't make either of them bad people."

"Neil, you're a psychiatrist, and I'm a cop. We both know that the people who do bad things often had something bad done to them. It's a vicious cycle."

If someone else had even suggested the possibility, he would be furious, but this was Amanda. "Did that detective tell you something? Do they have evidence?"

She shook her head. "It was nothing specific. But I can tell Hall is good at her job, and she knows I've been pulling every last string I can find to make sure they look for Riley. She said something vague about not letting my professional reputation get tied up in a personal friend's problems. And when she found out you were a psychiatrist and their childhood friend, she suggested the same for you."

"This is crazy. We're talking about one of our closest friends."

"Every single person getting arrested tonight is someone's childhood friend. That detective was telling me in no uncertain terms, Neil — there's another side to this story."

20

Melissa was listening once again to the fourth ring of yet another unanswered phone call to Charlie's phone. *Hi. You've reached . . .*

She hung up, knowing already that the voicemail box was full. Why were the messages not being checked?

She and Mike had no luck finding the woman from the park, but Melissa had a theory about her identity. Only Charlie had the information she needed to know if she was on the right track.

Desperate, she sent another text, her fingers trembling as she tapped at the screen. *Please call me back. I'm scared something has happened to you and Rachel now, too. What is going on?*

Her gaze moved to the muted television on the console table at the edge of the living room. So far, the local news had covered a drug bust in Riverhead and had now cut to footage of a fire at an apartment complex in Islip. According to the text at the bottom of the screen, all residents had been evacuated and two were being treated for smoke inhalation. Had they forgotten about Riley already?

She was trying to call Charlie and Mac again when a knock at the front door startled her so badly that she let out a sudden scream, piercing the silence of the empty cottage. She took a deep breath and settled her worn nerves, assuring herself it had to be Mike returning from JFK airport with their mother, until she realized they weren't due for another hour.

Charlie! It had to be him, after all of the unreturned phone calls.

She ran to the door, expecting to find him on the porch. Maybe he had lost his phone. Or the battery had died. He'd have an explanation. Of course he would. The alternatives were all unimaginable. By the time she reached for the doorknob, she was already berating herself for letting her imagination get the best of her. As she unbolted the lock, she even believed that Riley would be standing beside him, holding her daddy's hand. The police had found her. That explained why no one was answering their phones. They'd both be smiling, eager to fill her in on all the details.

This nightmare would finally be over, and they could all drive back to the city together — the three of them, going home as a family.

Her heart fell as she flung the door open. It was Detectives Hall and Marino.

She squinted against the glare of the pink-white sky preparing for sunset over the bay view in the distance, hoping they didn't perceive her expression as a glare. "Detectives, did you get my messages? I've been trying to reach you." The coffee cup. It would prove she was drugged.

"May we come in?" Hall asked. "There's a matter we'd like to discuss."

Of course there was. From the early minutes of this investigation, all these detectives wanted to do was talk . . . even though she and Charlie had already told him everything they knew. "I've been trying to call you all day. Do you know where Charlie and his sister are? I'm worried about them."

"When we saw them last, they were with his lawyer, Grant Macintosh," Marino said.

"I know how that must look," she offered, "but we felt like we needed help. We're all so exhausted, and Grant's an old friend from my days at the prosecutor's office." She wanted to explain it was all because of

168

Charlie's former in-laws, but she had no way of knowing how much Charlie and Mac had told them about the situation.

"We," Marino said. "You said *we* needed help, but as we understand it, Grant Macintosh represents your husband, Ms. Eldredge, not you. And we're here to talk to you, not Mr. Miller."

Her whole life, Melissa prided herself on her skill with words, but now she just wanted to scream. In her mind, she heard herself yelling, *Stop all this talking and find Riley!,* but instead, she looked away from the detectives to steel her patience. The sight of Riley's grin in the corner of the television screen suddenly became the only thing in the world that mattered. She leapt toward the remote control on the end table and unmuted the volume. How much of the coverage had she missed?

". . . where the three-year-old was last seen. But tonight News 12 has learned that the missing girl's father was remarried only last month, and, in an unexpected twist, his new bride — the missing girl's stepmother — was also abducted as a toddler in what was then a headline-grabbing national news story." Melissa felt a wave of panic wash over her as another photograph appeared on the screen. She recognized his face immediately. She'd seen the picture before. It was that man — that sick, disgusting man — walking out of a California courtroom forty-seven years earlier while her mother stood trial for the murder of her children, Peter and Lisa. Before Melissa was even born. Before the man in the photo resurfaced on the Cape, a little heavier, older, and balder, and living under a different name. Before he found their family. Before . . .

Words across the bottom of the screen blared, STEPMOTHER MELISSA ELDREDGE KIDNAPPED BY CARL HARMON 40 YEARS AGO. Her legs nearly gave out at the sight of her name next to the one she refused to ever speak aloud. Her stomach began to roil with a seasick feeling.

When she turned to look at Detective Marino again, he was facing the television, hands on hips. "That's what we're here to talk to you about. That's what we cops call a bit of a coincidence."

21

Melissa's legs felt rubbery and weak, as if she were struggling to balance on a boat crashing over rocky waves. A day and a half had passed with Riley gone and no hope of finding her, and now the police were wasting time asking about Carl Harmon.

She steadied herself by placing her hands on the back of the sofa. "My mother's first husband murdered their two children — Peter and Lisa. He was presumed dead, but when she started a new life in the Cape, he followed her there, abducted us, and tried to kill us, too. It was beyond horrific, but has nothing to do with Riley. The man who came after Mike and me died after he fell from an attic balcony into rock-filled surf. He was barely alive when they pulled him from the water. He confessed to everything before he died, but he definitely didn't survive, so he can't be involved in this. You can call the Adams Port Police to confirm."

Detective Hall was nodding sympatheti-cally. "That's a lot to go through as a three-year-old girl."

"Sometimes it's hard to believe it really happened."

Marino's back was to her as he browsed with new interest the handful of family photographs Melissa had placed on the fireplace mantel. "With your podcast and memoir, it's surprising that you haven't made more of the fact that you were a crime victim yourself as a child."

"My podcast is about unsolved cases or other injustices. My abduction was solved, and the perpetrator met his justice. And my book's not that kind of memoir. To be hon-est, I prefer not to talk about that incident at all. What does any of this have to do with Riley?"

"Just making sure we're not missing anything," Hall said. "It does seem very coincidental that you were kidnapped as a child, and now your stepdaughter has vanished at the same age, under similar circumstances."

"Did you get my messages about the woman at the park? I had an iced coffee near the playground. She must have drugged me. It's the only explanation for why I would be that tired. Mike and I spent all day combing the neighborhood. Maybe I could sit down with a sketch artist. There was another woman at the park who saw us talking. If we could find her, she could help, too."

"You wouldn't have noticed a woman slipping drugs into your coffee?" Marino asked skeptically.

"I left the cup on the bench when I saw her talking to Riley."

"You said you two exchanged words at that point, and then she walked away in the opposite direction," Marino said. "So, again, how'd she manage to sneak a drug into your cup?"

"She must have had someone help her while she distracted me. There's a wooded area right behind that bench." She was connecting the dots as quickly as she could speak. "Someone could have stepped from behind a tree and been gone in an instant."

"So now you're talking about a conspiracy of at least two people," Hall said. "You're a lawyer with a successful true crime podcast. Does it make sense that two people would kidnap innocent Riley, just to punish you for some unspecified wrong?"

No, it didn't. That was how Katie talked her out of her suspicion that Jennifer Duncan might be involved. "That's why I've been calling you," Melissa said. "Whenever I mentioned the woman in the park, we all thought I was the actual target of the malice, and taking Riley was the kidnapper's way of hurting me. But what if it's really about the woman in the park wanting Riley? She knew she could rattle me with those comments, either because she saw the TruthTeller posts, or wrote them herself. She drugged me so I'd blame myself for Riley's disappearance — and perhaps so you'd be here asking me all these irrelevant questions instead of looking for her."

"You're saying *she* and *her* as if you know who the woman at the park actually is," Hall said.

"I think I do, but Charlie needs to hear it from me first. It's important. And then he'll have the information we need to know if I'm right." The words were tumbling out so quickly that she tripped over some of them, causing a slurring effect.

"Well, Charlie's not here," Hall said. "If you think you know who has your stepdaughter, you need to tell us. Don't you care about finding Riley?"

Finding Riley was the *only* thing she cared about right now. "You think whatever happened to Riley has something to do with my family. But it's about *Riley's* family, which isn't just me and Charlie. You know that Riley's mother died by falling over a ledge into a waterfall, right? I've been trying to replay every conversation Charlie and I had about Linda's death. They were always brief. He was still so traumatized that I didn't press him for details, but I'm kicking myself now. I can't remember him ever talking about transporting her body back to the Pacific Northwest, or even spreading her ashes. Do you know how many people commit suicide by jumping from Niagara Falls? The water is so powerful, the remains are often never found. I need to speak to Charlie. Based on everything he told me, I think it's possible they never recovered Linda's body. She could still be alive."

They said nothing. She recognized the glance between Hall and Marino as another silent communication in their secret language, the equivalent of a shared eye roll. She couldn't stand it any longer.

"I am building your entire case for you, and you're treating me like I'm either crazy, stupid, or both," she said. "You want to know about that horrible experience I suffered as a child? An entire police force on the West Coast allowed Carl Harmon to frame my mother for killing her children, and my brother and I were abducted and abused as a consequence. You need to listen to what I'm saying. Charlie told me Linda was overwhelmed by motherhood. She may have been suffering from severe postpartum depression. She was the one who asked to go to Norway. She wanted to hike to the highest waterfall in the region. She could have faked her own death. Maybe she regrets it now and came back for Riley. Or she found out he got remarried. That might have set her off."

Detective Hall tried to wrap a calming arm around her shoulder, but Melissa flinched at her touch. "We're on your side, Melissa. You think Charlie's first wife faked her death only to reappear in a new place to abduct Riley? Meanwhile, your mother's first husband faked his death and then kidnapped you and Mike. See what we meant about too many coincidences? Think about it. How could Linda have possibly known when she plunged from that cliff that she'd survive the fall? And what are the odds that Charlie just happens to marry a woman who was abducted by a man who also faked his death? Coincidences stacked upon more coincidences."

She pressed her eyes closed. "Can you please just help me get hold of my husband?"

Her cell phone rang in her pocket. *Finally,* she thought. Charlie would have some explanation for not calling her all day, and she could ask him these questions herself. But when she glanced down at the screen, it wasn't her husband's name she saw. It was Patrick. At least she had changed his screen name from Future Husband after he had inexplicably dialed her number last month. She declined the call.

"Not Charlie?" Hall asked.

She shook her head, hoping they wouldn't ask a follow-up question. They obviously thought the worst of her. An incoming phone call from her ex-fiancé would not help matters. "If we talk to Charlie, he can tell us if Linda's body was ever located. Doesn't that seem important?"

She could tell from their expressions that they thought she was fabricating a fantastical theory to detract their attention from her. She wondered if they might leave without telling her anything else until Hall spoke up. "Were you having nightmares about Carl Harmon?" Hall asked pointedly. It was the kind of question a detective would ask only if she already knew the answer. "Our understanding is that people close to you thought you should go back to counseling but you refused. That kind of bottled-up emotional pressure can explode. We also heard you never planned to have children until you met Charlie."

"That's not true that I didn't want children. Who would say that, and why does it even matter?"

"You married Riley's father," Hall said, "but didn't adopt his little girl."

"I wanted to. I even called lawyers to set it up, but Charlie and I agreed to wait a year or two since we got married so quickly."

"Maybe *too* quickly," Hall said. "Maybe it was all a little too much. Everyone knows you wouldn't hurt that sweet child on purpose. People snap. We've seen it before. The regret can be impossible to live with."

"Tell us where we can find her body," Marino said firmly. "Charlie at least deserves closure, Melissa."

"Wait. You think . . . you think I *killed* Riley?" She was living inside a nightmare far worse than the ones she'd been having about Carl Harmon. Anxiety and agitation were causing her breaths to become harsh and labored. "No, I didn't *snap.* That's what happened to Linda. Don't you see? She abandoned Riley and must be the one who has her now. We just need to talk to Charlie. And we need a picture of her to see if she's the woman from the park." Her desperate pleas only made her sound more delusional.

"How long have you been researching the Evan Moore case?" Marino asked.

The name of the missing child from her latest podcast series felt like a jolt to the base of her spine. What did a child kidnapped eight years ago in Seattle, Washington, have to do with Riley? "I don't know. Six months, I guess. Why are you asking me this?"

"Because it's one more layer of coincidence," Hall said. At this point, it was clear they were trying to keep her off-balance. "The primary suspect in Evan's disappearance remains his stepmother. Some of her friends reported that even though she was madly in love with Evan's father, she never wanted to have children, and it turned out to be a lot more work than she ever imagined. Without Evan in the picture, she thought she could have her happily ever after, just her and her husband. Is there a specific reason you were interested in that case?"

"Because that poor boy's been missing for years, and that woman almost certainly killed him and got away with it."

Hall nodded. "She told the police she took a nap after going to the grocery and the gym. Problem is, her cell phone pinged to a tower on Camano Island, an hour north of the city. I believe your friend Mac even mentioned on your podcast that if she'd simply left her phone at home, she may never have been a suspect."

"You think I was somehow inspired by that case to harm Riley? You're twisting everything around. I knew about that case from one of my friends. Her name is Laurie Moran. She produces a true crime series called *Under Suspicion.* You've probably heard of it. Her husband is a federal judge named Alex Buckley. That's how Laurie and I first met, after she began dating Alex when he was still a defense lawyer. Laurie was going to cover the case but the stepmother refused to appear on-screen, which is the entire point of the show. When she found out I was starting my podcast, she suggested the case to me."

"And now Riley is missing, just like Evan."

"Except she's been missing a day, not eight years. And I don't know how to convince you, but you're wasting precious time here."

She could feel her blood pulsing hot through the veins of her neck as they asked her once again for yesterday's timeline — lunch at the Sip 'N Soda, a pit stop at Starbucks, the playground at the park, and then back to the cottage.

"No other stops?" Marino asked. "No sightseeing?"

She knew this tactic. They were locking her into a definitive account of her whereabouts. What she didn't know was why they were doing it. "You obviously don't believe me. Are you going to tell me why?"

Hall pulled a cell phone from her back pocket but didn't use it yet. "We got a call this morning from the captain of the Shelter Island ferry. You ever been to Shelter Island?"

"No. I've only been to the Hamptons a handful of times. I'm not even entirely sure where that is."

"Well, this footage would suggest otherwise." Hall held up the screen of her phone. It displayed a black-and-white video of cars slowly driving from a concrete road onto some kind of dock. "And right . . . here." Hall paused the video and zoomed in. "See this? That's a Volvo XC60, gray. Just like yours. And see this?" More zoom. "It's grainy but you can make out the basic shapes of the plate numbers. Looks a lot like that could be ATN9050, right? That's your plate."

"I didn't go to Shelter Island."

181

"Wait, there's more." Hall used her fingertips to focus on another spot on the paused image. The photo quality was bad, but the driver behind the wheel of the SUV appeared to be a woman. Her hair was light and curly, like Melissa's. "See her sunglasses?" Hall walked to the kitchen island and rotated Melissa's sunglasses to face the living room. "I noticed them when we were here yesterday. Nice. Chanel, I see."

"This is crazy. She may be wearing sunglasses, I grant you that, but there's no way to know that they're the same as mine. And I know that is not me in the video, and I know I did not hurt Riley — let alone kill her, which is just unspeakable. I was right here in the house. You heard what my brother said: I was in such a deep sleep he thought I was in a coma. And we need to have faith Riley's still alive if there's any chance of finding her."

Any hope she had that the police would be convinced was dashed when Detective Hall tapped her phone once again to play the video, this time without zooming in on the car's driver. "And . . . here we go." She hit Pause again. Melissa felt her stomach lurch as she stared at the phone screen. The woman was not alone in the SUV. She could make out the appearance of a child on the

182

rear passenger side of the vehicle, the same side she used for Riley's car seat. Despite the graininess of the photo, her memory filled in the missing pixels with punky pigtails and cherubic cheeks.

"Oh my God, that's Riley," she said. There was no question in her mind. It was the first time since this nightmare began that she thought they might actually find her. "That's exactly how she sits in her car seat. She sings to herself, making up songs based on what she sees outside the car window." She felt so close to Riley now, like she could reach out and touch her. Melissa could almost hear her stepdaughter's voice over her right shoulder in the car, making up nonsensical lyrics to pass the time. Her heart hurt thinking about it. How, how, how could they possibly believe Melissa would hurt that sweet child?

"Okay," Hall said, "so we agree that Riley's in the back seat of this car as it boards the ferry to Shelter Island, even though you insist that you were here at the cottage." Hall tapped her phone a series of times and then held it up again for Melissa. "Now this would appear to be the same Volvo on the return trip to the South Fork, forty minutes later."

Melissa could see it was a Volvo SUV.

Same horrible video quality. Same driver who might or might not have strawberry blonde curly hair and sunglasses like hers. Detective Hall hit Pause again, then used her thumb and index finger to zoom.

The car seat was empty. The child who looked just like Riley, making up her funny little songs, was gone.

22

Melissa wiped away the tears forming in her eyes. "That's not me. I swear on my life." The sound of her own voice felt distant, as if shock and fear were somehow clogging her ears. She needed the police to believe her, and she needed to find Charlie. "The video's not even clear enough to make out the license plate. That woman could be anyone with somewhat curly hair and sunglasses — on a sunny day, by the way."

"And yet with one look at the little girl in the car seat, you immediately said it was Riley," Hall replied. "Funny how that is, right? If you really know someone's essence, you can recognize them, even in the blurriest photos."

"Well, you don't know my *essence*. I do, and that woman driving the car isn't me."

"Don't assume we're the only ones who have seen these videos," Hall said flatly.

She placed a hand on her stomach as the

sting of Hall's words landed. Charlie. They had to be talking about Charlie. That was why he wasn't answering her calls.

"Search teams are spread out across Shelter Island right now," Marino said. "Searching the Peconic and the bays will take a lot longer. Do you know what a body looks like after decomposing in water? And they're talking about a summer storm sweeping over the Northeast tonight. The reports have spoken of gale warnings and heavy rains. If it gets bad out here, we may have to call off the search until the weather passes. You could help yourself out if you tell us where we can find her. By all accounts, you would only do this if you had a serious psychotic break. You're a lawyer. You know what that means in the state of New York. You'll be looking at manslaughter at the very most, maybe all the way down to second degree. You could even get an insanity defense."

"Except I'm not having a psychotic break," she shouted. "It has to be that woman from the park. She knew I'd be wiped out from whatever she put in my coffee. You need to test me right now, while the drug is still in my system."

"You told us yourself you were certain that the cottage doors were locked when you were here with Riley."

"I also told you I'm not entirely sure about the windows. We never had any reason to check them. And if I was the one to do this, why would I have locked the front door? I would have made it seem like anyone could have walked right in. Please, I am begging you, just ask Charlie if he's a hundred percent certain that Linda actually died in Norway. My gut's telling me they never found her body."

"You're not in a position to run our investigation," Marino said.

The phone in her hand pinged with new activity. On her screen, she saw an alert for a voicemail message from Patrick Higgins, followed by his text message: *I just saw the news. Please call me.*

She wondered if Marino had seen the name on the screen. She also wondered if they would know Patrick's prior role in her life. Unless she could find a way to convince them she was innocent, she had to assume they would search every message on her phone before long. She tapped a quick reply to Patrick. *I assume you're trying to help, but please stop calling. We haven't spoken for nearly two years.*

Her phone rang again with another call

from him almost immediately after she hit Send.

"You certain you don't need to get that?" Marino asked. "It seems like someone's eager to talk to you."

"It's that news report, I'm sure," she said, rejecting the call again. "Friends are obviously worried. I'm only leaving my phone on in case Charlie calls."

She pecked away furiously at her screen. *I need you to stop. Really.*

Another message appeared simultaneously. *Call me. It's important.*

She could feel Marino's eyes on her, increasingly curious about the current text exchange on her phone. She started to shut it down, but could not risk missing a call from Charlie. Instead, she tapped the photo above the name *Patrick* on her screen — tan and smiling beneath the brim of a Cornell University baseball cap on their one trip to visit Mike in St. Maarten. She hit the Block button and then tucked the phone into her back pocket. "Look, I can't find that coffee cup anywhere. I'm assuming whoever took my car disguised as me also got rid of the cup. But whatever they drugged me with is almost certainly still in my system. You need to give me a blood test, before it's too late."

"Again, you're not calling the shots here," Marino said. "And we have no authority to drug test you."

"You don't need authority if I'm volunteering. And your refusal to do the very easy things I'm suggesting will be proof I can use down the road to show that you were never really interested in finding out the truth. I'll argue that you were blinded by your bias against me because of the nature of my professional work."

"Okay, so are you done with your rant?" Marino asked.

"It's not a rant, just a statement of facts. One final thing: if you don't test me, I'll drive down to emergency care and get it done myself."

Marino's lips moved into a slight smirk. "Speaking of driving," he said, "where's your Volvo? We didn't see it outside."

"My brother's picking our mother up from JFK. They should be here any second."

She saw them exchange another look. Hall gave a slight nod, and Marino pulled a folded document from his back pocket and extended it to Melissa.

"That's a search warrant for your car. And if you'll sign a consent form, I'll get a tech in here now to get that drug test from you."

By the time Melissa heard the familiar

sound of her car pulling into the driveway, a tow truck was parked at the curb in front of the cottage, and a Suffolk County police officer trained as a phlebotomist was drawing blood from her right arm. As soon as the test was done, she ran to the front door. Her mother and brother were on the front porch. She heard the rumble of thunder in the distance.

Please, she thought, *please do not let the storm hit out here.* She had been checking the weather reports between phone calls to Charlie and Mac. The heaviest rain and wind gusts were supposed to be through New York City and then moving north, but Long Island wasn't completely out of the danger zone. Right now, helicopters, small seaplanes, and ground search parties were still at work, but if gale warnings were issued for the area, the air search would be called off, and the volunteers on the ground would seek shelter. She couldn't bear the thought of Riley out there on her own during a storm.

"What's going on here?" her mother asked, spotting the gloved police officer at Melissa's side.

Melissa could hardly believe the words as they escaped from her mouth. "Mom, they think I killed Riley."

23

Melissa wasn't sure if her mother had been holding her for five seconds or five minutes. In recent years, Melissa had noticed how much smaller her mother had gotten with age, but at this moment, Nancy Eldredge felt as solid as an oak tree.

Only yesterday morning, she was excited with the anticipation of welcoming her mother to her new house, proud that she and Mike had worked together to make the cottage feel like home. She allowed herself to be wrapped in the security of her mother's embrace, knowing that when she let go, she would have to return to the awful truth.

She finally brought herself back to reality when the police officer who had drawn her blood coughed to get her attention. He had packed up his kit and needed to walk past them to leave the cottage.

Through the front window, she watched her SUV being pulled away by a tow truck.

She knew from the warrant they had served upon her that her car would be impounded at the police station for a complete forensic search. Her thoughts flashed to the list of items specified in the search warrant: latent fingerprint evidence, hair, blood — including inside the trunk. The thought of it was horrifying.

"How in the world could those people possibly suspect you of harming Riley?" Her mother's usually gentle voice sparked with anger.

Mike's brow furrowed as he looked at their mother with grave concern.

"I'm sorry I upset you, Mom," Melissa said. "I shouldn't have been so dramatic. I'm sure I'm not really a suspect. The police are just being thorough, checking all the boxes."

Mike was already in the kitchen, heating a kettle on the stove, reaching in the cupboard for the herbal tea that had been part of their grocery run only forty-eight hours earlier. "Melissa's right," he said. "Those detectives practically did a stakeout on me last night until they realized I was looking at boat outfits all afternoon with two locals." He tried to deflect their mother's worry with a light chuckle, but the attempt at levity fell flat.

"The two of you are treating me like some kind of geriatric invalid, and, frankly, it's insulting. I will never forgive myself for leaving you alone in the yard that day, even for a few minutes, and I know all too well the harm you suffered as a result. But I think you forget what I went through. Do you know that I dove into the ice-cold lake, frantically grasping for you beneath the water? When I couldn't find you, I was convinced you had drowned and I would never find you. Your father found me on the freezing sand, my sopping clothes clinging to me. I was clutching your little red glove to my cheek, Melissa. At first, the police were supportive. Sympathetic. Even compassionate. But once they learned my true identity — that I was the notorious Nancy Harmon — everything changed. They were convinced that when I found out my secret was going to be exposed, I had a psychotic break and did the same thing to the two of you that I supposedly did to Peter and Lisa."

Psychotic break, the same term Marino had used.

Melissa had never heard her mother speak so candidly about what she experienced when they were abducted. "I'm so sorry," she said. "We both know this must be terribly traumatic for you."

"Stop it!" her mother snapped. "You're such a bright woman, Melissa. The teachers all said you are literally a genius. But you are missing my point entirely. I, of all people, know damn well what was going on at this house when we got here. I could sense it immediately from the way the detectives looked at us when you opened the door. Did they even bother to comfort me about the fact that my granddaughter is missing? No. They couldn't get out of here fast enough, because they probably see me as some frail little old lady, too, and didn't want me to know the truth. So stop trying to protect your mother."

"Fair enough," she said.

Mike reappeared with a cup and saucer, the tea bag still steeping. "May I give this to you, or are you too gangster for herbal tea now?"

Their mother accepted the drink with an amused eye roll. "Now, both of you, sit down and tell me everything."

For the next half hour, Melissa forced herself to step outside of her own body and recite the bare facts as if she were a lawyer summarizing a case for a colleague. It wasn't until she heard the evidence in her own words that she realized why she was the natural, predictable, even inevitable suspect.

What had the detectives called it? *Coincidences stacked upon more coincidences.* Melissa was the last person known to have seen Riley, the only one entrusted with her care that day, and the doors of the house were locked when Mike came home to find Riley missing. Her lifestyle had suddenly morphed from that of a single professional to a woman juggling a career, social life, husband, and toddler. She had spent months researching an unsolved case where police suspected that an unhappy woman murdered her young stepchild so she could have freedom beyond the confines of caretaking. She was recorded on her podcast agreeing that the stepmother never would have even been a suspect if she had been smart enough to leave her cell phone at home when she drove, as police suspected, to a nearby island to get rid of the body.

And then, the piece of evidence that probably explained both the search warrant for her car and the many unanswered phone calls to her own husband — the videotape of a woman driving a child to a nearby island in an SUV that looked just like hers, and then returning to the South Fork alone.

At some point during her monologue, the

protection of her unemotional, lawyerly objectivity had failed her. She pressed her face into her hands and squeezed her temples as if she might literally control the direction of her thoughts. Why hadn't she seen it earlier? She knew from her own work that people who had never even gotten a traffic ticket could commit horrible acts under intense psychological pressure. Many of them were so shocked by their own conduct that they repressed the crimes entirely from their consciousness, claiming to have experienced either amnesia or a blackout.

How many times had Mike warned her that she couldn't keep ignoring the damage that had been done to them? He warned her that the trauma would find a way to make it to the surface. Those terrible nightmares were her subconscious's way of telling her that the illusion of normalcy she had so carefully constructed over the years was beginning to crumble. She remembered the look of worry — *no,* she thought in retrospect — the look of *pity* on Charlie's face when he found her in the middle of the night, wrapped in a towel, staring at the water gushing into the empty tub. And just two days earlier, she had wandered out to the beach before dawn, crying out like a toddler for her mother, with no memory of how she got there.

What else had she blocked out?

She finally realized where the flashes of thoughts were leading. "What if —" She removed her hands from her face, but couldn't bring herself to look at her family. Her arms began to tremble involuntarily as if her very bones were trying to tell her the truth about what had happened in this house the previous day. "Oh my God, what if . . . they're actually right? This is all because of me. I tried so hard to make the past go away — like, *poof,* it never happened. *Happiness is a choice?* How arrogant and stupid I was. But it's exactly what you said, Mike. Eventually that trauma is going to find a way to express itself. What if, what if . . . Poor little Riley. Oh dear God, no. Please don't let it be possible."

Beside her, her mother placed her cup decisively on the table and then shifted on the sofa to grab Melissa's hands. "Look at me, Melissa."

Melissa's gaze remained on her lap as she shook her head. In a weak voice she barely recognized, she said, "Maybe if I go to Shelter Island, something will look familiar. Maybe I'll remember. I just need to remember. If I did this, I have to tell them —"

Her mother's voice grew even more firm. "Please, my beautiful, compassionate, generous, brilliant, and *very stubborn* daughter. I need you to look at me right now."

Melissa complied as instructed.

"I have been where you are. You and your brother didn't want me to know the truth about what's going on because it would dig up all that pain I suffered — that *we* suffered — forty years ago. Well, you were right, and that's exactly why you need to listen to me. Everything you said just now, I heard in my own voice. Back when I was in California — before you were born, before I met your daddy, when I was being held for trial after Peter and Lisa were killed, I used to pray every morning and every night in my jail cell. *Peace . . . give me peace. Let me learn to accept.* I knew there was no way I could have hurt my children. They were me. I felt like I died when they died. And yet my prayer to God was to help me accept that they were gone, and to also accept my punishment, because I blamed myself. Did I ever tell you that I've listened to the tape recordings with Dr. Miles?"

Dr. Lendon Miles was an esteemed psychiatrist who had been deeply in love with Nancy's mother before she died in what police initially believed was a tragic car accident shortly after meeting Nancy's new fiancé. After Mike and Melissa were kidnapped, Dr. Miles was determined to help the family of the woman he had never stopped loving. When their mother claimed not to recall the events surrounding her children's abduction, he questioned her under an injection of sodium amytal to relieve her of what he suspected was a form of amnesia resulting from a psychologically catastrophic experience.

"When I agreed to let Lendon give me the injection," her mother said, "it was out of desperation. I would have done anything to help find you. But once the drug took effect, I fell into a manageable state of calm, at least compared to the state of shock in which I had spent the rest of the day. Does that make any sense? It felt like a sudden awakening."

"Are you suggesting I find a psychiatrist to help me remember what happened yesterday?"

"No, because I don't think you repressed anything at all. When the injection Lendon gave me wore off, I felt a newfound certainty. Your father said he'd never heard me sound so forceful. I was absolutely confident that I could help the police get you back home. After hours of wallowing, I got myself off that sofa and out of my bathrobe. I never would have had the strength to pull you from Carl's arms as he fell from that balcony if I hadn't made a decision to believe in myself. That little voice of doubt that you've allowed to whisper in your ear? *What if I did something awful?* That's not because you did anything wrong, Melissa. It's because you love that little girl like she's your own heart."

Melissa had been trying to identify the helix of emotions she'd been spiraling through for the last two days. Fear. Anger. Helplessness. But one feeling remained constant and overwhelming: guilt. Deep in the pit of her gut she knew that she was responsible for Riley's disappearance and any other harm that came to her. "I feel paralyzed by this crushing pressure of guilt. What if it's my subconscious telling me that I actually did something bad while I was blacked out?"

"There would be something wrong with you if you *didn't* feel guilty," her mother said. "I think you feel just like I did after I left Peter and Lisa in the car while I ran into the market, only to find them missing when I returned. And then I swore when your father and I decided to have children that I would never, ever, ever take the smallest risk at your expense. But that's impossible, don't you see? That horrible day, I took my eyes off the two of you for the tiniest moment when you were playing in the yard. Part of me will never forgive myself, but I have learned that I didn't belong in prison for it. Carl Harmon did, and he eventually paid the ultimate price. Now, you know you can tell me anything in the world, and I will still love and stand by you without conditions. Do you really think there's any chance at all you did something to hurt Riley?"

Melissa pressed her lips together and felt a rush of blood to her face. She shook her head, grateful for what felt in that moment as an unquestionable and fundamental truth. "Never," she said. "It's absolutely impossible."

"Okay, then. Consider that to be my equivalent of Dr. Miles's truth serum, the clarity you needed. Now, we need to get to work finding Riley."

Melissa placed three more back-to-back calls to Charlie. His outgoing voice message announced that the mailbox was full.

She moved on to another call to Mac and was surprised when he actually answered. "Hi."

That's it? she wanted to scream. *HIIII?!*

Instead, she thanked him for answering. "I don't know how much they've told you, but I need to talk to Charlie. Where are you guys?"

"As of right now, I'm in your mom's driveway. Can I come inside?"

24

Grant Macintosh felt his pace slow with each step toward the cottage porch. Last night's phone call had caught him completely off guard. His girlfriend Sarah had planned what she called the "perfect city Sunday," beginning with brunch in the Meatpacking District before a visit to the new floating park on the Hudson River, followed by a walk up the High Line to hit golf balls at the Chelsea Piers driving range. As they were popping into the Met Museum on the Upper East Side, Sarah was gloating about hitting the 20,000-step mark on her Apple Watch for only the second time in her personal history. By the time they had settled into their favorite table at Neary's for dinner, all Mac wanted was a prime sirloin and some red wine, followed by a good night's sleep.

And then Melissa had called.

Maybe if he had followed Sarah's advice

and let it go to voicemail, he wouldn't have learned until today that Riley had disappeared. That news was shocking enough, but Melissa didn't stop there. The police were treating Charlie and her family like suspects, following her brother to a park and asking questions about Charlie's first marriage. When Melissa began explaining that Charlie's former in-laws suspected foul play in his first wife's death, he knew where the phone call was headed. Charlie needed a lawyer.

He also knew he had no choice. In the years he had known Melissa, he had never heard her sound so distraught. Her stepdaughter was missing, and the police were wasting precious time digging into matters that had nothing to do with Riley's disappearance. Of course he had to help. That's what you do for your friends.

Now, only a day later, he wished he had a time machine so he could turn back the clock and make another decision. He could have told Melissa he was too busy, or that Charlie needed an attorney who didn't have a personal connection to them. But it would have felt heartless. Then again, a day ago, he didn't know what he knew now.

What he was about to do to Melissa was going to be so much worse.

With trepidation, he rang the doorbell.

Mac's regrets deepened when Melissa flung the cottage door open to greet him. His friend's usually rosy cheeks were sallow, and her eyes were puffy and bloodshot. She reached out with one of her usual bear hugs, but he managed to shift sideways and slip inside the house instead, closing the door behind him. He was relieved that the cottage curtains were all drawn. The police or the press could be watching the house, and even the slightest sign of favor could be misconstrued as collusion with Riley's stepmother.

Still, he could not bring himself to push her away when she gave him a quick hug in the living room. "Thank you so much for being here," she said. "I've been crawling out of my skin all day, wondering where you and Charlie went after the police station, and why no one was returning my calls. And then Detectives Hall and Marino came over, basically accusing me of driving Riley to Shelter Island and killing her. Mac, I can't even describe the feeling — it was . . . unimaginable. Please tell me that Charlie doesn't actually believe I could do something like that to our daughter."

Our daughter. The words sounded so

genuine as they rolled from her lips. A day ago, he would have sworn that they in fact were. But could he really be sure? When he was a guest host on her podcast, he was so quick to riff on his knee-jerk reactions to the most granular details of a true crime case, but now that he was involved as a lawyer, and the suspect was someone he knew, he was questioning everything.

He had expected that morning's sit-down with Charlie and the detectives to be pro forma. Charlie had been on an international flight yesterday — as solid as an alibi could get. He was by all accounts a doting father who adored his daughter. The tension with his in-laws was problematic, but Mac was confident he could persuade the police that it was only natural that a couple who had lost their only daughter in a tragic accident would resent the son-in-law who chose to move to the other side of the country with their grandchild.

But when Mac spoke with Charlie privately before going into the police station, Charlie was adamant that if detectives were going to call Linda's parents, they'd have to locate the contact information themselves. If Mac had learned one thing as a prosecutor, it was that law enforcement was always most interested in whatever information they couldn't have. When a suspect consents to a search of his car, except for the glove box? You can bet something's in the glove box.

Mac was prepared to spell out Charlie's concerns to the detectives, but then the questioning began. Was it true he'd known his wife for only ten months before they got married? Had she wanted children before she met him? Did she seem overly consumed by the case of Judith Moore, the woman long suspected of killing her stepson and hiding his body on a nearby island? How much did he know about her childhood trauma and the ways it had affected her?

And then they played the video from the Shelter Island ferry.

Mac had wanted to rise to his feet and pound the table as if delivering the most adamant closing argument of his career. Melissa Eldredge was one of the finest people he had ever known. They were fools to believe she was capable of committing a crime, let alone one so heinous as the murder of a child. But that would be Melissa's friend talking, and, thanks to Melissa, Mac was now her husband's lawyer.

"Mac?" Melissa said now, staring at him expectantly. "What's going on?"

This was why he hadn't wanted to come here. He had a professional obligation, though, to protect his client and not his friend. He knew how it would look if Charlie appeared to care more about protecting his new wife than the safety of his own daughter. And given the choice words Charlie's sister, Rachel, had had for Melissa after viewing the ferry video, he thought any future contact between the two women would be better suited to a bad reality television show than actual life.

"You said the detectives were here," he finally said. "What did they tell you?" *The video. Did they show you the video? Please, Melissa, explain the video.*

"They had this grainy video from the ferry dock. I'm assuming they showed it to Charlie and that's why he's not calling me back. Did you see it? That driver could be anyone, Mac. Come on. You need to explain that to him."

He tilted his head and held her gaze. She knew better than this.

The last time he saw her, she had invited him to stay at her apartment after the podcast recording for a drink. He had lied and said he was supposed to meet his sister. The reality was he was going out for happy hour with the old gang from the DA's office. There was a reason that he and Katie were the only former coworkers Melissa was still in touch with. The truth was, people were jealous. While everyone else was handling garden-variety thefts and drug cases, Melissa got tapped to serve as what they had called the "third chair" on a murder trial — and a high profile one at that: Jennifer Duncan, the former model accused of killing her wealthy older husband. For the entirety of the trial, she was spared the usual grunt work so she could be the right-hand woman to two senior homicide prosecutors.

That initial envy was the stuff of normal interoffice competition. Any lawyer who was going to last in the office was eventually asked to work on a murder case. Katie served in a lesser capacity on that same case, handling any initial inquiries from the general public or the victim's friends or family members. Then, two months later, Mac was third chair on the office's next big murder trial.

But then two years ago, Melissa hit the jackpot, successfully overturning the conviction obtained by the very first homicide trial she ever worked. Splashy headlines, cable news, daytime talk shows. She was no longer a mere lawyer. She was a *personality.* Mac and Katie joked that if it had to happen to someone other than them, they were glad it was Melissa. Their former colleagues were less accepting.

If they could see her now, they wouldn't be jealous.

He let out a puff of air, bracing himself for what needed to be said. "You know I love you, right? We were each other's people from day one at the DA's office."

"Of course. You, me, Katie. The Three Musketeers. We're family."

They each had a personal reason that drew them to the office. A county prosecutor who volunteered in the Big Brothers Big Sisters program had practically been Mac's surrogate father as a child. Katie had a cousin who was permanently incapacitated by a drunk driver in a hit-and-run that was never solved. And, although Melissa never spoke in detail about what had happened to her and her family as a child, she had told them once that she thought it had led her into criminal law.

"You're the best lawyer I know, Melissa. Your book about your own career explains how the system only works when we don't stray from the ethics of our assigned roles. And, ethically, I'm Charlie's lawyer, not yours. You called me for a reason, and now I have to do the job you chose me for."

"And that means you can't tell him to call his wife so I can explain that I didn't do this?"

"Look, I know this is horrible for you. But to be blunt, the police looking at you instead of Charlie is what's best for my client. And if he appears too cozy with you right now, how is that going to look? He has a rock-solid alibi. You don't."

The pain in her eyes meant that she understood the point. Charlie could not have killed Riley himself. But it was certainly possible that he and his new wife had planned the crime to rid themselves of a toddler neither of them wanted. The only way for Charlie to ensure he was not also a suspect was to distance himself from Melissa.

"But he has to know that I didn't do this, Mac. *You* have to know. We have to get the police on the right track so they can find Riley."

"They're looking for her, Melissa. Don't you hear those helicopters? Whether it was you behind the wheel of that SUV or someone else —"

"Seriously?"

"You know what I mean. The point is they're searching all over Long Island." Mac's phone rang in his pocket. He noticed the time on the screen. He'd already stayed here longer than he should. "Look, this is Charlie."

Melissa's eyes suddenly brightened. "Please, let me talk to him. I'm begging you."

He hated seeing her so vulnerable. She was normally the person who always had the right answer, the Wonder Woman who could fix any problem. Now, she had no control at all.

He accepted the call and told Charlie to hold on.

25

I finally might have a lifeline, Melissa thought. Charlie had called Mac's phone, which was only inches away. If she could simply speak to him, he would understand she was innocent. Of course he would. She was certain of it. They would find Riley no matter how long it took. They would survive this nightmare together.

She reached out her hand for the phone and felt her heart sink when Mac held it out of reach.

"Here's the deal, Melissa. Charlie was the one who insisted on talking to you, against my advice. I'm saying way more to you than I should, but I can't have phone records showing the two of you speaking directly right now, so I said one call, through me. That was the compromise."

She nodded her acceptance, and he handed her the phone.

"Charlie, thank God. That's not me in the

video. It has to be the woman from the park. I had the police test my blood. It will prove I was drugged. I'd bet my life on it."

"Mac will kill me if he finds out I said this, but I believe you, Melissa."

The words felt like a gasp of fresh air when she had previously been suffocating. "You have no idea how relieved I am to hear that."

"My God, of course I believe you. And if anyone is strong enough to go through this, it's you."

"What do you mean? Go through what?"

"Didn't Mac talk to you? The police — we think they suspect you, not me."

"That's why I've been trying to call you. We have to prove that —"

"No, Melissa. No." She could hear the pain in his voice, but it was not the sound of weakness. She could tell he had reached some kind of decision and that it was final. This was the reason for the phone call. "I love you. I love you more than anything or anyone — except Riley. She has to be the only one that matters to me right now, and I know you'll agree with that."

"Of course. I feel the same."

"And the only thing keeping me from jumping in front of a speeding truck right now is the hope that I'm going to get her back. Riley is out there — alive and healthy and waiting for me to find her. I have to keep believing that, and I have to get her home, okay?" She started to agree again but he cut her off. "If that happens — *when* that happens — I know what's coming next. Linda's parents will try to take her from me again. They'll say I'm unfit to care for her. And even though I know down to the very core of my being that you are not to blame, they will twist everything around and say I put my daughter in danger by leaving her with you while I traveled off to another country for work. I love you, Melissa, but if you love me even half as much, you will understand the position I am in. Mac is adamant that I not see you until this is over."

The logical part of her brain realized that she'd probably give Charlie the same advice if she were his attorney, but she was also jumping out of her skin from the frustration of all her unanswered questions. "Did you get my messages about Linda?"

She could barely hear Charlie due to voices crossing behind him at the police station. He muttered something about almost being ready before returning to their conversation. "It's been too hectic for me to listen to all the voicemails. I didn't understand why you were asking about her."

"Did they ever recover Linda's body? Maybe she didn't really die in that fall. She could have found out you got married and changed her mind about Riley. She might be the woman in the park."

"Melissa, Linda is dead. How could I possibly have moved across the country and gotten married if I wasn't absolutely sure?"

"So they found her after the fall?"

She heard a woman's voice in the background. It was Rachel. The only words she could make out were *Charlie* and *almost ready.*

"Melissa, I'm sorry, I have to go."

"No, no, just one more second. Don't hang up."

More voices in the background.

"I love you," he said quickly. "No matter what happens, please, don't forget that."

"Charlie, wait. What do you mean? That sounds so . . ."

She was about to say *permanent* before he cut her off. "I have to go. Mac set this thing up. He can explain. It's for Riley. We're going to be okay, once we have Riley back. I'm so sorry."

The sympathetic look in Mac's eyes as she returned his phone made her feel small and pitied. "He said you set something up for him."

216

"A press conference. For what it's worth, it's exactly what you would do." He made his way to the coffee table, picked up the remote control, and turned on the television to News 12 Long Island. The words at the bottom of the screen announced that the father of missing toddler Riley Miller was about to address reporters.

"I should be there for that," she said. "So should you."

"Rachel's with him. So are Hall and Marino. He can't be seen with a defense lawyer. These are the optics he needs right now given where we are with the police."

Right. As the new wife he met only a year ago, she was an *optics* problem.

"Is that why you came here?" she asked. "To give me my one phone call before I get thrown under the bus?"

Mac turned his head away before speaking. "Charlie needs his suitcase. He won't be coming back here until they find Riley. I'm sorry. I really am."

"Will you please ask him whether they found Linda's body after the fall? It's the least you can do for me."

He had the nerve to squeeze her shoulder before making his way upstairs uninvited.

26

Nancy knew this cottage was the right house for her the very first time she saw it. It was one of only three she had walked through when she made the trip to Southampton. The local realtor was highly recommended by Taylor Summers, the agent to whom Ray had turned over his business when he retired six years ago. She loved the open floor plan and the oversized windows that allowed sunlight to flood across the rooms. It reminded her of the gut feeling she had when Ray first brought her to the house on the Cape that she would then rent for herself until it eventually became their family home. She just knew that she would stay.

What sealed her decision to make an offer on this cottage was the view from where she stood now, by the railing above the staircase. The large window over the landing allowed views of the bay at the end of the road. She would be able to begin every morning with a glimpse of the water. Right now, however, what she appreciated was the echo from the living room up to the second floor from which she eavesdropped while her son stood next to her, shoulder to shoulder.

"Can you believe this?" she whispered. "He's keeping Melissa from talking to her own husband, when *she's* the one who hired him as their lawyer in the first place. I thought I liked Mac, but this is ridiculous." Melissa had asked to speak with Mac alone, but this was Nancy's house. If he continued speaking to her daughter that way, she would tell him to leave if she had to. Until he showed up, she had Melissa sounding confident and optimistic. She did not want to find her brilliant daughter broken and vulnerable again.

Instead of responding, her son shushed her. "Wait, I can't hear."

"I'm seventy-two years old. How can your hearing be worse than mine?"

"Obviously all those years of the devil's rock-and-roll music, but really, Mom. Shhh." He had always been able to maintain his dry sense of humor.

She heard the ring of a cell phone from the living room. *Charlie,* she thought. Maybe Charlie was calling Melissa, despite his lawyer's heartless advice. Or it could be the police, saying they found Riley. She remembered how every ring of the phone and every knock on the door while her children were missing felt like it might be the end of the nightmare — or confirmation of her worst fears.

The ringing stopped and was soon replaced by the sound of Mac's voice. *Look, this is Charlie.*

She and Mike listened carefully as Mac explained why Charlie was calling Mac's phone instead of Melissa's. Beside her, Mike shrugged. The rationale did make sense from a lawyer's perspective.

But then she heard the desperation in her daughter's voice as Melissa took the phone to speak to her own husband. *Charlie, thank God. That's not me in the video . . . What do you mean? Go through what? . . .*

Nancy knew what it felt like to be a suspect. Oh, did she know. She could still feel the burn of Adams Port Police Chief Jed Coffin's hostility when he walked into their house. It was exactly like the first time, after Peter and Lisa. Knowing her past, he thought he had the entire case solved before he'd asked a single question. She had seen the newspaper article revealing that local wife and mother Nancy Eldredge was actually the notorious Nancy Harmon, long

220

suspected of drowning her children in California and getting away with it. Certain that the new life she had built on the Cape was about to implode from the revelation, she must have gone "berserk," in Coffin's words, and did to Michael and Missy what she had done to her first two children.

Despite her shock, she could sense at a visceral level that Ray was defending her. Chief Coffin had asked to speak with him privately, as if she didn't even matter. Instead, Ray had made the chief wait while he placed his hands on her shoulders until she stopped shaking. He had rested his cheek against hers to calm and reassure her before leading the chief into the next room. The mere way he carried himself — tall, unflinching, and self-possessed — made it clear that despite Coffin's authority, he owed their family a modicum of respect. Even when Coffin read Nancy her Miranda rights and the Boston news outlets parked outside of their house, barking questions that clearly assumed Nancy's guilt, Ray never faltered.

She could tell from both Melissa's words and her tone that Charlie was no Ray in this moment when his wife needed him.

Charlie, wait. What do you mean? That sounds so . . .

Melissa stopped midsentence. *So . . . what?* Nancy wondered. Cold? Indifferent? Selfish?

Long seconds of silence followed before Melissa spoke again. *He said you set something up for him.* Her daughter's tone had changed. She was addressing Mac again. *To give me my one phone call before I get thrown under the bus?*

She noticed Mike's jaw was clenched and his hands were balled into fists. He had always been so protective of his little sister.

Charlie needs his suitcase, Mac said. *He won't be coming back here until they find Riley. I'm sorry. I really am.*

They heard footsteps approaching in their direction and Mike stood upright, appearing ready to block Mac by force.

"No, do not," she said firmly. "If Charlie wants to take his things with him, then good riddance." By the time Mac hit the staircase, she was already in the guest room. A roller bag of men's clothing, not yet unpacked, was open on top of the dresser. She zipped it and placed it in the hallway.

Mac looked at her awkwardly from the landing. "I'm sorry. I don't expect you to understand, Nancy."

"Well, good. Then I don't need to worry

about failing to meet your expectations."

Mike emerged from the guest bathroom and thrust a leather shaving kit against Mac's chest, harder than he needed to. "Dude, you should go."

Immediately after the sound of the front door closing, the volume of the downstairs television quickly went from a murmur to a roar. It was a woman's voice, with the professional tone of a seasoned correspondent. "We're waiting here in Southampton on Long Island for an update from the father of missing toddler Riley Miller."

27

We're waiting here in Southampton on Long Island for an update from the father of missing toddler Riley Miller.

Melissa was on her feet, remote control in hand, when her mother and brother joined her in the living room. She could tell with one look that they had eavesdropped on every word of her conversation with Mac. She allowed herself a moment of satisfaction as she imagined the subsequent interaction that must have taken place upstairs before Mac hightailed it out of the house with Charlie's suitcase.

Despite the sting of Mac's betrayal, his words echoed as she looked at the television screen. Microphones surrounded a temporary lectern positioned in the police station parking lot for the anticipated press conference. *For what it's worth, it's exactly what you would do.*

He wasn't wrong. More than 600,000

people are reported missing every year. Many of them are never found, and only a few of their names will ever be heard by the public. Both she and Mac knew that a missing-person case can't become a national search without the obligatory press conference featuring heartbroken family members pleading for their loved one's safe return.

As the News 12 correspondent recited the same basic facts that had been reported all day, Melissa recognized Hall among the group of people milling behind the lectern. The detective whispered something to another officer, who took on a confused expression before departing from view.

The camera cut to the on-scene correspondent. "Margot, we're hearing now from the police that the timing for this might be more fluid than previously announced. We'll turn it over to you as the search for Riley Miller continues in eastern Long Island."

"What do you think that was about?" Mike asked.

"I don't know," she said, muting the television. "Mac set up a press conference with the police for Charlie and his sister. Maybe there's new evidence. Or maybe they found Riley." *Please,* she prayed, *let her be alive — located unharmed.*

She called Charlie yet again. It went straight to voicemail, making her wonder if he had turned off his phone in anticipation of the press conference or had gone so far as to block her incoming calls. A call to Mac also went unanswered, so she followed up with a text message: *Charlie needs to get out there in front of the cameras. He can say whatever he wants to about me, but they need to keep the search going. That storm is still a possible threat, too.*

She pulled up Rachel's number next and hit Enter. After three rings, she was ready to leave a message, but to her surprise, her sister-in-law actually answered. "Hi." Her voice was low, and Melissa could hear crosstalk in the background.

"Oh God, Rachel, thank you for picking up."

"Look, I'll be honest, I really don't know what to think about you right now, Melissa."

"All I care about is finding your niece. What's going on with the press conference? Did something happen? Did they find Riley?" She braced herself for the worst possible news.

"No. Of course we will tell you if that happens — *when* that happens, God willing." She paused as if wondering whether to say more. "It's Charlie. He had a total panic attack when we started to walk outside. I'm trying to calm him down to go out there, but he's a mess right now. First Linda's death. Now Riley's gone. I'm worried this is just too much for him. He's shutting down. He's even worse than he was right after he came back from Norway."

"Let me talk to him —"

"Wait. Mac's here now. Let me see —"

She couldn't make out the conversation taking place beyond the phone line, but Rachel's voice was soon replaced by Mac's. "Seriously, Melissa. Do not come here. If the reporters see you, they're going to want to know why you weren't here before, and why you're not standing by Charlie's side once I finally get him out there. You won't be helping anyone. Please, let me handle it."

"But Mac —"

"I've got to go."

"Don't forget to ask Charlie about Lin—"

The line went silent.

"Did that jerk hang up on you?" Mike asked. He had obviously inferred enough from overhearing her side of the conversation. "I thought that guy was your friend."

And so did I, Melissa thought. Looking down at her darkened screen, she felt empty, wondering if she had lost both her husband and her friend.

28

Alone in her guest bedroom, Melissa typed another search into her laptop. *Linda Mother Oregon Waterfall Norway.* It was a variation of all of her other attempts.

Again, nothing helpful.

She realized now how little she knew about Charlie's first wife, not even her last name. She was certain it wasn't Miller, because when Melissa had talked to Charlie about keeping her maiden name, Charlie readily agreed, mentioning that Linda had done the same. Charlie must have told her Linda's full name at some point, but her memory kept coming up blank.

She knew that Charlie and Linda met in their freshman year of college at the University of Washington. She searched for *Charlie Miller Wedding Announcement Linda Washington.* Again, nothing.

She pulled up the web page for the alumni relations office of the university. It was still business hours on the West Coast. A female voice, young and friendly, answered on the third ring. "Alumni office. This is Kelsey."

Melissa was about to fabricate an elaborate cover story for the questions she wanted to ask, but decided nothing would be more compelling than the truth. She was four sentences in when the woman on the other end of the line said, "Wait, this is Melissa Eldredge as in, like, *Justice Club* Melissa?"

"Oh, you've heard of it?"

"Um . . . yeah! My roommate and are like totally obsessed with the Evan Moore disappearance. It happened when we were in middle school. We were literally just listening to your podcast last night. So you're working on another missing child case? How long has the girl been missing? You said her name's Riley Miller?"

Melissa had not gotten to the part yet where the missing child was her own stepdaughter, or that the alumnus about whom she was calling was her own husband, but she could tell that Kelsey was already inclined to help. She explained that the abduction had occurred only yesterday and she was trying to locate information about the girl's biological mother. "All I know is that her first name was Linda, and she married a classmate named Charles Miller. Oh, and her hometown was Portland, Oregon." She also provided the year of their graduation.

"Oh wow, I have no idea how I could help you with that. I'm just a student employee here. Maybe call the registrar's office?"

"Do you have archives of the alumni announcements?" she asked. Melissa's own college sent out a quarterly magazine, and she always skipped directly to her class year to look for any names she recognized. "Perhaps they reported the news of their wedding."

"Oh sure, I could do that." She could hear keyboard tapping on the other end of the line. "Hmm, I'm not seeing anything yet."

"What about donations?" Melissa suggested. "Your office must keep track of that."

"Oh boy, do we," Kelsey said with a chuckle. "I love this. It's like I'm helping you be all sleuthy. Okay, so I'll search for . . . Charles . . . Miller. Hey, that worked. I've got him! His first donation was the year after he graduated. Only fifty dollars, but most new alums don't give anything. And then it looks like he was a regular donor every year, increasing the amounts over time —"

"He and Linda got married three years

after graduating. She should be there as well."

"Nope, I don't see a Linda. They're just under Charles Miller. But, oh, this is weird."

"What?"

"Well, he was sending in $200 a year annually, but then the donations suddenly stop twelve years ago. Nothing since."

Charlie had never mentioned a reason he may have stopped contributing to his alma mater. It was possible that Linda had begun sending in the donations instead, but without her last name, there was no way to know. And in Melissa's experience, donations to a college from married alumni were always credited to both names. Regardless, she had hit a dead end.

"Kelsey, thank you so much for trying to help. If there's any way you can keep researching this on campus, it might be really important to saving this little girl. Maybe one of the older professors or administrators would remember them. Charlie Miller was an environmental science major, if that helps."

"I'll keep looking into it," Kelsey said after they exchanged numbers. "I promise."

With no other options, Melissa continued with her searches for news stories about Linda's death.

Charlie Linda Miller Norway Fatal Fall
American Woman Charlie Linda Waterfall
Died
Charlie Linda American Mother Died Selfie
Oregon woman dies waterfall Europe
Linda

Still nothing.

Feeling her mother's eyes from the hallway outside her room, Melissa looked up from her computer.

"I didn't mean to interrupt," her mother said. "Watching you there, I was picturing the way you always lived in another world with your homework, happy on the floor or your bed, your legs crisscross applesauce, just like that."

Melissa allowed herself a small smile. When push came to shove, she still preferred working like this to sitting at a desk. "Dad was always telling me I would ruin my back. And then years later, I was the one who pressured the two of you to sign up for Pilates." A year since he had passed, and she was still trying to adjust to her father's absence.

"Can I ask what you're doing up here in front of your computer?" Her mother's eyes were filled with worry. "You can't possibly be trying to work right now."

233

"I feel so helpless about Riley," she said. "I just can't set aside this feeling I have in my gut about Linda's fall in Norway. I'm looking for the details of her accident, to make sure she actually died, but I keep coming up empty-handed."

In grief counseling, Charlie had moved quickly in Melissa's mind from *the guy who sits near the coffee urn* to her trusted confidant. Even though he had lost his wife, and she was coming to terms with the death of a parent, they found a deep connection as they both learned how to grieve.

"This is so frustrating. I don't even know where precisely in Norway they were visiting when Linda fell."

Next to her on the quilt, Melissa's phone buzzed with a new text message. It was from Mac. *I asked Charlie about Linda.*

She watched her screen as a series of dots told her that he was still typing. Then the dots stopped. She waited.

Mac . . . come on, she texted. *What did he say?*

More dots. *Linda was cremated in Norway.*

She immediately began composing a reply. Did he see her body? Was it somehow possible that Linda had enlisted the help of local officials to help her fake her death?

Another message from Mac appeared. *Be-*

fore you ask all your follow-up questions, I already did. Charlie had to identify her body after they pulled her from the water. He spread the ashes with Linda's parents in the Pacific Ocean off Cannon Beach before everything fell apart with the in-laws. So whoever took Riley, it's definitely not Linda.

Her shoulders slumped three inches with the news. She had been so certain she was on the right track.

Is he doing the press conference? she asked.

I got the information that you wanted. I have to go now.

"Is there news?" her mother asked hopefully when Melissa set her phone down.

She closed her laptop and pushed it away. "Well, I can apparently stop my endless Google searches. That was Mac. Charlie saw Linda's body with his own eyes after the fall. So much for that theory." She realized how desperately she had wanted to be right. If Riley's own mother had been the one to take her, it would have been to reunite with her. Riley would at least be safe.

"Come downstairs. Your brother's concocting some kind of supper. You at least need to eat."

"Did you eat while Mike and I were missing?"

235

Her mother pursed her lips, accepting the reply. "Fair enough."

"Can you please let me know if the press conference comes on? Charlie's sister is worried he won't be able to handle the pressure of this."

Her mother shook her head in frustration, but then simply said, "Of course."

Left alone in her room, Melissa opened her computer again and typed in another search. *Melissa Eldredge stepdaughter missing.* She hit Enter, even as she knew it was a mistake to look. The first hit was to Net-Sleuths, a true crime message board that Melissa regularly frequented for potential cold cases for her podcast. She wasn't surprised to see that many of the NetSleuth users were aware of both her and *The Justice Club.* While most of the comments on the thread expressed sympathy for Melissa and hope that Riley would be found soon, a vocal minority seemed convinced that Melissa should be considered the primary suspect.

She was on the third page of comments when her phone buzzed with a new text message. *Jennifer Duncan.*

There had been a time when that name popped up on her screen multiple times a day, but it had been more than a year since their last communication.

Melissa, I am so sorry. I had no idea of your connection to that poor missing girl until a friend just called me. I didn't realize you had gotten married or had a stepdaughter now. I would have sent my best wishes. You'll recall how much I always wanted a child. I can't imagine what you and your husband must be going through. I know we parted on a sour note, but I am still so grateful for everything you have done for me. Please let me know if I can be there for you in any way, even if it's as a sympathetic ear. I am in Sag Harbor for most of the summer. Sending prayers, Jen.

Melissa pulled up Instagram on her laptop and then searched for Jennifer Duncan's account. The most recent photo, posted early this afternoon, showed her on a boat, smiling behind aviator sunglasses, her long honey-blonde hair blowing in the wind. *Even Monday Can Be Sun Day. #SagHarbor #Boatlife #Beachlife #Bestlife #wearyoursunscreen*

Jennifer was in nearby Sag Harbor?

She reread the message at least three times, and with each review, the words became only more ambiguous. At face value, it was a compassionate and supportive note from a former friend and client during a time of crisis. Or if Jennifer really did despise Melissa — enough, perhaps, to be the voice behind the TruthTeller posts — the message could be read as a subtle attempt to rub salt in the wound. *I didn't realize* might be a passive-aggressive reminder that they had cut off all communications. *Sending prayers.* Did she mean this as a sincere condolence, or with the Twitter-like tone of sarcastically wishing disfavored people "thoughts and prayers" when it becomes clear they're experiencing something unpleasant?

And then, most ominously of all, *You'll recall how much I always wanted a child.*

Melissa texted a response before she could change her mind. *I really could use a friend right now. And I need to get out of the house, but also don't want people staring at me.* She jumped from the bed, slipped on her sandals, and trotted down the stairs before Jennifer had replied. She went to grab her car key from the kitchen island but then remembered the police had it.

A new message appeared on her screen. *I totally understand. Why don't you come to my place?*

Melissa clicked on the address that followed. "Mike, I need the keys to the U-Haul." The rental truck was now long past overdue, and would have to remain that way.

"Sure, I think they're in my room." He turned the stove burner down to low beneath whatever he was cooking and headed up the cottage stairs.

Her mother rose from her chair in the corner of the living room. "Are you going down to the police station? Let me go with you. Maybe Charlie will listen to me. I can tell him what it felt like to have all those people suspect me of something so awful. Maybe he'll come around."

She shook her head. "No, Mac's actually right. If I go there, it could turn into a total spectacle. I need to get some air."

"You can't get air in a moving van," her mother admonished. "Why don't we all go for a walk together — just a loop around the block?"

"After those news reports, I don't want people watching me."

"Then let's sit upstairs on the deck off of my bedroom," her mother suggested. "That's private, and there should be a nice breeze off the bay."

Mike cleared his throat as he reentered the living room. "I know what it's like to need to be alone," he said. "She'll be fine, Mom."

Nothing was going to stop Melissa from finding out where Jennifer had been all weekend.

29

According to her phone's GPS, it would be a nineteen-minute drive to Jennifer's house.

Melissa hated lying to anyone — especially her family — but Mike and her mother would have tried to stop her if she had told them where she was going, and, more importantly, why.

Melissa suspected that Jennifer might be the person behind the TruthTeller posts, but had brushed off a possible connection to Riley's disappearance. All of that changed with one sentence in Jennifer's text: *You'll recall how much I always wanted a child.*

Melissa had initially begun second-guessing Jennifer's motives for shooting her husband when she was so adamant about inheriting the entirety of his estate once her conviction was set aside. Money, however, was only one possible motive that prosecutors explored during the original trial. Investigation into the couple's marriage revealed that Jennifer had undergone two unsuccessful courses of in vitro fertilization with her husband. Curiously, though, the autopsy of Doug Hanover's body made clear that he had gotten a vasectomy, and his medical records established that the procedure had been performed shortly after he graduated from business school — two decades before he met Jennifer.

Taken together, the evidence suggested that Hanover not only misled Jennifer about his ability and willingness to have additional children, but also permitted her to put herself through a physical and emotional process that was doomed to end in disappointment. Where the prosecution fell short was their inability to prove that Jennifer ever learned the truth about her husband's vasectomy until after the autopsy. The evidence also portrayed Hanover as a cruel and selfish man. Melissa was not surprised when the two prosecutors trying the case made the decision not to use the evidence, and that was the last time she'd given much thought to it — until now.

Once she made the turn at Water Mill onto Scuttle Hole Road, she knew there'd be no further turns until she passed the golf club and winery on this road. She steered with one hand while she pulled up Katie's number on her phone with the other.

Katie picked up almost immediately. "Oh, thank heavens you called. I didn't want to interrupt when you must be getting ready for this press conference, but what's going on? It sounded at the top of the news like it was about to happen any second, but now they've moved on to other stories."

"It's Charlie. He's having some kind of a panic attack. His sister thinks he's shutting down from the trauma of this on top of Linda dying."

"What do you mean, a panic attack? He needs to get out there. Can you call Neil and see if he can do something for him? Maybe call in a prescription out there, just to calm his nerves. Or can you and Rachel do the press conference together, and he can just stand there? What does Mac think?"

The barrage of Katie's questions made Melissa realize how desperately she wanted to be with Charlie, to see with her own eyes what he was going through. She was certain she could help him through it, the way her mother had gotten her to climb out of the pit of her own guilt so she could refocus on the search for Riley.

"I don't actually know," she said. She felt the burn of shame in her cheeks as she explained that the police obviously believed she was lying about what happened yesterday and that Charlie was distancing himself from her on Mac's advice.

"Are you kidding me? Melissa, I am so sorry. I'm the one who told you to get him a lawyer."

"Stop, it's not your fault. I'm calling you for another reason." She told her about the message she received from Jennifer Duncan and its possible significance.

"Wait. Jennifer is out on Long Island? Did you tell the police?"

"No, it would seem like a desperate attempt to shift their attention from me. I saw the way they looked at me. They really think I did this. I don't even have my car anymore, so I'm driving this stupid U-Haul. I'm going over to Jennifer's place right now."

"Alone?"

"That's the only way this works. I told her I needed a friend to talk to."

"*I'm* the friend you talk to in your time of need," Katie said, "not a woman who may or may not be a murderer and a kidnapper."

"I see you haven't lost your sense of humor."

"Seriously, this sounds too dangerous, Melissa. If nothing else, we know she's capable of pulling a trigger under the right circumstances."

"If she wanted to kill me, she could easily have done that already. If she is the one who took Riley, it's because she actually wants to raise her as her own. She desperately wanted children, and Doug took that away from her. She could come up with some kind of private adoption story and hire lawyers to make it stick. She could even move to another country and disappear. Reaching out to me might be a tactic to avoid being a suspect — the way killers attend their victims' funerals. Or maybe she hates me enough to want to see me in agony. Either way, as long as I don't let her know I suspect her of anything, she has no reason to hurt me."

The silence on the other end of the line signaled Katie's continued disapproval. "And yet you called me specifically to say you were going to that woman's house. You see the irony in that, right? You know this is dangerous."

"Just on the off chance something goes wrong. If you don't hear from me in an hour, call the police."

"I don't like this."

"You don't have a choice." She gave her the address. She was almost there.

30

Through the pulled-back edge of a drawn living room curtain, Nancy watched until the taillights of the rental truck disappeared around the corner.

"She really shouldn't be alone," she said. "I should have stopped her."

The smell of garlic and tomatoes escaped the kitchen as Mike lifted the lid from the pot and gave it a quick stir. She'd had no idea her son knew how to cook so confidently. "Melissa's tough as nails, Mom. She finally admitted she's been having nightmares about what happened to us as kids. She remembers more than she ever let on. And now Riley. It's a lot to handle. Give her some room."

"What do you mean, nightmares? When I noticed how tired she's been, she said she was having insomnia. I assumed it was pressure from all her work, plus moving Charlie and Riley into the apartment."

He shook his head. "It's more than that. Remember when she was out on the beach early Friday morning, supposedly saying good-bye to the view? She wandered out there in her sleep. Riley told me she was calling out for her mommy, saying she didn't want to get in the bathtub. She's been reliving everything we went through in her dreams."

Nancy knew from the police interviews after the children were rescued that Carl had abused them in the bathtub among other locations. In the early years of their marriage, Carl used to insist on bathing Nancy in the tub. The way he had touched and examined her. She was too young and inexperienced to realize it wasn't normal. It was one of the many ways he had exercised power over her.

It pained her to know that her beautiful, brilliant daughter had been suffering, pulled into that horrific trauma from the past during her sleep. Nancy herself had been plagued for years by nightmares. How many nights had she jolted upright in bed, picturing Peter and Lisa the way they had been found, with the wet seaweed and bits of plastic on their faces and in their hair? Their bodies swollen in death. The nightmares always began the same way: she was in a police station being questioned and then she was taken down a long corridor to the mortuary and made to identify her children.

And when she would wake up, as she had so many nights, she would slip out of bed and go in to see Missy and Michael and cover them. Only then could she crawl back into bed, trying to be soft and quiet so as not to wake Ray and alert him to the darkness that she could never escape. But even in sleep, he would always sense her worried next to him, reaching out and pulling her close into his arms. Against the warm scent of him, she'd be calmed and find sleep again.

Nancy did not realize how connected a married couple could be until she wed Ray. Carl had been so cold. As eager as he had been to marry her quickly at such a young age, he stopped touching her after the children were born, trying instead to "treat" her so-called illnesses with medicine. Only after Dr. Miles questioned her under the influence of sodium amytal was she finally able to let herself remember her worst fears about Carl. She realized that Carl was the one making her so tired and complacent with those drugs . . . and the reasons why. Keeping Nancy drugged, in a weak, child-like state, had been one of the many ways

Carl had isolated her while leaving him free to spend time alone with Peter and Lisa.

By recovering her repressed memories, she was also able to remember that Carl had staged the fatal car accident that killed her mother. She was still a teenager, but had no friends after Carl swooped into her life. He wanted her all to himself, which was why he found a way to take her mother from her.

"Did Charlie know about the nightmares?" she asked. "What has he been doing to help her through this? Did she talk to Katie about it? She should not have had to carry the weight of such a thing on her own."

"Knowing Melissa, she thought she could make it go away all by herself. And I think it's pretty obvious right now that Charlie doesn't do much of anything to help anyone but himself. It's like he took over Melissa's life the minute he met her. She dated Patrick for years, and then suddenly marries this guy in a matter of months? Sorry, but I can't shake the suspicion that Riley going missing has something to do with her father. He could owe a loan shark a million dollars for all we know about him."

While Mike cooked, Nancy went to her bedroom and tried to occupy her thoughts by rearranging the clothing that the kids had brought down in the moving truck. Nancy had been so certain the first time she walked through this house that she would spend the next phase of her life here. But now danger had found her family again, before she had even arrived. She was half tempted to begin packing everything up again. Instead, she sank into the pillow top of her new bed, realizing how tired she was. She tried allowing herself a brief rest to close her eyes, but could not put aside Mike's observations about Charlie and his influence on Melissa's life during the last year.

After Patrick had abruptly broken off their relationship, Melissa closed herself off, focusing only on her work and a few trusted friendships. Nancy had worried endlessly that her daughter might never be willing to trust her heart to another person. But then she met Charlie. They both needed someone to lean on, and he had that sweet little girl in need of a mother. Nancy had been so happy about Melissa's willingness to love again that she had not noticed the ways that her daughter's new relationship had monopolized her priorities.

Nancy had never heard her daughter sound so desperate as when she was begging Charlie to simply speak to her. If Ray had distanced himself from her that way for even a glimpse of a moment when Mike and Melissa had been kidnapped, she never would have survived. That wasn't speculation. She was certain of it.

Mike called out that dinner was ready. She was about to go downstairs when a ping sounded quietly from her purse. She slipped the smartphone that the kids had bought her last Christmas from the outside pocket of her bag. There was a new text message. It took her a moment to register the name. *Dear Nancy, I am so sorry to contact you during such awful circumstances. I need to talk to Melissa, but she seems determined not to hear from me. At the risk of putting you in an awkward position, can you please let me know where I can find her? It's urgent.*

Her accomplished, confident, caring daughter had been reduced today to questioning her own sanity, wondering if she might have hurt a little girl she loved as her own heart. She needed support now — support she wasn't getting from her own husband.

Before she could rethink her decision, she dialed Patrick's number.

31

Melissa's GPS announced that she had reached her destination. Gravel crunched beneath her tires as she pulled into the U-shaped driveway. Jennifer would certainly hear the arrival of a rental truck in front of her house. There was no turning back now. She made her way to the front door, where the porch light was waiting for her. She typed a text message to Katie — *I'm going in now.*

She was reaching for the brass knocker when the door sprang open. Jennifer pulled her into a tight hug, and Melissa immediately recognized the familiar scent of her ever-present perfume — not sweet, but bright and floral and fresh. Would she have noticed the smell if Jennifer had been lurking in the woods behind the park bench yesterday?

As Jennifer led the way from the foyer through the living room and then into the den at the back of the house, Melissa searched for any sign that Riley might have been here. A sippy cup or plush toy or one of the Cheerios or Goldfish crackers she managed to leave behind everywhere she went. Nothing.

Jennifer gestured to a pair of overstuffed white armchairs. Melissa settled into one as Jennifer poured iced tea from a pitcher.

"I didn't realize you had a house out here," Melissa said as she accepted a glass. She waited until Jennifer took a sip from her own tea before doing the same.

"I don't — not yet, at least. I took this place as a rental. I'm going out with my broker to look again this week, but house hunting's the last thing you need to hear about right now. How are you holding up? How is your husband?"

"We're both struggling to keep it together." Melissa was searching for a way to ask Jennifer where she had been yesterday afternoon without confronting her directly. "How long have you had this rental? It's beautiful."

"I have it for the whole summer, but I've been in the city for the last two weeks. I just got back this morning. I'm glad you took me up on the invitation to come over. It shouldn't have taken something so awful to put everything in perspective, but I hate that we fell out of touch. I know I was hard on you when you wouldn't be my lawyer for the probate mess. It was my fault, but if it makes any difference, I was convinced I would never be able to get anything done without you. That's how important you've been to my life, Melissa. And it pains me to see you going through this. I'm so terribly sorry."

The apology sounded sincere, but Melissa was more interested in what Jennifer had said about her arrival to the beach house. "You came out today? You didn't want to take advantage of the weekend?"

"I would have, but I didn't want to miss the fundraiser for the Wrongful Conviction Project last night. I left the city at the crack of dawn to make sure I could make it to a friend's boat party. He insists on doing them on Mondays to have the water to himself. If only I had a clone, I could be in two places at once."

"Right, the fundraiser . . ." Melissa said, her voice drifting.

"I was sort of hoping I would see you there," Jennifer said. "Find a way to extend an olive branch after everything that happened between us. Now here we are together again, but under such horrible circumstances."

"I had to miss it because my brother and I were helping my mother move." She was desperate to know whether Jennifer was telling the truth about her whereabouts yesterday. "I'm sorry, but can you point me to the powder room?"

Once she was alone, Melissa pulled her phone from her back pocket. She opened Instagram and searched for the New York Wrongful Conviction Project. The most recent photographs were from last night's fundraising dinner. The fourth picture showed Jennifer in a navy-blue gown, standing at the lectern as an image of her in handcuffs and prison scrubs was projected onto a screen behind her. It was definitive proof that Jennifer was not on Long Island when Riley was taken.

When Melissa returned to the living room, Jennifer was smiling at her sympathetically. "I'd love to know more about your husband and stepdaughter. I wish I had been around to see you fall in love again."

Melissa realized that she wished Jennifer had been there, too. Over the years, they had become far closer than a lawyer and client. One night, after a little too much wine with dinner, Melissa had confessed to Jennifer that she did not think she could ever open herself to another relationship after the pain of losing Patrick. She and Jennifer were real friends, and then, suddenly, they weren't. She had missed her. "I met Charlie in grief counseling. I started going about a year ago, after my father passed away."

Jennifer held a hand to her chest. "Oh, Melissa, I am so sorry. I didn't know. I missed so much."

Melissa waved away the apology. "We were helping each other to heal, and I just knew that he was the person I wanted to talk to every day for the rest of my life, and then I met his baby girl, and I was absolutely in love with them both." She took another sip of iced tea to keep her voice from cracking. "Is it awful that I want you to talk to me about literally anything else right now? I think my brain needs a break or it's going to shut down entirely."

"Okay, let's talk about anything you want."

"Well . . . someone on the internet keeps threatening to out me as a liar and a hypocrite. I finally blocked whoever it is. I know social media comes with the territory for my work, but sometimes I think my skin is too thin to keep at it."

"I've seen a couple of those posts," Jennifer said. "That's another example of when

I should have reached out to you as a friend. Of all people, I know what it's like to be vilified. It plays with your mind and your self-esteem. Even if the information is wrong, you start to internalize a sense of shame and embarrassment."

Melissa was thinking through the parallels to what her mother had said earlier that night when her phone pinged from her pocket. It was a text from Katie. *Making sure you're still alive. I still can't believe you went over there alone.*

When she was done typing her reply — *all good here* — she felt Jennifer's eyes on the screen and looked up. It was clear they both knew Jennifer had read the message.

"Sorry," Jennifer said, breaking the awkward silence. "I really didn't mean to spy. It was just an automatic reaction. I hoped it was news about your stepdaughter."

She hit the Send button on her text. "Nope. Just Katie."

"Is there a reason she didn't want you to come here?"

"Okay, it's my turn to come clean. Those social media posts I've been getting? After everything that happened between us, I wondered on occasion if it might have been you."

Jennifer's eyes slowly widened, and Melissa braced herself for another round of the rage Jennifer had unleashed the last time they spoke. Instead, Jennifer let out a sudden cackle.

"Oh my gosh, I'm so sorry. That was . . . definitely not appropriate. But, no, I'm not your internet troll, and, in any event, you wouldn't have come here tonight only to ask me about some anonymous posts. Did you actually think I might be involved in the disappearance of your stepdaughter? Is that why you asked me how long I've been out here?"

"Jennifer, I don't even know what to say. You have no idea what an emotional roller coaster this has been. I've had a hundred different theories. If it helps, I spent all day convinced that my husband's first wife might have faked her own death on the other side of the world only to reemerge yesterday to kidnap Riley. I'm not exactly operating at peak cognitive capacity right now."

"Please, you don't need to apologize to anyone with what you're going through." She fanned her eyes with both hands, still recovering from her laugh attack. "Well, I was nervous about seeing you again after how poorly I behaved the last time we saw each other. I certainly did not expect it to come to this."

"I can't tell you how mortified I am," Melissa said.

"Then can we call it even and forgive each other? I am still very ashamed about how I treated you, after everything you did for me. I probably came across as a money-hungry monster. I was so angry about the years that had been taken from me that I never even told you why I was so consumed with Doug's probate case."

"I saw the news that you eventually won. I suppose congratulations are in order."

"His finances were so tied up in real estate, it will probably be years before any money actually gets distributed, but it does feel good to be vindicated by another court. Did you mean it when you said you needed a distraction? Because I'd like a chance to explain my side of the story if you're up to listening."

Melissa nodded, realizing she really did want to hear it.

"Brace yourself, because it sounds like something out of your podcast. Let me be blunt: Doug's children are lucky they're not in jail."

32

Jennifer paused to pour herself an inch of whiskey from a bar cart in the corner of the den. Melissa declined the offer.

"Doug told me the whole story not long after we met. Rebecca and Brian — those are his kids — pretty much stopped talking to him not long after he split from their mom. He knew he had poisoned his relationship with them through his own conduct, but when he started making money, he did everything he could for them financially, not expecting anything in return. They'd go right through it and always come for more, and he still kept writing the checks, figuring it was owed to them. And then one day, they announced that they were ready to try letting him back into their lives. It started with a couple of dinners together, and then they suggested a family trip to Maui. Doug said he was thrilled, finally hopeful that he might be able to mend things with his kids. They were out on a day trip on a motorboat they chartered, and Doug eventually nodded off. He said he only halfway woke up, and figured it was a combination of sun and seasickness that put him out. But then he heard his daughter say something about whether it was time yet. His son then said they should find a spot with shallower reefs. He assumed they were talking about going snorkeling since reefs can be fish habitats, but when he sat up, they apparently looked at him as if he'd risen from the dead. They immediately started asking how he was feeling and joking around that he had too much to drink, even though he was sure he only had one glass of wine because he didn't want to take a chance on doing anything to mess up their trip."

Melissa could see where the story was going. "As if they didn't expect him to wake up?" she asked.

Jennifer raised a finger toward Melissa, confirming the point. "I still remember Doug describing the sense of panic he had — out there on the water, alone with just the two of them, and he was absolutely certain that his own children were going to murder him in a staged swimming accident. He played along, saying that he had learned

261

a valuable lesson about combining wine and boats. When they got back to the hotel, he ordered room service for dinner, claiming to be exhausted from the boat trip. He was that worried they would try again. Then the next day, he feigned a work emergency so he could stay locked in his room until they flew home the following morning. He couldn't prove what they were planning, but he knew he wasn't going to risk them having a second chance to kill him. The day after he got back to New York, he called a lawyer to take the kids completely out of the will, then sent them each a final check for $250,000 with an explanation that he had disinherited them. He said they both claimed to be confused and hurt, but he said that, if anything, their reaction only confirmed his belief they were dangerous."

"So you weren't the one who convinced him to change the will," Melissa said.

Jennifer shook her head. "No, this all happened long before I met him. He did rewrite his will after we got married, but his ex and their kids had already been taken out years earlier. He had amounts set aside for the housekeeper, his barber, and a few longtime friends and employees, but the remainder would have gone into a charitable foundation."

"I hope you know I wasn't judging you when I said I couldn't be your probate lawyer. It's not my field. I might have lost the case if I tried to handle it."

"At the time, it felt like one of the only friends I had in my life was abandoning me, and I was hurt. I understand now, though. You were being a good lawyer, which was also being a good friend."

Melissa realized that Mac was in the same position today. She felt like he was abandoning her, but he was trying to be the best lawyer he could be for Charlie, which was what Melissa had asked him to do.

Jennifer was still talking about her husband's will. "The probate battle was never about the money. As you know, I could make millions in a book deal if I ever need to. The reality is that Doug's children are sociopaths who plotted to kill their own father, and I'm convinced the reason their mom wouldn't testify about Doug's abuse was because she wanted me to rot in prison while her children got his money. And once I do get the money from the estate, I plan to distribute large gifts to the people Doug loved — the ones listed in his earlier will before our marriage. I know this sounds weird, but even after everything that happened, I have never wanted the people who cared about Doug to remember him un-kindly."

It wasn't the first time Melissa had noted the sadness in Jennifer's voice when she discussed her deceased husband. "You still love him, don't you?"

Jennifer shrugged. "Depends on which Doug we're talking about. The one who made me coffee every single morning no matter how busy he was, who called me his angel? Who got up at a piano bar and belted out 'We've Only Just Begun' on our fifth anniversary, even though he was a terrible singer?" She smiled at the memory. "Yeah, I still miss him. He was the love of my life. The man I hid from in that laundry room cabinet? No, I'm not in love with him any-more."

Melissa was more than familiar with the incident. To help Jennifer build the self-defense claim in her wrongful conviction case, they had argued that as a result of a pattern of abuse, Jennifer was able to predict when Doug was going to behave violently toward her, even before he raised a fist. One of the many episodes she described was a day when she could tell from his side of a phone conversation that a major real estate deal was falling apart. Trying to preempt the inevitable, she climbed inside a laundry room cabinet to hide from him. The bruises he left on her after he found her there kept her from leaving the house again for the next three days.

And even though Jennifer had seen the absolute worst in her husband, she never actually wanted any harm to come to him. On the final night of his life, she had only grabbed his gun to scare him, hoping it would be the wake-up call he needed to get help. But then he charged at her violently. There was uncontroverted evidence that she had tried desperately to resuscitate him after he was shot.

Melissa found herself thinking about her parents. When they met, her mother was living under an assumed name, hiding from the fact that most of the country believed she had murdered her own children and gotten away with it. Despite that, her father had fallen in love, started a new family with her, and would have taken his wife's secret to the grave with him. When Mike and Melissa disappeared and their mother's true identity was revealed, she was the glaringly obvious suspect. But not once did their father doubt her innocence. Instead, he risked the ire of the entire community with his passionate defense and loyal protection of her.

But Charlie? One grainy video of a woman on a ferry boat, and he was treating Melissa like a total stranger — or worse.

She heard echoes of her brother's voice, wondering why Charlie was so eager to marry after losing his wife and asking her how well she really knew him. She had met Charlie while she was still devastated and heartbroken after Patrick ended their relationship so abruptly. It was the one time in her life when her motto of choosing to be happy had utterly failed her. She had told herself that she would never allow herself to be that vulnerable again, but then Charlie had come along. Maybe her undying need to be happy had convinced her that Charlie was the solution.

Charlie claimed to be keeping her at a distance because Riley was all that mattered right now, and yet he still had not gotten in front of the cameras, which might help make the search for Riley more than a local story. None of the decisions he was making right now made any sense.

She had been spent the entire day consumed with learning more about Riley's mother. But Riley had a second parent.

"Honey, are you okay?" Jennifer was looking at her sympathetically. "You checked out there for a second. I know that feeling.

Like all of a sudden, it hits you, and you can't even believe this is really happening. If anyone knows that your worst nightmare can come true, it's me."

"Yes, that's exactly what it's like," Melissa said. Was it possible? Like Jennifer said, the worst nightmares can come true. "You know, I'm really worn out. I should get back home. Thank you, though. I needed this. Really. I've missed you."

Jennifer pulled her into a final hug after walking her to the door.

Melissa called Katie as soon as she was in the truck. "Have you been watching the news? Did Charlie do the press conference yet?"

"I've been watching the whole time. They keep saying they expect one, but nothing yet. What did Jennifer say —"

"It's a long story, but it's definitely not her. She was in the city yesterday."

"But how can you know —"

"I saw pictures of her at an event. I'm positive. Katie, I need a really big favor. Can you go to my apartment?"

"Of course. Anything you need. I'm in Jersey right now finishing this big cupcake delivery, but then I'll go straight to your place when I'm done."

Melissa didn't recall Katie mentioning the

delivery before, but she had spent the last two days in a half daze. "Where in Jersey?"

"A place called Saddle River. I'm only a couple miles away from the venue."

Saddle River was thirty miles outside of the city. Between the delivery and the return trip, it would take Katie nearly two hours to get to Melissa's apartment.

"I can call Neil and Amanda instead," Melissa said.

"What's going on?" Katie asked with concern. "You sound panicked."

"It's Charlie. I'm starting to wonder whether he's been telling me the truth."

33

The sound of Metro-North slowing on the tracks shook Jayden Kennedy from his semi-sleep state on the train. It was his stop, the Wassaic station. A glance at his phone told him that the train had managed to arrive two minutes early, despite the downpour that had come with this current storm. Even a brief wait outside would leave him soaked. As he lined up to exit behind a young couple loaded down with shopping bags from New York City, he peered between them to check out the small parking lot beyond the platform.

He recognized her little Mini parallel-parked at the nearest possible waiting spot. The glow of an electronic device was barely visible behind the windshield. Of course, Julie was there already. Since the day he first met her, she had never let him down. He suspected that as long as they lived, she never would. His phone pinged in his jacket pocket, the pocket of the new suit he had managed to buy and have tailored just this morning. It was Julie. *You're here! I'm right out front. Welcome home! Let's celebrate.*

The celebration would wait until he changed out of his suit, the bottom of his pants drenched. He draped the pants over the shower curtain rod in Julie's bathroom. Even if the suit was permanently ruined, the trip into the city had been well worth it. The potential new client had offered him a consulting contract right there on the spot before the arrival of the lunch check. It wasn't simply a one-time training for staff, which was his usual gig. He would be a year-round consultant on global strategy for a multibillion-dollar fund that had decided to make socially responsible investing a core part of its mission. He would end up earning more than he ever had on Wall Street — worth the price of a new suit, indeed.

He found Julie in her kitchen — more of a kitchenette, really. She dumped icy water from a martini glass and replaced it with the contents of a frosty metal shaker. She inserted a toothpick of olives that she had already prepared. A perfect gin martini to join the one she had already made for herself. She held her glass up for a clink. "I am so proud of you," she said. "You believe in your beliefs — and yourself. And it is paying off. Congratulations."

He took a sip, and it immediately took away the damp feeling of the storm. "It smells so good in here."

"Coq au vin," she announced. "I normally only make it in winter, but tonight called for comfort food. It needs to simmer for a bit, I'm afraid."

"I'd be happy to wait here with you and this cocktail forever."

He was giving her a more detailed play-by-play of that day's meeting when a loud beeping noise erupted from his phone. He recognized it as an alarm from his house's smart-home system. "Oh, this is not good."

"What's wrong? It's not about your new client, is it?"

"No, it's my house. There's an excess moisture alert from the basement. There must be leaking, enough to set off the alarm, and this rain isn't stopping anytime soon."

He pulled on a pair of sneakers.

"Where are you going?" Julie asked.

"To check on the house." He was not about to risk major property damage to his house to accommodate the oddities of an emerging vacation-rental company. "The renter won't be inconvenienced at all. I can get to the basement though the egress window. She won't even hear me, but I'll text her through the Domiluxe app to let her know I'm on my way, just in case."

"I'll go with you," she said, turning off the stove.

"But this is going to ruin your beautiful dinner."

"It will be fine, and you said you were willing to wait forever, remember? If you do happen to disturb the renter — and she is in fact a woman there writing by herself — it would be better if I'm with you."

By the time they reached his house, the renter still had not responded to his message on Domiluxe. He was hoping to find the house empty, but the white car in the driveway and glow of lights across the first floor told another story. When the outline of a person moved across the living room window on the right side of the house, he was certain she was home.

"At least the front curtains are drawn," Julie said. "Where's the basement entrance?"

"In the back. I can run along the left side while she's in the living room." He pulled up the hood of his rain jacket and jumped into the torrent. It wasn't until he slid open the egress window that he realized Julie was right behind him, standing at ground level, water dripping onto his shoulder as she peered over it. He shook his head disapprovingly before stepping inside, making room for her to do the same. He held up his cell phone to help light the path.

"What if she hears us?" Julie asked.

"The entire basement's concrete," he whispered, "and we'll be quick."

Using the light of his phone, he quickly found the source of the leak, a small basement window that had blown open during the storm. He secured the window, and then used the mop and cleaning rags he stored in a closet at the foot of the basement stairs to sop up most of the standing water. It would have to do for now.

They were about to climb back outside when they heard footsteps on the floor above them. She had moved from the living room to the kitchen. Once they were outside, he pointed to the right, indicating that they would circle back to the front of the house from the opposite side.

As they ran past the rear windows lining the back of the house, he noticed that the curtains were open. On the opposite wall, his television was on. *I'm never renting my house again,* he thought as he ran through the downpour, dreaming of a new set of dry clothes and perhaps another martini.

From the safety of the main road back to Julie's, he finally allowed himself to push back the hood of his raincoat. "Spy mission accomplished," he said with a smile.

"Is it crazy that I think that was actually fun? Did you notice what was on the TV?"

"No way, I just wanted to get out of there."

"It was a cartoon," she said, her voice full of excitement.

"So maybe Helen brought her kids after all."

Her eyes widened. She was clearly prepared with a rebuttal. "Except *'Helen'* " — she used air quotes to emphasize her point — "told you she had two teenagers."

Indeed she had. He had forgotten. "Maybe she likes cartoons for relaxation?" Jayden suggested.

"People don't rent vacation houses using cryptocurrency and untraceable messages to watch children's television." He could tell she was deep in thought, conjuring up an alternative explanation. "I bet it's someone with a double life. I heard a story about this guy who had not one, not two, but *three* wives. He was a pilot with different families in three separate area codes. I bet your renter is a man with multiple families, and his secret child was the one watching *Peppa Pig* before bedtime."

"Peppa Pig," he repeated. Something about the name of the cartoon rang a bell for some reason, but he couldn't imagine what it could be. "I don't understand why anyone would want to juggle a life full of lies." He also couldn't imagine wanting to spend his life with more than one partner. With the small window of free time he had between today's meeting and the next train home, he had stopped at Tiffany and selected an engagement ring.

Once this nightmare rental situation was over, he'd find the perfect way to ask her.

His phone pinged with a new message. It was from Helen through the Domiluxe app. *ABSOLUTELY DO NOT COME HERE!!!*

"I told you," Julie said, a knowing gleam in her eye. "Secret family."

A second message soon followed. *I checked the basement and saw no leak. Must be a false alarm. Please do not violate the terms of the rental agreement.*

In the morning he would try to convince the college friend who started Domiluxe that his business model was a terrible idea.

34

At the same time, in Southampton, New York, a woman named Wendy Keller was bouncing between News 12, the Weather Channel, and a weather-tracking app on her phone for the latest updates on the storm. The consensus was that the worst of it was heading north of the city. So far on Long Island, it wasn't even raining, but the red banners flashing high-wind alerts across the screen had her worried. Winds up to fifty miles per hour. She was no meteorologist, but that sounded bad.

A friendly-looking announcer on News 12 was advising people west of Amagansett to prevent property damage or even physical harm by securing outdoor items that might be thrown by the wind. She looked out the sliding glass doors to the back deck. The grill. A glass-topped table with four chairs. Two ceramic planters. Now she wished she had let Tom take it all when he had left.

Any one of the items could be a problem if blown through the glass doors or windows.

This was the kind of thing Tom used to take care of. The sandbags and heavy-duty cables they were suggesting on the television? He would have gone to the hardware store yesterday to prepare. Wendy, on the other hand, was the type who rarely watched the news and, when she did, thought they blew everything out of proportion, all in the interest of ginning up ratings.

She decided better safe than sorry and dragged the table and chairs inside, stacking them in the corner next to the sliding glass doors. She rolled the grill to the opposite side of the yard where it couldn't hurt anyone if the wind decided to move it. As for the big planters, she tried to reposition those, too, but to no avail. If this wind managed to throw those monsters around, they were in much bigger trouble than even the news was predicting.

Her chore for the night completed, she felt the pull toward her computer. Six months ago, on a blustery night like this, she would have cooked a luxurious dinner, read to Anna before bed, and then curled up with Tom on the sofa to read or perhaps stream a movie together. They were happy then. Or at least, she was.

Everything was different now. She needed to vent, and that's what the computer was for. From the sofa, she flipped her laptop open. The screen of her browser was already open to Poppit, an anything-goes message board that allowed users to post whatever they wanted without a registration process. It was completely anonymous. She hit the link to enter her only saved community: the First Wives Club.

A friend at work had told Wendy about the online group when she finally admitted that the reason she had returned to the sales floor at the dealership was not because the "stay-at-home mommy thing" wasn't for her, but because Tom had left her, and there wasn't enough money to support two households. Half of what she made went to Anna's daycare, and until she started first grade in September there was nothing she could do about it.

She clicked on the box to begin a new message, using her usual handle, Anna's Mom. *How long before being alone feels normal? Just when I think I have it down, something sneaks up out of the blue and wrecks me all over again. Tonight, it was a high wind alert on the news. My immediate reaction was to ask my ex what to do. So now I have dirty patio furniture in the corner of my living room and a sore back from trying to move planters that could apparently wipe out small villages. But mostly I have another reminder that he's gone and is never coming back.*

It felt good to pour out these negative feelings, but even more addictive was the immediate feedback from other group members.

He would have brought more than dirty furniture into your life in the long run. Things will get better.

This is not permanent, AM. Hang in there. You'll be happy again. I promise. Keep your head up for your little girl.

I'm sorry, AM. I know how stressed you were about this weekend. Anna will be home tomorrow (am I remembering that right?), and you're still going to be her mommy, no matter who else comes and goes.

And therein was Wendy's actual problem. Not the weather. Not the back deck. The problem was that Tom had announced he would be introducing their daughter to *her* over the weekend. She refused to speak her name. The other woman. The reason Wendy now lived half of her nights alone and spent hours talking to anonymous strangers in the identical position. She had tried to convince him it was too soon for Anna to meet her.

She was only five years old. It would confuse her. Tom replied by saying Wendy had "no role in the decision" and that he'd only told her in the interests of "healthy co-parenting."

She didn't know how she would have gotten through the last months without the support of the First Wives Club. Most of the users popped in only sporadically, but Wendy was one of about thirty "super-users" who posted daily, usually multiple times. These women were still unknown to her, but at this point, they felt almost like family.

Most of the messages were quick rants followed by the ensuing pep talks, but First Wives were also known to help each other in more concrete ways.

Just yesterday, Wendy had agreed to do a little dirty work herself, too.

She felt a pang of guilt — or was it shame? — as she recalled the scared and shocked expression on the woman's face after Wendy had confronted her. It was a step too far. Wendy never would have agreed to it if she weren't so upset about her own situation with Tom.

From now on, she would stick to messages only.

On the television, News 12 had moved

from the wind warnings to an alert about a missing toddler and the search that was still underway under the threat of the impending weather. *See,* Wendy thought, *this is just like the news. One disaster after the next.* If she had to guess, the child wandered off while playing outside and her parents had overreacted.

She allowed her eyes to leave the computer screen long enough to gaze up at the television. Scrolling text announced, SEARCH ONGOING FOR MISSING SUFFOLK COUNTY TODDLER. Informational bullet points filled the screen. Her name was Riley Miller. She may have been carrying a Peppa Pig plush toy. She was last seen yesterday wearing blue *Frozen* pajamas.

Yesterday. So it was more than just a child wandering off. Wendy could not even imagine the terror of having anything bad happen to Anna. She needed to remind herself more often that there were worse things than losing a husband.

The bullet points were replaced by a photograph of a smiling, heart-shaped face gazing up at the camera. She had blonde hair and strawberry-pink lips. Such a cute little girl.

Wendy was starting another message board post when her eyes darted involuntarily to the television screen again, but the missing child's photo had been replaced by footage of a warehouse fire in Islip.

She searched for *missing girl Long Island* on her browser and hit Enter.

"Oh no," she said aloud, alone in her living room. "No, no, no, no, no."

It was the girl from the park yesterday. What had she gotten herself into?

35

On the other side of a FaceTime video call, a grinning seven-year-old named Ricky Keeney joyously held up a ten of clubs to the screen. "Uncle Neil, Aunt Amanda, is this the card I showed you before?"

In their New York City living room, Neil and Amanda Keeney applauded vigorously, feigning a sense of awe. "How in the world did you do that?" Amanda asked. They had of course pretended not to notice when Ricky's hands had slipped beyond the view of his mother's laptop camera.

"A magician never tells his secrets," Ricky declared proudly.

Of the four Keeney siblings, only Neil's sister Kit had remained in Hyannis Port where they were raised. Dierdre was a professor at Brown University in Providence, and Jimmy — who went by James now — was a teacher in Boston. Ricky was Dierdre's son, and she had taken her family to the Cape for the weekend for Ricky to visit his grandparents and cousins.

Ricky was asking if he could perform one more card trick when Neil's mother asked if he could show Grandpa instead in the family room while she spoke to Uncle Neil and Aunt Amanda in private. He raced off, happy to comply. Ricky was named for Neil's father, Patrick, and absolutely adored his grandfather and namesake.

Even though Neil's mother was now alone at the kitchen table, she kept her voice in a low whisper. "I just got off the phone with Nancy Eldredge. Are you aware of what's happening there? I had no idea until now. We were just at the oyster bar together yesterday with your sisters and the kids. I don't know how Nancy can even handle this right now. Sometimes, I think that poor woman is cursed."

Amanda looked to Neil to answer. "Melissa called us right after it happened," he said. "The police were at the house immediately. There's a massive search underway on Long Island."

"They say on all those shows I watch that the first forty-eight hours of an investigation are the most important," she said fearfully. "Isn't that right, Amanda?"

"That's not always true, but yes," she

conceded, "time is obviously of the essence."

"And Riley's barely three years old. She can't be off by herself all this time. And Nancy told me that Charlie has basically walked out on Missy and won't tell her anything about what the police are up to. Can't you do something to help her?" Even on a computer screen, it was clear she was looking at her daughter-in-law the police officer.

The discomfort that had been growing between him and Amanda throughout the day felt palpable now. Out of respect for his wife's wishes, he had refrained from getting too closely involved in whatever was happening in Southampton, knowing that it could put Amanda in an awkward position if the police believed he and his NYPD wife were interfering in their investigation. He had been rationalizing the decision because there wasn't much they could do to help, and Melissa's entire family was together and could support one another.

"What do you mean Charlie walked out on her?" he asked.

"I guess Missy hired one of her fancy lawyer friends, but now he only represents Charlie, and Charlie sent the lawyer to Nancy's house to pick up his things. Nancy's really worried about Missy's state of mind right now. And I think the whole situation is digging up some very difficult memories for Nancy. What is it that people say now — *triggering*? I think Nancy's prior trauma is being triggered. And probably Missy's, too. Oh, that poor family."

"I didn't know about Charlie. Let me call Melissa now and see if there's anything we can do."

"I'm going to St. Francis now." Neil's mother was a daily communicant at St. Francis Xavier Church, just down the block from the family home. He knew that she was certain in her belief that only prayer had made the rescue of Missy and Mike possible forty years earlier. She said she loved them both before ending the Face-Time call.

He was about to pull up Melissa's number on his phone when her name appeared on the screen with an incoming call. Perhaps his mother's work was already kicking in.

"Melissa, we were just about to call you." Next to him, Amanda was nodding in support. He no longer detected her reluctance. He tapped the screen to change the audio to speaker.

"I need a favor," Melissa said. "Can you go to my apartment?"

36

Detective Guy Marino remembered a time when he used to dream of being a singer or a comedian or a celebrity chef. When none of those fantasies materialized, he landed a gig as private security with a popular boy band. Now, a decade and a half later, he was a police detective on Long Island.

He was a long way from the days of watching A-list public relations campaigns in action, but he knew that something was off with Charlie Miller. His top-tier criminal defense lawyer had arranged for a high-profile press conference, but instead, Miller was hiding in the coffee room of the police station, huddled with his sister and lawyer.

His partner, Heather Hall, was on the phone, but once she was done, he was going to propose that the chief of police hold the press conference without the family. The reporters had already complained about being gathered outside given the expected storm. They wouldn't wait much longer.

After Hall ended the call, her face was pale and her gaze was distant.

"You okay?" he asked.

"That was the sergeant working with the search teams on Shelter Island. They found a child's tank top on the beach. It's the Princess Elsa pajamas. It's hers, Guy. It's Riley's."

He could tell from her response to the information that this wasn't an optimistic development. "Where on the beach?"

"Washed up onshore off the sound. It definitely came out of the water." There would be no reason for a suspect to throw the girl's clothes into the sound. More likely, if her body had been weighted down, a garment like a loose tank top could float away with the tide. "I got to be honest, Guy. I don't know if I can handle this. Whenever I think about that poor little girl, I just want to go home and hug my Milo."

"Hey, we both know you're tougher than I am, so if you can't take it, there's no hope for me. Okay? And we still might find her. I'm not ready to give up yet."

"We need to tell the dad, though."

"Once we do, there's no way he'll be able to pull himself together for those cameras."

"The chief's going to want to pull the plug

on that anyway," she said. "Finding the pajamas changes things. We're not ready to announce that yet. So let's go talk to the chief first," she said, thinking out loud. "Then we tell the dad. And we can ask him about the medications before we break the news."

The initial toxicology screen had come back from Melissa Eldredge's blood test. The only substance found was the active ingredient in a prescription sleeping pill that neither detective had heard of until today.

After they met with their chief, Guy tapped twice on the door before entering the break room. He could tell from the lawyer's expression that he was growing impatient with his client. "We're still not ready here," Mac said. "Maybe you should go ahead without us —"

"Sure, we can talk about that," Guy said, "but in the meantime, we could use your help on something. You mentioned to me yesterday that your wife's been having some sleeping problems. Was she taking anything for that, by any chance?"

"Yes, she had a prescription." The brand name was a match for the substance in Eldredge's blood. She could have had detectable amounts in her system from prior use, or she may have taken a pill after coming home from Shelter Island, either to calm herself down after whatever she did to Riley, or so she would be found asleep by her brother. In any event, the only drug in her system was one that they could tie directly to her.

Hall gave him a look that said it was time to tell Charlie about Riley's pajamas. To his surprise, she was the one to break the news.

Charlie stared at them blankly, struggling to process the information, but his sister immediately covered her mouth in horror, choking back a sob. As Charlie registered Rachel's reaction, the color drained from his face. Guy worried he might become physically ill.

"So that was my daughter in the ferry video," Charlie said vacantly. "And it must have been Melissa driving the car."

Rachel reached for her brother's hand across the table. "I'm so sorry, Charlie."

Mac held up both palms. "Let's not jump to any conclusions, okay? What's the next step, Detectives?"

"Let's not worry about this press conference tonight," Hall said. "We're going to have divers begin searching the sound, but that's going to have to wait until we have light in the morning. Do you have a place to stay tonight? I gather you won't be going back to your mother-in-law's house."

Charlie placed his head in his hands. "I don't know. I'll get a hotel, I guess. We'll figure something out."

A knock on the door was followed by the appearance of the on-duty desk sergeant. "Hall, Marino, I've got a walk-in wanting to talk to you." A quick look to the station house with wide eyes suggested that the matter was urgent. Guy nodded his understanding.

"Why don't you guys try to take a break and regroup in the morning," Hall said.

"Try not to give up hope," Guy said. "We haven't. I promise you that."

After they walked the Millers and their lawyer to the back door of the station house to avoid the cameras waiting in the parking lot, Hall asked if he meant what he said about believing that Riley Miller might still be alive.

He didn't answer. "Sarge, who's this person looking for us?"

"All I got is a name — Wendy Keller," the desk sergeant said, glancing down at a notepad. "And she says she talked to Riley Miller right before she disappeared."

They found the woman waiting in a nearby interview room. She abruptly stopped chewing her left thumbnail when they entered. Guy guessed she was about his age, which would make her forty years old.

"We understand you've got information about Riley Miller?" Guy asked.

"I do. But I'm having trouble making sense of any of it. I'm really scared about what I may have gotten myself into." Her voice was shaking and her hands trembled as she spoke.

"Okay, start by having a seat," Hall said, pulling out a chair at the table to emphasize her point. "Take a deep breath. You're here voluntarily. Any information you can offer is important. You told the desk sergeant you think you spoke to Riley Miller yesterday?"

The woman exhaled audibly and nodded.

"So why don't you start there," Hall said.

"But I need to explain something else first or it won't make sense," Wendy said. "I'm part of this chat group online. Oh, this is just so embarrassing. And pathetic."

"A little girl is missing," Hall said firmly.

Wendy nodded. "And that's why I'm here, but it's still hard. So this group is called the First Wives Club. It's totally anonymous, but we are women who, to be blunt, were unceremoniously dumped by our husbands. It's basically a support group where we can rant and maybe try to comfort each other."

"I don't think that's embarrassing at all," Guy said gently, hoping that it would encourage her to share the unvarnished truth.

"Okay, but sometimes members of the group do more than just send messages. So if your ex-husband's new girlfriend blocks you on Instagram, maybe another member of the group will go to their profile and get screenshots for you."

"Harmless enough," Guy said.

"But on occasion it's more than that. Two weeks ago, a lurker who had been reading messages but not posting disclosed that she suspected but was not certain that her husband's supposed business trip to Washington, DC, was in fact a liaison with an old high school girlfriend. A fellow First Wives Club member who lived in Arlington volunteered to make a trip to the hotel where he was staying. Do you get the idea?"

They both nodded sympathetically, but Guy could see that Hall was beginning to lose her patience.

"So where does Riley come in?" Hall asked.

"Last Monday, a user who called herself *Jilted* said that her ex was taking their three-year-old daughter and his new wife for a vacation in the Hamptons over her objections. She was looking for a member in the area who might be willing to check on them to make sure the woman was at least being nice to her daughter. I direct-messaged her saying I was willing to help. But then once we started to message back and forth, the conversation sort of escalated to where she asked me to confront her instead. It was so mean. I still can't believe I did it."

Guy still did not understand where this story was going. "Confront her in what way?" he asked.

"The conversation started innocently enough. I told her that her daughter was really cute and looked just like her. She seemed nice enough and said something like that was sweet, but the girl was actually her stepdaughter. And that's when I turned on her. I almost chickened out, but then I justified it because the woman had broken up a happy home with a little girl involved. So I said what Jilted told me to — that she wasn't taking good care of the girl because she was only a stepdaughter. And then I said *I know all about you* and called her a fraud and hypocrite. She seemed so rattled. I rushed out of the park, feeling ashamed."

"Wait, was this at the park on Pond Lane? At the playground?" Guy asked.

"Yes. And I'm almost a hundred percent

sure that little girl's the one you're looking for now."

"So the woman in the park really exists," Hall said once they were alone again. She wiped at her eyes. He had never seen his partner look this exhausted. "God, is it possible Melissa was actually telling the truth? Someone tells this poor sad woman a story to get her to distract Melissa at the park, then slips sleeping pills into her coffee?"

"You mean the obscure brand of sleeping pill that just happens to be sitting at home on her nightstand? No. Not possible. My guess is this person called Jilted is none other than Melissa Eldredge. Shoot, she's probably the one posting all those other threats on her own social media. It's one distraction after another. She keeps us chasing down the lady in the park, pressures us to drug test her. It could all be part of giving herself a cover story."

"That's awfully elaborate."

"Well, as you pointed out from the start, the woman's a defense attorney. She literally writes a podcast talking about how people could have committed their crimes better. Think about it: every time we talked to her, she kept pointing us toward the woman at the park. At the end of the day, we've got her on video coming and going from Shelter Island."

"Plus the pajama top," Hall said dejectedly.

"So we wait for forensics to come back on her car. And the divers start searching the sound tomorrow. Go home and hug your little man Milo."

37

Melissa eyed the clock at the top of her laptop screen. The twenty minutes since Neil and Amanda had left for her apartment felt like an eternity. She was back on her laptop in her mother's guest room, trying to learn more about Charlie's clients. She couldn't find any mention of his work online, but that wasn't surprising. He was a one-man operation who got most of his consulting work as referrals from two of his former colleagues at one of the larger geology firms on the West Coast, where he worked right after college. If she could remember the name of the company, maybe they could point her in the right direction.

She immediately picked up when her phone rang with an incoming call from Neil. "Hey, did you get in okay?" She had called Louie, the doorman on duty, to let him know that friends were coming over and would need the front desk's copy of her apartment key.

"Yeah, we're here now," he said. "I've got you on speaker with Amanda. What exactly are we looking for?"

"I don't know. Anything. I just know something isn't right. Maybe he's wrapped up in something dangerous. Someone could have taken Riley to put pressure on him. Maybe he owes money to the wrong kind of people? Or his work got him entangled in something shady? Somebody could be blackmailing or threatening him." If Charlie believed Riley had been kidnapped to influence his behavior, he might have chosen to distance himself from Melissa for her own protection. It would also explain why he was reluctant to hold a press conference.

"So we'll start with his desk?" Amanda said.

"We set up a workspace for him in the corner of the den," Melissa said. She realized the Keeneys hadn't been over to the apartment since Charlie had moved in. In retrospect, she hadn't seen many of her friends much at all since she had met Charlie.

"His most recent job was in Antigua, consulting on the build of a new resort. I tried finding it online, but the only announcement I could find was for a project three years ago that has already been completed. Maybe look for any information about that."

She could make out the sounds of drawers being opened. "Is this the right desk?" Neil asked. "White with a glass top?"

"Yes, that's Charlie's."

"There's nothing here," Neil said.

"Nothing about Antigua?"

"No, I mean nothing at all."

"The drawers are all empty," Amanda added. "Like completely cleaned out."

"Oh my God. Did he move out? Can you check our bedroom?"

She waited as she heard the sounds of them walking through her apartment, followed by shuffling in the background.

"There's men's clothes in the master bedroom closet," Amanda said.

"And in the dresser, too," Neil said, "but not a lot. There's definitely extra room in the drawers."

"He's not entirely moved in yet," Melissa said. "He still has most of his stuff from his house in Oregon in storage. Keep looking around to see if you find anything that might be relevant. I'm going to call the doorman. If this has something to do with his work, someone could have gotten into our apartment and taken everything from his desk."

Louie answered on the second ring, not bothering with polite greetings. "Ms. Eldredge, I just heard the news from one of the residents. Is this true about Riley being missing?"

"It is," she said, still trying to absorb the reality of the situation. "But I have a weird question, Louie. Has anyone else come to our apartment in the last few days? Charlie and I have both been out of town." The building logged every key checkout into a computerized record.

"No, the only key authorization I see recently was from you for your two friends. They're still upstairs."

"Are you aware of any other visitors that my husband may have had to the apartment?" She realized Louie was probably wondering why she could not ask Charlie these questions, so she explained that he was at the police station looking at photographs of possible suspects. "We're trying to make a list of any possible suspects who might have taken Riley, which could include anyone coming into the apartment — maybe a workman, or someone who came by to meet with Charlie."

"No one I know of," he said. "Well, his sister, of course."

"Yes, that's Riley's aunt Rachel. She lives in Brooklyn but has come by a couple of times to take Riley for visits."

"A couple of times?" he asked, the register of his voice upticking.

Melissa counted the number of visits in her head. There was the pick-up and drop-off when Rachel kept Riley during their honeymoon. And then the delayed birthday celebration, followed by the day she babysat last month while she and Mac had knocked out the Evan Moore episodes for her podcast. "I guess four to be exact," she said. "Why do you ask, Louie?"

"Um, perhaps I'm confused. It's not for me to say. My wife teases me that my brain's been getting cloudy lately."

"Please, Louie, it's gravely important."

"Well, from what I have seen, Miss Rachel is at your apartment all the time. She has her own key and we wave her up whenever she comes over. Come to think of it, maybe it's only when you're not home. You don't know about this?"

38

Melissa's brother was pacing behind the living room sofa, his hands balled into tight fists. "I knew I should have done more to shake you back into your senses," he said. "I was convinced you wouldn't listen and would only become more stubborn about going through with the wedding. When I find him, I'm going to get some answers out of him, no matter what it takes."

She always knew that Mike had a temper that he was careful to hold at bay. She had not seen him this outwardly angry since she had told him about her sophomore homecoming date pretending to have a stalled car engine on the way home after the dance. When she saw her date at school the following Monday, he was sporting a black eye and a heartfelt apology.

"Let's not jump to any conclusions," her mother said, holding up her palms. "A clean desk at a home he just moved into isn't a sin. You said Charlie works primarily from his office, and most of his personal belongings are still in storage."

"But he was obviously hiding the fact that his sister spent so much time at the apartment — *Melissa's* apartment, by the way," Mike added. "What else is this guy hiding?"

"It was no secret that Rachel thought they were moving too fast. The woman refused to attend the wedding, for heaven's sake. But she is still Charlie's sister. You don't turn your back on your family over a disagreement." It was obvious that their mother was referring as much to Mike and Melissa as Charlie and his sister. "When Riley lost her mother, Rachel was the only one helping Charlie until Melissa came along. Mind you, I'm not taking his side. Once I fell in love with your father, I never kept a secret from him. But he may have been trying to keep Rachel as a constant presence in Riley's life without provoking a confrontation between his wife and sister. Honestly, even though he should have told you, I don't see why you're both so upset about his only other family member coming to the apartment when all she has done is try to help with her niece."

As her mother and brother debated the relative degree of Charlie's betrayal, Melissa replayed everything she knew about Charlie in silence. The distance he'd placed between them. The icy tone in his voice during their last conversation. The first time he had placed his hand on the small of her back as he walked her to her car after counseling. The way he'd leaned in and whispered "You look amazing" as they were about to exchange vows at their wedding.

She was trying desperately to come up with some rational explanation for everything she knew about him — every moment they had spent together — but she kept coming back to one fundamental, horrifying question: If he loved her, how in the world could he leave her in this kind of pain and confusion? She could feel the rational part of her brain trying to tie disparate threads of information together, but something was blocking her mentally.

She flinched at the sound of the doorbell. Maybe it was Charlie, coming home to offer all of the answers he owed her.

Her breath left her briefly as she registered the face on the other side of the door. Even through the fog of the peephole lens, his hazel eyes managed to connect to hers immediately. His face was slimmer and more sun-kissed than the last time she'd seen him — when he'd suddenly broken off their engagement — but it was definitely him.

She cracked open the door. "You can't be here, Patrick. Please, I told you on the phone not to contact me anymore. You dump me and now show up like this when a child is missing?"

A white Tesla was in the driveway. He had been dreaming of buying one before they broke up. Maybe the car had made him happier than she could. "How did you even know where to find me?"

She saw him glance quickly into the house before bracing one arm against the front door. One look at her mother's face confirmed Melissa's suspicions.

"I won't leave," he said. "I'm absolutely convinced this is important."

"*This?* This has nothing to do with you."

"I need to talk to you about your husband."

39

How many times had she imagined what she would say to him if they ever ran into each other at a party or one of the favorite restaurants they had frequented over the years? *Stomp on any hearts lately?* Or maybe she'd ask him how many other women he had proposed to recently. Or, best of all, she would take the high ground and be gracious and content in his presence, and he would realize what a mistake he had made, giving up the life he could have had with her.

But now Patrick was here in her mother's living room, and none of that mattered anymore. From the chair beside her mother's, he had their full attention.

"Okay, this is embarrassing and makes me sound awful, but I won't waste any time skirting around it. After we broke up, I couldn't let you go. I'd wake up wondering where you were and what you were doing and whether you were okay."

Mike started to rise from the sofa, his purposeful scoff summing up her own feelings.

"Wait," Patrick said. "I promise, I'm not here in some grand attempt at reconciliation. My point is that I tried to keep track of you, even though we weren't together anymore. I've listened to every episode of *The Justice Club,* and, well, I probably check your social media on a daily basis."

Mike half-muttered, half-coughed the word "stalker."

"Pretty much," Patrick conceded with a shrug. "So, I saw your post with the curlers in your hair. You looked beautiful, by the way. Happy. And the caption said something about *taking the leap.* I figured if it was what I suspected, Katie would be there, and then I saw that she had posted a photo of a wedding cake at a winery down the road from the Cape house. I put two and two together, but I had to know for sure. I called the town clerk up there and confirmed it. And then I got curious about your new husband, but it turns out there's a lot of Charles Millers on the internet. Oh man, this is so embarrassing. I wound up calling the vineyard where you got married and talked the event planner into giving me the information on the business card that Charlie had given her."

"Are you kidding me?" She could not believe what she was hearing.

"Like I said, this is embarrassing, but that's how strongly I feel that you need to know this."

"So, what did you find out?" Mike asked.

"That there's *nothing* to find out," Patrick said. "The website for his firm? The domain name was bought only a year ago, even though his online business profile says he's had his own outfit for six years. And the lease on his office was signed only a week later."

Patrick was an experienced programmer who specialized in building web applications for businesses in the private sector. She wasn't surprised that he could trace the history of Charlie's website. "You checked on his office lease?" she asked.

"I know I sound crazy, but I've done work for that building management company. I only asked because his website information didn't add up. That office space is a tiny hole in the wall in a rundown walk-up in Hell's Kitchen. Have you ever even been there, Melissa?"

The one time she had been nearby and wanted to meet for lunch at Chez Napoléon, he had been waiting for her on the corner nearest to his building even though she had planned to go upstairs and see his firm's offices. He explained that he was starving and wanted to eat as soon as possible. Then afterward, he said he needed to go back to the office alone for a conference call, blaming the time crunch on the flambéed crepe they had shared for dessert.

Feeling her family's eyes on her, she asked to speak to Patrick alone. Once they were in the privacy of the dining room, she didn't even pause to sit down.

"You had no right to pry into my life that way, especially after the way you derailed it. Did you want me to be alone forever, pining for you? I was crushed, Patrick. Utterly devastated. And then when my father died, all you did was send flowers? You couldn't even call? I was a wreck. And then I met Charlie. I made a decision to be happy."

"And that's why I've kept my concerns to myself. I picked up the phone so many times to call you, only to change my mind at the last second. I convinced myself there had to be some explanation and that I was only looking for an excuse to get back into your life."

"As for all this sleuthing, you have no idea what you're talking about. Charlie's a widower. He had to move across the country after his wife died, raising a baby girl alone. He dropped almost all of his work. So I'm not the least bit surprised about the timing of his lease or that he'd need to start with a humble space."

"Okay, but you have to trust me on this, Melissa. He would not have let his domain name go. That business he supposedly runs? I would bet everything I have that it did not exist — if it exists at all now — before last year."

She asked him for the date the website was set up. It was two weeks before she met Charlie in counseling.

"And now this child is missing," Patrick said. "And your mother would only tell me so much, but it doesn't sound like this guy Charlie is acting quite right."

Melissa rubbed her eyes, determined not to cry in front of him. "I have the information now," she said coolly. "Is there anything else you unearthed?"

"No, but is that all you're going to say? What should we do about this?"

"There's no *we,* Patrick. You were the one who chose to stop being the person I turned to with important decisions." She could see the pain in his eyes, and softened her tone. "I do appreciate you coming all the way out here to tell me this, but I need you to go now."

"Missy —"

She shook her head. He didn't get to call her that anymore. "I'm serious. You need to go." She was nearly shooing him toward the front door as he argued. "You really cannot be here. Riley's not only missing. The police obviously think she's dead, and that I'm the one who murdered her."

His face contorted with confusion, and Mike and her mother looked away. "Let me help you. Please." He reached for her, but she pulled away.

"Patrick," she said sharply, "do you have *any* idea how horrible it will look if the police find out that my ex-fiancé is here with me right now? You told me to listen to your expertise on that website, and I did. Now it's time to listen to me. You *have* to leave. Now."

He held her gaze and then nodded, muttering an apology as he left.

Melissa's mother immediately sprang from her chair. "Oh, Melissa, I am so sorry. It was my fault for telling him to come. I was trying to help."

"Mama, it's fine."

"But you were right," her mother said. "What if the police are watching the house and this becomes something else they use against you?"

"Then I'll handle it when the time comes."

"Can we go back to what matters most here?" Mike asked. "Not cool that Patrick basically stalked you, but that stuff he found out about the website and the lease was weird. I'm telling you — something is seriously wrong here."

"I know," she said, finally wrapping her head around the truth. Charlie could have been lying about everything since the day they had met. She had to rethink every assumption she had ever made about him. What did she actually know, and what had she simply chosen to believe?

Riley. She felt a pain in her heart at the thought of her name. Riley was real. That much was certain.

Linda. When she had been searching for proof that Linda was actually dead, she never found any evidence that an American woman had taken a fatal plunge from a waterfall in Norway. She had never even seen a single photograph of Charlie's first wife. He kept postponing going through the belongings that were supposedly in storage, but wouldn't a father leave out a single photograph of his daughter's mother so Riley might remember her?

"Maybe you can try his sister," her mother said. "Rachel picked up the last time you called."

Her mother's suggestion — at that specific moment — allowed her to see what she had been blocking out mentally. She replayed the sound of Louie's voice when he said Rachel was at the apartment all the time, the doorman sounding almost sympathetic.

She heard Riley's cute little voice the morning of their wedding, asking if she could find her daddy in the *bucky-ord*, adding that she wished her mommy could be there. All those other days that Neil reassured her it was normal for Riley to say that she still talked to her mommy all the time.

It was all so clear now. "What if Rachel's not his sister?"

40

The words were tumbling from her mouth so quickly that Melissa had to force herself to take a deep breath and spell out her suspicions to Mike and her mother methodically, as if she were detailing the facts for a jury or her podcast listeners.

"I was so focused on finding out whether Linda had really died that I never stopped to consider the basic question of whether she even existed. This has to be why Charlie refused to tell the police how to contact Linda's parents. The entire family is a fabrication." Between the fatal fall that may or may not have been suicide, to the custody battle his former in-laws had threatened to launch, to their suspicions that he may have pushed their daughter to her death, he had buried Melissa in details that kept her too preoccupied to scratch beneath the complicated surface. "I should have realized as soon as I called Charlie's university. If the

two of them graduated together, the donations he made to the school would have
been listed under both names once they
were married, but there was no mention of
his wife."

Her mother and brother were still catching up with the implications of her conclusion. "So if there's no Linda, who is Riley's
mother?" her mother asked.

"Rachel," Mike explained. "That's why
Rachel refuses to see Melissa in person.
She's Riley's mother."

Her mother sucked in her breath sharply.
"Oh, now I see. That's why you said she's
not Charlie's sister. Oh my goodness. Is that
possible?"

But Melissa was too busy tying her own
thoughts together to answer her mother's
question. She wasn't ready to move on from
the issue of Charlie's college donations. Kelsey, the student who worked in the alumni
office, had said that the regular pattern of
annual donations had come to a sudden halt
twelve years ago.

She was trying to pull up Kelsey's number
when her phone rang. It was Katie.

"Well, at least I know you're alive," Katie
said after Melissa picked up. "Didn't you
see my texts?"

"I'm sorry," Melissa said. "It's been wild

here. I told you Jennifer had a rock-solid alibi. You didn't need to worry."

"Except the last time we talked, you wanted me to check on your apartment because Charlie was lying to you about something. I was so caught off guard. I'm kicking myself for not throwing the cupcakes out the window and turning around."

"Neil and Amanda already went to my place." Her theory about Charlie and Rachel was going to sound even stranger out loud. "I've been trying to dig into Charlie's background and here's the thing: I don't think he really had a wife who died. Linda may never have even existed. And Riley's mom might actually be Rachel. The whole thing is a fraud."

"What?" Katie gasped. "Why would they do something like that?"

"Money, I assume. You know I didn't ask for a prenup."

"Do you want me to drive out there? I'm here for you always," Katie said.

"No, thank you, but I need to run. I have to call his college on the West Coast before it's too late. I'll let you know if I need anything."

"Promise? You know I love you."

"Love you, too," Melissa said.

Kelsey picked up almost immediately

when Melissa hit her number. "Melissa! I was just scanning some pages of old *Chronicles* to send you."

Melissa was surprised by the sudden response. "I was checking in to see if you'd found anything else about Charlie Miller and his wife, Linda," she said. "I'm particularly interested in the fact that Charlie suddenly stopped donating."

"That's why I was going to call you," Kelsey said. "I've been digging around, and I found an old announcement in the college paper. Charlie Miller was hit by a car while he was out on a weekend bike ride. It was a hit-and-run, probably by a drunk driver. He never recovered."

Her knees nearly buckled as a wave of heat rushed to her face. "Wait, so the Charlie Miller who graduated from there is dead?"

"No, not dead. At first he was unconscious at the hospital, and then in a coma, but he ended up in a vegetative state. It sounds like it was a bad situation. Initially, it seemed like he might wake up, but over time, any hope was lost. But technically he was still alive."

"How recent is this information?" Melissa asked.

"The crash was twelve years ago. The article was a few months later, announcing that his college class was setting up a scholarship fund in his name. It looks like contributions have petered out over time. I guess it's possible he's either dead or awake now, but we haven't published any kind of update."

"You said you were scanning information to send," Melissa said.

"Yes, his first-year class photo in the freshman yearbook that goes out to the entire university. And I also have the article about his bike accident. I will email them to you now."

Melissa made her way to her laptop.

"What else have you learned about him?" she asked as she opened the new message from Kelsey.

"Nothing, except the article about the accident mentions his family."

Melissa finished reviewing the attachments to Kelsey's email. According to Charlie's parents, he was their only child. They were praying for him to return and would never stop fighting for his life. No mention of a Linda. No mention of a Rachel. And, most importantly of all, the young man in both photos could definitely pass for an early version of Charlie at a superficial glance, but she knew Charlie beyond the superficial.

She could feel the truth at a cellular level. There was no Linda. No plunge from a waterfall. And no Charlie Miller. At least, not the one she thought she knew.

Her husband didn't even exist.

41

Jayden Kennedy was still walking on clouds, excited for both the new job he had landed and the diamond ring he had brought home from New York City. As inconvenient as the Domiluxe rental of his house had become, it also turned out to be a blessing in disguise. He and Julie had never spent this much uninterrupted time together, and he was even more convinced that he wanted to spend the rest of his life with her.

He was trying to think of the perfect place to pop the question. The hiking trail where they had first met? The restaurant where they had their first date? Or should he wait for Greece? They'd been talking about making the trip together.

He suddenly felt Julie behind him, her arms wrapped around his waist. "Do you want me to turn the TV off?" He had insisted on cleaning up after dinner, and she was catching up on the news while he washed the dishes. "I can always tell when your thoughts drift to some faraway place. You're not worried about the new client, are you?"

He dried his hands on a dish towel and turned to face her. Her smile had a way of grabbing his heart. "Not a worry in the world. I was actually dreaming about that trip to Greece."

"Oh, I like the sound of that." She squinted at him, reading his expression. "Now why are you grinning like a Cheshire cat — like you have some kind of secret?"

"There's no secret," he said. After he proposed — and after she said yes, he prayed — he would remind her of this moment and congratulate her for always being able to read his mind.

They had both sat down on the sofa, watching the meteorologist explain why the rain would only be getting worse over the next few hours, when Julie's cell phone beeped on the coffee table. Her eyes widened and her lips parted as she read a new text message. "My friend Kara's out in East Hampton and says that Melissa Eldredge's stepdaughter is missing. Apparently, they've got search teams all over the Hamptons looking for her."

"Is she sure? That's so weird. Didn't

Melissa even say in her podcast that if her stepdaughter went missing, she wouldn't behave the way Judith Moore did when Evan disappeared?" Something else about that podcast episode was tugging at the back of his memory.

"Wait, Kara just texted a link to an article." Julie scrolled through her screen as they read together.

"Peppa Pig." They said it nearly simultaneously.

"Yes, that's what she said on the podcast," Jayden said. "She said she loved her stepdaughter so much that she could now recite the plot of every episode of *Peppa Pig.*"

He felt his chest contract as he processed the possibility.

"Your renter," Julie said as she raised one hand to her mouth. "I thought it was a man with a secret family on the side, but . . ."

"When she first contacted me, she asked about that old swing set out back. I said it was for children, and she made this odd comment about it being perfect. She clarified that she meant the house itself, but the text seemed strange at the time. I'm going over there."

"And do what? Get yourself killed? No. You can't. Please."

"So, we'll call the police," he said, reaching for his phone.

"But they won't be able to do anything," she said. "Think about it. All we saw was a cartoon playing on a TV screen. We didn't even see a child, let alone this particular one."

"But the cartoon doesn't line up with the story my mystery renter fed me. Plus, there's the complete overreaction when I said I was going into the basement to check on the leak."

Julie was chewing her thumbnail, deep in concentration. "Okay, I think I've got it. I'll call the police from a payphone and say I was just near your house — which is true, after all. And I can say I heard about this missing girl. And that the owner of the house is a single man who lives alone, but I saw evidence that there's a child in the house now, who was watching *Peppa Pig,* and it made me wonder. If you see something, say something, right? And then I give them your name and number so they can follow up."

"And then when they *do,*" he said, picking up her train of thought, "I can tell them about the anonymous rental and all the ways it seems suspicious."

"That way, it will seem like they have two independent sources of information," Julie said. "They'll go to the house to check. I'm sure of it."

"You are some kind of smart," he said, reaching for his rain jacket. "Let's go. There's an old payphone at the diner."

42

The Southampton Town Police station was a short, squat, flat-roofed building tucked behind a dense thicket along the road. As Melissa pulled into the parking lot, she expected to find it full of news vans and reporters waiting for the press conference about Riley's disappearance. Instead, she spotted one sole woman walking toward her car, a press pass dangling from her neck.

Melissa fumbled in her purse until she located her own press credentials, obtained for her by the media company that sponsored her podcast. She kept her thumb across her name as she flashed it toward the stranger. "I just got here. What happened with the press conference?"

"They called it off," the woman said. "The chief said they weren't prepared to share any details beyond what we already had. Everyone packed out of here right away, but I stuck around trying to find out what actually changed."

"Did you get anywhere?" Melissa asked.

"I wouldn't tell another reporter if I had, to be honest, but no. Just a gut instinct that canceling the presser could mean the case took a bad turn. I've got a daughter at home not much older than Riley. I was really hoping to have good news before going home. These stories take a toll, you know?"

Melissa choked back a sob. "Sorry. Yes, I obviously agree."

Inside the police station, she was met with a frenetic energy closer to a big-city precinct than a small beach-town department. She recognized Riley's face on a stack of flyers one uniformed officer was passing to another. She stopped a man wearing a tie and sports coat as he was about to rush past her. "Excuse me. Are you a detective here?"

"Yeah, what do you need?"

"I'm looking for Detectives Hall and Marino. It's about the Riley Miller case."

"We got an information line set up for that, or you can make a report with the desk sergeant right there," he said, pointing to the front desk.

"They're the ones overseeing the case, though," she said. "They've spoken to me already multiple times. I was one of the last people to see Riley before she went missing."

"Ah, I got it. Last I heard, Hall went off duty, and Marino was heading to Shelter Island. I was rushing out on my own thing, so let me find someone else to —"

"I need to get to Hall or Marino as soon as possible. I'm Riley's stepmother."

His casual demeanor immediately stiffened. Whispers of her guilt had clearly spread through the department. "Funny you didn't mention that immediately. Let me see if I can track them down for you. Can I put you in a waiting room until then?"

She did not want to risk a "waiting room" that might actually be a holding cell. "No. I'd rather wait in my car. I will also call them. But, please, they need to look into my husband's background. He's not who he claimed to be." She reached into her bag and retrieved the pages she had printed at the house — the college photograph of an eighteen-year-old Charlie Miller and the university newspaper's announcement of Charlie's bicycle accident. "This is the man I thought I married, but it turns out he's now in a vegetative state on the West Coast. My guess is that if you research my husband's driver's license, you'll find that he has stolen this man's identity. The current photograph won't be an exact match, but there's a close enough resemblance that he was probably able to just renew the license with an updated picture and then get a new license once he moved to New York."

The detective took the papers reluctantly, his eyes darting between the exit door he had been heading toward and a door that probably led to the detectives' division. "Okay, yeah, let me find someone. Can I please get you into a waiting room? You'd be free to leave if that's what you're worried about."

"I'd prefer to wait outside," she said firmly. "I'll be easy to find. I'm in a U-Haul."

Once she was back in the truck, she found Detective Hall's business card and called the cell phone number she had scrawled on the back. By the time she finished spelling out everything she had learned about Charlie's lies and the real Charlie Miller's identity, the voicemail system told her that she had reached the system's time limit. She hit the pound key to send the message. She was in the process of dialing Detective Marino's number when her phone beeped with a new call.

It was Charlie. She answered immediately.

"You called," she said, forcing herself to

sound relieved and grateful, as in love with him as she was convinced she was when he had left the cottage that morning.

"I got your messages," he said. "All of them. I finally had time to listen."

"So you didn't block me?" she asked. She sounded pathetic, just the way he must have wanted her to feel.

"Of course not. I would never do that. I was trying to follow Mac's advice, but it doesn't feel right to lock you out this way," he said. "I can't imagine how deserted I made you feel today, and, honestly, I can't get through this without you. You're still my wife."

Was she? Their marriage license said Charlie Miller, but he wasn't Charlie. Who was she actually married to?

"I know you've been lying to me," she said. She allowed silence to hang over the connection.

She expected him to lie again — to offer all the same, complicated stories. But when he finally spoke, she could hear utter exhaustion in his voice. "I promise you there's an explanation."

"Will you even tell me your real name? Because I know it's not Charlie Miller."

"I've been trying to protect you."

She scoffed, shocked at the ease with

which he admitted to lying about something so fundamental. "So, you admit you were lying."

"About some things, yes. Not everything. It's about Linda's parents."

"Stop it. There's no Linda. Charlie Miller is in a hospital somewhere in a vegetative state. And he was never married."

"No, he wasn't, but I was. And then my wife died, and I had to start over again, but with a new name to hide from her family. Please, I can explain. I swear. Just give me a chance. I am begging you. I love you. And I'm terrified for my baby girl right now, and I don't know how I'm going to survive if you aren't in my life."

Happiness is a choice. It would be so easy to allow herself to believe him. But she didn't. There couldn't be happiness without the truth. "I don't want to think that our entire relationship has been some kind of lie."

"And it's not. Please, let me talk to you, one on one, okay? I promise that it will all make sense. Hell, I'll even sign away the rights to my story and you can use it for your next podcast once all of this is over."

She could almost see his smile, another part of the act. "Where should I meet you?"

She could lie, too.

43

Melissa held the phone away from her ear as Katie's volume suddenly escalated. "First Jennifer, now Charlie? Are you trying to put me in a grave from a heart attack? Maybe we can share a burial plot since you seem to have some kind of death wish today."

"I have to do this," Melissa said. "I thought about just calling the police with the address, but he already has a lawyer — thanks to me — and Mac definitely won't let Charlie talk." She felt a pain in her stomach every time she spoke that name, knowing it was never real. "They could charge him with getting a fake ID, but it won't answer who he actually is or why he and Rachel targeted me this way. And I still need to find Riley."

If there was any possible silver lining to having her heart ripped out again, it was that she believed more than ever that Riley wasn't actually abducted. Whatever game

Charlie and Rachel were playing, Melissa believed that Riley was safe — at least physically.

"Did you tell Mike and your mom where you're going?" Katie asked. "I'm surprised they didn't tie you to a chair to keep you from leaving."

"No, they'd never allow it. They forget I used to go on callouts with police at the DA's office. I do have a plan. He thinks I'm meeting him at the hotel, but there's no way I'm going into his room. I looked up the address. The places out here were all sold out, so he's staying about an hour away near Riverhead. It's called the Riverhead Sunshine Motel. There's a diner across the street. I'll call him from there so we'll meet in a public place. I'll have my phone set to record. I'll pretend to believe every word he says and then go straight to the police with it. He won't tell me the complete truth, but I'll at least have proof that he's lying, and hopefully he'll give me some hint where Riley is."

"Is there any way I can talk you out of this?"

"No. I'll have my phone right on my lap under the table. I should be there in about fifteen minutes and will text you when I arrive. If you get any kind of weird message from me after that, call the police and tell them I'm at the Golden Spoon Diner in Riverhead. Also call them if you don't hear from me again within twenty minutes."

"Now you're really scaring me," Katie said.

"Trust me. I'll convince him I'm on his side and that he's bought himself some more time. I'm the girl who chooses to be happy, remember? I'm going to use that to my advantage."

As she made her way north on Flanders Road, she imagined an alternative reality where she would be enjoying the bucolic setting on this two-lane country road connecting Montauk Highway and the Long Island Expressway, relatively untouched by the forces that had redefined the Hamptons over decades. Instead, she used the time to rehearse her plan, hoping to engrain the mental version of muscle memory. By the time she pulled into the parking lot of the Golden Spoon Diner, she was fully prepared for her role. Trusting. Loyal. Eager to be fed a story that would keep her happy and in love. She would pretend to be the woman she had been only hours earlier.

The strip of parking in front of the diner had a few open spots, but none large enough for the U-Haul. As she continued to the side parking lot, she found more than enough room in the far corner. She pulled into a spot directly beneath a light pole. If she was really nervous after she met with Charlie, she could probably persuade one of the diner employees to walk her to her car as a precaution.

She cut the engine, pulled her cell phone from the cupholder where she had stashed it, and began typing a text message to Katie.

Just got to —

The truck's passenger door suddenly opened. She managed to hit the Send button by the time he was in the cab.

"Why are you driving a U-Haul?" It was the man she knew only as Charlie Miller, and he was holding a gun.

44

Eighty miles north, in the Western District Headquarters of the Connecticut State Police, Lieutenant Floyd Anthony watched the rain pour outside his office window. When he first started on the job, his training sergeant told him rain and snow might be bad news for sun lovers, but great news for law enforcement. He swore that inclement weather kept criminals indoors, which meant less work at the station house.

Twenty-two years in, Floyd wasn't ready to bet the farm on conventional wisdom. High winds and broken branches could set off home security systems, creating callouts on the job. He'd caught a guy once who used the false alarms as a cover to commit real burglaries. And people rushing from their cars through the rain could be lazy about locking up, leading to overnight car prowls. So to Floyd, rain was simply . . . rain.

He heard the rap of knuckles against his open office door and swiveled his chair to see Officer Janelle Jackson. She was an Army veteran, two years on the force now. He was pretty sure she'd end up chief of police someday, whether here or somewhere else.

"Lieu, my understanding is all search warrant requests go through you?"

"As a final stop here before we call a judge. But warrants usually come to me from the detectives, Officer Jackson, not a swing-shift patrol officer."

"Yes, sir, but time is of the essence on this one. There's a three-year-old girl missing from Long Island, New York. Riley Miller." He had seen a BOLO alert at the start of his shift. "Dispatch got a call from an anonymous tipster that traced back to a pay phone in West Cornwall. The woman said she saw the news about the missing child and connected it to one of her neighbors. The man's name is Jayden Kennedy. Single male, thirty-one years old, resides alone. But she said she saw evidence that there's a child currently present at the house, and a show called *Peppa Pig* was playing on the television. And reportedly that's something the missing girl loves."

"That's a stretch, Jackson. Bachelors who

live alone have friends with children. Neighbors. Nieces. Cousins. What have you."

She nodded. "I'm aware, sir. I thought about driving by to check out the situation, but in the unlikely event a child is being held against her will, I did not want to set off a dangerous situation. What I did instead was call this Jayden Kennedy, the homeowner. I told him that we had received noise complaints about a party, but with the acreage out there, the precise location was unknown. I said a neighbor provided his name and number, and we were checking to see if he had heard anything."

He was right about her. She had good instincts. He nodded his approval.

"It turns out that Jayden Kennedy has a renter in his house right now. It's through a new app that promises complete anonymity. He has no idea who the person is, and people pay extra in digital currency to be untraceable."

Anthony sighed loudly and shook his head. "These tech people get rich making our jobs even harder."

"Kennedy told me he had texted the renter earlier to say he needed to check the house for a possible leak with this weather, and the person got irate and told him not to come over under any circumstances. He said he found the response peculiar and was wondering what the renter might be up to. And that's why I'm here."

Floyd knew that Judge Chandler was on duty tonight. She'd never sign a warrant based only on what they currently knew, and he didn't want to waste precious time on a futile request. "There's something called a public welfare check. I'll go with you. And we'll bring backup."

"One more thing." She held up a gleaming key with a brass finish. "The homeowner dropped this off in case we need it."

45

"Why are you driving a U-Haul?" Charlie's voice was filled with contempt and rage. If Melissa could close her eyes, she would not know that the person speaking to her was her husband.

"I don't know. Why are you holding me at gunpoint?"

His eyes narrowed as one corner of his mouth tilted into a half smile. "I always admired your skill for a quick comeback, but you're not in a great position to mouth off right now." He had immediately jabbed the muzzle of the gun against her ribs once he was in the passenger seat of the truck, and now he demanded that she leave the diner parking lot to head back to the South Fork. They were on the same isolated two-lane road that she had taken to Riverhead. She scoured her memory, hoping to recall an open gas station or roadside bar where she could possibly escape, but came up with nothing.

"Where's Riley?" she asked.

"Why don't you tell me?" He looked pleased with himself. She wondered if his face had always been so smug, or if he had somehow managed to alter his physical appearance. "Because from what the police have told me, you drove Riley to Shelter Island and drowned her because you never wanted children and could no longer handle the pressure."

"Why are you doing this to me?" She hated the pleading sound of her own voice, like an unfed animal teased with a dangling piece of meat. "Is it money? We don't have a prenup. You could get a windfall out of this without staging a kidnapping and framing me for it. You made up this elaborate story about Linda and Norway, and then signed up for group counseling so you could find an easy mark. Of all the people in the group, why me?"

The half smile returned. He was enjoying the fact that he knew everything, and she knew nothing. "I almost pulled the plug after a few months of knowing you."

"Is this the part where you tell me that it started out as a con, but then you really, truly fell in love with me?"

He shook his head. "Sorry, babe, but

nope. It's always been a con, if that's the word you want to use. I almost pulled the plug because you're too smart. Even watching a show on Netflix, you've got the whole thing figured out by the third episode. Thanks for spoiling all the endings, by the way. But when it comes to real life — at least, *your* real life — you don't see the truth at all, do you? Guess it's all that *choose to be happy* nonsense."

Her phone rang on the dashboard in front of him. She could see her brother's name on the screen.

"Don't even think about it," he hissed.

She kept both hands on the wheel as one unanswered ring after another sounded.

When the truck cabin fell silent, she asked, "So, what's the truth that I'm missing?"

He jabbed the muzzle of the gun into her ribs even harder. "No more questions."

She prayed that the partial message to Katie had gone through. Katie would call the police. They would find her, and then they would find Riley. *Please, God, I don't want to die.*

46

Mike saw the disappointment in his mother's eyes when he clicked End on the call. "She didn't pick up," he said.

"She left for the police station almost two hours ago. I knew we should have gone with her."

Melissa had been convinced that the police would be more likely to take the evidence about Charlie seriously if she could present it to them in person. "She's a lawyer, Mom. And a good one. She has more credibility with them if she's not bringing her mom and brother around in tow."

"Except now she's gone without a single update. For all we know, they arrested her." She was swiping at her phone frantically. "We need to go to the police station and see what is happening there. I cannot believe they took your sister's car."

"Mom, what are you trying to do with

your phone?"

"Get one of those Uber rides. Or I'll call for a regular taxi. They must still have those here, right? Not every problem has to be solved with an iPhone."

On any other day, he would have had a grand time ribbing his mother about this, and she would pretend to be insulted by his teasing while she laughed at every word. Instead, her rant about the cell phone triggered a memory of the conversation he and Melissa had as they were leaving the Cape.

He tapped his own phone screen.

"Are you getting a car?" his mother asked.

"I'm checking something. Melissa set our phones to share locations while we were driving here, but it might have expired by now." A round circle with his sister's photograph popped up on a road map. "No, it worked. I can see her, right here. She's between us and the police station. She must be on her way home."

"Oh, what a relief. The idea of her being arrested. I don't think I could handle it. Can you show me how that works? I want to see for myself where she is."

He explained that Melissa had insisted that the two of them share locations in case they got separated on the drive to the cottage. "With everything that's been going on, neither one of us thought to turn off the tracking."

"Thank goodness for that," she said, squinting at the screen. "Okay, I see her. And where are we?"

He zoomed the map out until she was able to pinpoint the location of the cottage. "Oh, yes, she is quite close, isn't she?"

They both watched the screen together, entranced by the real-time movement of the little circle containing Melissa's photograph. The welcomed moment of mental calm was broken as the dot continued south past the expected turn toward the cottage.

"Is that working right?" his mother asked. "She's driving too far. Where is she going now?"

He forced himself to stop watching the screen to call Melissa. There was no answer. When he pulled up the map again, she had made her way all the way down to the beach and was heading west again. According to the map, she was on the sole road that ran through a narrow strip of land with ocean beaches to the south and Shinnecock Bay to the north. The road dead-ended at a park that fronted an inlet. He could not imagine any reason why his sister would be going there.

"I need to go find her," he said. It was too

far to try to run after her on foot. His mother was making a phone call. "A cab's going to take forever out here in the summer."

His mother held up a finger as she waited for an answer. "Patrick, it's Nancy Eldredge. Where are you?"

47

Lieutenant Floyd Anthony pounded his fist against the door again. *Boom boom boom!* "Connecticut State Police. We got a call about a problem in the neighborhood. We're doing a wellness check. It won't take but a minute." This was the third unsuccessful try. "Anyone home?" he yelled.

No response, as expected by now. The homeowner, Jayden Kennedy, had told Officer Jackson he thought the tenant might be driving a white rental car. The lights on the first floor were on, but the driveway had been empty when they arrived.

Beside him on the porch, Officer Jackson shrugged. "Okay if we look through some windows?" she asked.

"Sure, if you've got X-ray vision. Curtains are all drawn."

"Figured we could walk the perimeter, this being a welfare check and everything. It's not like we're going inside."

It was a safe call. A court would uphold a cursory inspection if their conduct were challenged later.

At the back of the house, they found one set of windows on the south side with the curtains open. A television hanging on the far wall was on, playing some kind of cartoon. Jackson pressed her forehead against the windowpane, cupping her hands around her periphery to get a better view. "I can make out the kitchen from here. There's half a chicken on a platter on the counter and dirty dishes. I can see a sippy cup and a bright pink plastic plate. Something a child would use."

She stepped away from the window and looked at him expectantly.

"No car but all the lights are on, plus the TV," he added.

"Exactly — as if someone may have left here in a hurry. They could have seen us coming up the main road and taken off," she said. "Or gotten wind that a neighbor had tipped us off."

He followed her train of thought to the necessary conclusion. "It's possible the child's in the house alone given the perp was in such a rush to get away. That's a dangerous situation."

He radioed the three patrol cars waiting

at the end of the driveway for his call. Once the officers were on site, he slipped the homeowner's key into the front lock. "Go!" he yelled, slamming the door open with force.

His team moved quickly and methodically through the house, weapons drawn, checking closets and behind doors. Looking for blind spots, clearing them, and moving on. It was a textbook safety sweep.

"I've got the kid's room," Jackson called out. He followed her voice to a bedroom at the end of the upstairs hallway and found her standing over a duffel bag next to a child's portable playpen. "How much do you know about little girls and their favorite things?" she asked.

"Next to nothing if you ask my three grown daughters. And I like you, Jackson, but I don't like quizzes. What am I missing?"

"The missing girl, Riley, was last seen wearing *Frozen*-themed pajamas. See these little blue snowflakes? Those are Princess Elsa snowflakes." She pulled a pen from her uniform chest pocket and carefully used the tip to find the label inside the pajama pants. The brand was Disney. "She was here, Lieutenant."

48

In her periphery, Melissa watched Charlie continually tap his phone for updates with his left hand, managing never to lose control over the gun that was aimed directly at her head with his right. He had ordered her to come to a stop when they dead-ended in a beach parking lot. In the minutes that had passed, she had waited in silence as he kept checking his phone.

"Is this where you meant for us to end up," she asked, "or is this like when we got lost on those winding roads in Italy and you refused to ask for directions?"

He glared across the truck cab at her, but then allowed himself a small grin. For a moment, he looked like the man she thought she would spend the rest of her life with. "I enjoyed your company more than I should have on our honeymoon."

"Wow, you don't just want to con me. You really hate me, don't you?"

He shrugged. "Me? No. Not personally."

"But *someone* does," she said, noticing the inflection in his voice. "Rachel, I assume." She couldn't imagine why the woman posing as Charlie Miller's sister would despise her so intensely. "Did I prosecute someone in her family when I was at the DA's office or something?"

He shook his head as if they were playing a round of Twenty Questions that had gone on too long.

"We do know each other at some level," she said. "Tell me why we're here. And why do you keep checking that phone?" She could tell from looking at the device that it wasn't his usual phone.

"Good lord, you really are acting like we're married." He used his left hand to mimic a mouth prattling on. "You want explanations? Fine, I'm checking my phone because I'm waiting for the exact wording of your suicide note. We were working on it at the hotel but then I had to leave to meet you. And we're here because you're despondent and depressed and are going to wade into the water, weighed down by your clothing, and will drown . . . just the way you drowned your poor stepdaughter."

After everything she'd learned about him in the past few hours, she obviously had not yet absorbed the depths of his depravity. He was utterly devoid of humanity.

"Every case I've covered on my podcast was about someone who was smart and yet still made a mistake. How are you going to get out of here? You're at a dead end on a beach. You can't leave with my U-Haul because then where will you park it? I suppose Rachel will pick you up." She remembered saying goodbye to Charlie only this morning as he was leaving the cottage to pick up Rachel from the train station. She assumed now that Rachel had already driven to Long Island long before Riley disappeared. Rachel had to have been the one who had drugged her coffee and then snuck into the cottage to take Riley, posing as Melissa in Melissa's car for the ride to Shelter Island. "What you said before about my being smart in the abstract but not about my own life? You're not wrong. Bravo for convincing me that Rachel was your sister and not Riley's mother. You really did have me convinced."

He held her gaze for a few seconds, but she could not read his expression. "It's funny. In another world, this would be a great case for your podcast, because I'm the one who didn't make a mistake. Ironically, you may have been the one to help me with that. I learned a lot watching the way your mind works. Too bad no one will ever figure out the truth."

Her eyes squinted at the reflection of headlights in the rearview mirror of the U-Haul.

"Did you see that car?" she asked. "That's at least one mistake."

The car pulled a quick U in the empty parking lot and disappeared. As it turned, she could have sworn that it was a white Tesla.

"Nice try," he said.

"If something happens to me, the driver of that car will remember seeing this rental truck. At the angle we're parked, with his headlights on, it would be obvious there's someone in the passenger seat."

"No way. Besides, did you see how quickly that car turned around? A Tesla driver without a care in the world. I'm sure he missed a friend's address up the road. He didn't notice a thing here and is probably arriving at his party by now."

So, she had not been mistaken. The car was a Tesla, which meant it could have been Patrick. He had been worried about her. It was possible he'd been following her since she left the house. After insisting that he keep his distance from her, she was praying that he had ignored her instructions. If so, she needed to buy herself time.

"Your name isn't Charlie Miller," she blurted out.

"Yeah," he said dryly, "no news to me."

"I'm not the only one who knows. Before I drove to Riverhead, I told someone everything I know. They know I was leaving to meet you. You didn't attend the University of Washington. There is no Linda. I saw a picture of the real Charlie Miller, and it's obviously not you. They'll figure out how you stole his ID. You won't get away with this, and you and Rachel will spend the rest of your lives in prison, and Riley will grow up without a mother and father. If you stop now, you really haven't even committed a serious crime. Kidnapping your own child isn't illegal."

The phone Charlie had been checking finally rang, and he answered immediately. "It's almost done," he said, never breaking eye contact with her. "She thinks she has an upper hand because she supposedly told someone about *the real Charlie,* as she calls him. She's not as smart as we thought."

She forced herself to take even breaths, even though she felt like a minnow circled by a great white shark. "I love you, too," he said.

She suppressed a rush of nausea as he ended the call and rubbed his palms together. "It's go time," he announced. "I've got your script ready to go." He hit the Record button on her phone while he held up his own screen with words ready to be recited.

She scanned the first paragraph. "I won't do it," she said.

"You will," he said firmly. "If you don't, I'll kill your mother and your brother. I did my research. These are the rockiest waves close to your mother's cottage. I can get to your family in seven minutes. I'll make it look as if you shot them before committing suicide."

"Can I ask just two questions?"

"Maybe. Depends what they are."

"Is Riley safe?"

"Yes."

"And you drugged me and then used my car to make it look like I took her to Shelter Island."

"That's probably two questions technically, and not *me* personally — I was actually in Antigua — but yes, you fell asleep because a few of your sleeping pills ended up crushed in your iced coffee."

She was about to ask him how Rachel had managed to get inside the cottage, but quickly remembered how he had volunteered to run a few of the errands on her to-do list the previous week. "You were the one who picked up the keys from Mom's realtor in the city," she said.

His smile was gleefully smug. "You always say how much you love it when I take jobs off your plate. Here's a bonus piece of information for you. The video footage from the ferry? Your car, your sunglasses, but obviously not you. I'm told Riley had the best time on the car ride. On the way off the island, she pretended she was a turtle in the back seat, tucking herself into the footwell beneath her blanket, just the way she was asked. She really is a great kid." Melissa remembered finding the heart-printed blanket by the front door after Riley disappeared. Rachel must have tossed it to the floor when she returned the car keys and glasses before locking the front door behind her.

"So, who was that woman at the park who distracted me?"

"Some lonely, bitter woman we found on the internet. She had no clue what was going on. That's enough chitchat. It's time for you to record what we'll call your final podcast."

Melissa began to read the script that had

been typed into a message on Charlie's phone. *Traumatized. Stress. Psychotic break. I held her under the water.* It was exactly the story that had been fed to the police after Riley disappeared.

She continued to follow the script as he scrolled through the message. "My anxiety was also heightened by dishonest decisions I made in my professional life. My seminal wrongful conviction case — the supposed exoneration of Jennifer Duncan — is a complete fraud and a miscarriage of justice. Once she was out of prison, she admitted to me that she murdered her husband in cold blood for the sole purpose of inheriting —"

She came to a sudden stop and turned to look at Charlie in silence.

"Are you kidding me?" he yelled, slamming the truck door with his arm in anger. "Now we have to do it all over again. Read it word for literal word."

"Or I won't," she said. "And *that* will be your mistake. Why do you even care about that case? It's not enough to kill me? You have to tarnish my reputation, too?"

"Stop thinking you have any power." He raised his gun for emphasis. She craned toward the driver's side window as he moved to press the gun's muzzle into her forehead. "I will give you one more chance to get this right. If you mess it up, I will type it into your phone, kill you, and then torture everyone you love for kicks before I finally put them down."

Melissa was four seconds into her supposed confession, reading the predetermined words aloud, while the rest of her mind tried to figure out what she was missing. *Fraud.* The word TruthTeller invoked over and over again.

Melissa Eldredge is a phony and a fraud.

You're a liar and a fraud. It's all going to come out.

The woman in the park had called her a *fraud* and a *hypocrite.*

Why did he and Rachel care so much? Was it possible . . . ?

"Hey," he yelled, raising his hand as if to pistol-whip her. "Why did you stop reading again? We were almost done."

It was the only explanation. "Now I know why you looked so proud of yourself that I hadn't figured it out yet. Rachel *is* your sister. You're Doug Hanover's children. This is entirely about the estate lawsuit. Your father disinherited you, but you had a shot at getting the money after Jennifer Duncan was convicted of his murder. You want leverage to go back to probate court before the assets are actually transferred."

Charlie waved his hands with mock excitement. "Ding ding ding, we have a winner. See, I knew you were smart. I inherit what you have as Charlie Miller, while our lawyer goes back to probate court to get us the real money."

"But Riley calls you and your sister mommy and daddy," Melissa said. "Does that mean —"

"Don't be gross. That mommy and daddy stuff is automatic when they're little. Once we came up with this plan, we just didn't correct her."

"So, one of you is her parent, right? Does that mean she's really safe? Is Riley even her true name?"

He looked at her and shook his head. "Wow, you actually do care about her, don't you? Do you really want to know?"

She nodded eagerly, desperate to know the truth about the girl who now felt like a piece of her own heart. She had told herself she was only buying time in case Patrick had been following her, but reality was setting in. She didn't want to die, but if she had to, she wanted to know that Riley might have a life waiting for her.

"Yes, her real name is Riley. She's Rebecca's kid. Well, you know her as Rachel, but her name's Rebecca. Once you're out of the picture, Riley will go back to live with her mom like before. It won't be long until she forgets all about you or the way she used to call me daddy."

"Who's her father?"

"Your guess is as good as mine. My sister never told me and refused to put the guy's name on the birth certificate."

"And *your* name?" Melissa remembered Jennifer describing the absolute cruelty of her husband's two children, but if she had mentioned their names, Melissa could not recall them.

For the first time, Charlie looked a little sorry for her. "Brian. We were born with the last name Hanover, but our mom changed it to Bloom after our dad left. I guess raising kids without their crummy fathers runs in our family."

She repeated the name to herself in silence. Brian Bloom. The man she married. The man she thought she had loved. The man who was going to kill her.

"Okay, I mean it, this is your last chance. Read the entire note into the phone. If not, I'm moving on to Plan B. You're not helping yourself. Or Mike or Nancy."

She hated the sound of her family's names on his lips.

For the next three minutes, she read the

words that had been scripted for her. Even though she tried to alter her usual inflection so the people closest to her might know she was under duress, Charlie looked satisfied as they ended the recording.

"Get out," he commanded. He marched her at gunpoint to the edge of the parking lot, where he ordered her to take off her sneakers. With the gun at her back, she made her way through cool, soft sand toward the sound of waves swelling at the end of the beach. For once, the weather forecast had been right. The wind was whipping the surf into steep surges. She watched a lone nighthawk zagging turbulently, struggling to make headway against the gusts.

Her eyes darted wildly as she searched for any possible way to escape. She felt herself mentally reaching for the glint of a broken bottle washed up on the sand, but she had no way to make contact with it physically. Her heart fell as she stepped past it.

When she could walk no further, she understood why Charlie had brought her here. Beyond the sand was a rocky beach of stacked, slick cobbles, where angry white-caps churned and crashed, ricocheting against the backside of the inlet.

"Keep going," he ordered as he came to a halt on the sand, waving the gun for emphasis. "Walk out there, onto the rocks."

As she took one perilous step after another, she stared at the tumultuous beating of the water on the stones beneath her bare feet. She imagined the water pouring over her face, gushing into her nostrils and mouth. She would be sucked down by the violent undertow and rolled back to sea. All of her fears, however repressed, had kept her from learning how to swim. If she slipped into the surf, her death would be certain.

She turned to face him, searching the horizon behind him, hoping for any sign that the white Tesla had in fact been Patrick, but saw nothing. She tried to tell herself she had made the right decision, waiting to resist his commands until she was here in the open air, instead of trapped with him inside the truck or on the narrow beach path. Here, she could at least have freedom of movement if he started to shoot, but he was on solid ground on the sandy beach, while she was balanced precariously, trying to avoid falling into treacherous waves that would be well over her head.

"You won't get away with it," she said.

"I believe you told me that," he said, unperturbed. "Your hypothetical friend knows the truth."

"Not just a friend," she said. "The police. I told them, too. I went to the Southampton precinct. I left documentation. I called the University of Washington alumni office. I have proof. The real Charlie's in a vegetative state. The police will trace his driver's license and passport. You managed to renew them but the pictures won't match. You're going down."

The smug, pompous look on his face melted away. He wasn't Charlie. He wasn't her kidnapper. He was someone else now.

She flashed back to her days at the district attorney's office, when cocky defendants knew she had them in a corner. For all the professional gratification she had found from vindicating innocent people as a defense attorney, she realized she also missed being on the other side.

In the seconds when Charlie paused, she noticed movement in the sand behind him, giving her a glimmer of hope. Maybe it was her partial text to Katie, or the message she had left at the police station, or the white Tesla taking a U-turn in the parking lot. She had to hope that one of her lifelines had come through. If she was alone here with this man any longer, she was going to die.

She had bought herself all the time there

was to be found. She had to act.

She pictured herself lunging toward him, somehow making her way off these slippery rocks, and then reaching him on the sand, where she'd go for his gun. She had no doubt that he would pull the trigger to stop her. If his first attempt missed, she might have enough time to get to him before he could fire off a second bullet. Even then, how could she possibly take that weapon from his control?

But as risky as it was, it might be her only chance at survival.

As she took a deep breath to steady her nerves, she suddenly heard a voice cry out from the beach. "Melissa!" Even beneath the howl of the violent ocean winds, she was certain the voice that was calling her name belonged to Mike.

Charlie turned his head away from her for a split second. She squatted low and charged at him with all of her strength. His eyes widened, displaying his shock before she barreled into his abdomen. As he tumbled backward, he fired off an uncontrolled gunshot. She had never felt so large, forcing herself to fall flat, pressing all of her weight against his body.

As his left hand caught in Melissa's long hair — caught and twisted and held — she suddenly imagined her three-year-old self reaching out toward her mother from that icy, narrow balcony as the railing began to crumble. Like a permanent imprint on her sensory nerves, she could still feel her mother's hands in her hair as she fought to take hold of her baby while Carl Harmon grabbed at Melissa's legs as he began his fall into the angry, rock-filled surf below.

She would fight as hard now to save herself as her mother had forty years earlier. Once Charlie was on his back, she dug her elbows into his forearms while she jabbed at his lower body with her knees. Spotting the gun still in his right hand, she focused all of her weight in that direction. If it hadn't been for the sand, she might have broken his arm.

Charlie managed to bend his wrist enough to aim the muzzle of the gun toward her belly. She wrapped both of her hands around the barrel of the handgun, pinning her shoulders and torso against his upper body, struggling to steer the gun in another direction. As she saw the muzzle aimed directly at her face, she bit down on his forearm, eliciting a vicious growl. Once he released his grip on the gun, she batted it onto the slippery rocks behind them.

She clawed her way through the sand, trying to make her way to the broken glass she had spotted before. Charlie was grabbing at her ankles when she managed to land a solid kick in his chest with the heel of her flexed foot. When she heard a deep grunt as air was knocked from his lungs, she thought she might have a chance. She threw herself forward and extended her right arm. A dark shadow emerged beneath the moonlight as her fingertips located the piece of cold, smooth glass on the damp sand.

She rolled onto her back just as Charlie — Brian Bloom — dove on top of her. He screamed as she sliced the glass across his shoulder, cutting his shirt open. She was about to cut him again when his body weight suddenly lifted from hers. Mike and Patrick were on either side of him, flipping Charlie onto his back. He winced as the three of them piled on top of him, pinning him to the ground, but he would not stop squirming.

"Stop fighting," Mike yelled, "or your head's going to find itself in a fight with those rocks over there."

Charlie continued to resist, trying to move his left hand toward his back pocket.

"Gun!" Patrick screamed. "He's reaching for a gun."

Melissa got to Charlie's pocket first. His

body went limp at the sight of his phone in Melissa's hands.

"Rachel was the last person to call him. He was probably trying to warn her off."

She tapped on the number of his last incoming call. One ring and then an answer. "Did you do it? Is she dead?"

She recognized the voice, eager and elated. It didn't belong to Rachel.

49

An hour and a half later, Melissa sat with Detectives Hall and Marino in the back of an unmarked van across the street from the Riverhead Sunshine Motel. Melissa had finally convinced them that they needed her at the scene. She was, after all, the one who had set this plan in motion with texts sent from Brian Bloom's phone. If everything went according to plan, all of the adults in Riley's life would be spending the night in a jail cell — except for her.

She was the one who had scrambled onto the slippery rock beach to secure Bloom's gun. Recalling her one training session years ago at an NYPD shooting range, she had aimed the gun directly at Charlie from a safe distance while Mike called 911. Detectives Hall and Marino arrived only minutes behind the responding patrol officers. By that time, they were aware of the information she had left for them at the station about Charlie Miller. They had also spoken to the woman in the park, who came forward after recognizing Riley on the news. And the Connecticut State Police reported that they believed Riley had been held at a rental house in West Cornwall, but that it appeared the occupants of the house had left with her. The homeowner believed the renter had been driving a small white sedan.

Melissa found herself wondering whether the departure from the house had been planned all along, or was a panicked response to Melissa's growing suspicions about her husband. She took a small amount of pleasure, imagining the three of them scrambling to cover their bases as she continued to peel away the layers of their lies.

She kept her eyes on the door to Room 106, looking away occasionally to search for any cars turning off the main road toward the motel parking lot. The police had already confirmed with the front desk that a Charlie Miller had rented two rooms for the night using his driver's license and credit card. The other name on the booking was Rachel Miller, but the clerk had not required the second guest to show identification.

Melissa had been using Bloom's cell

phone to continue his text message threads. When his sister asked if he was finished yet, she had replied, "Yes, all done." She had led both of Bloom's accomplices to believe that a large group of high school kids had begun to gather by the inlet for a bonfire party, so he was walking back to town along the shore to avoid contact with them. He promised to text his location when he was ready for a ride. In the meantime, the person who had called Bloom right before he tried to kill Melissa said that she was almost to the motel, where she would drop off Riley before meeting Bloom at his destination. She ended with the message *I love you so much,* followed by a heart emoji.

"Heads-up," Detective Hall said as a set of headlights turned toward them from the main road. As the car passed their van, Melissa could see it was a small, nondescript white sedan. She sucked in her breath as she made out a small silhouette in a car seat in the back. That had to be Riley. They were here. Her hopes escalated as the car turned again into the motel parking lot.

It was time. She looked to the detectives for confirmation, and they both nodded.

She tapped her own phone screen to make the call, leaving her phone on speaker. She thought she saw the faint glow of a screen in the rental car before there was an answer on the other end of the line. "Oh, thank God, Melissa, I was hoping you'd call. Where are you? Are you okay?"

"Did you get my text?" Melissa asked frantically. "Did you call the police?"

There was a long pause, followed by a weak explanation that her phone reception was bad and that she hadn't heard what Melissa just said. Melissa pressed her eyes closed. Some part of her wanted to believe there might be an explanation, but she was certain now.

"I asked whether you called the police like we discussed."

"Yes, I called them as soon as I got that weird message, but when they went to the diner, they couldn't find you or Charlie."

"Charlie got into the truck with a gun and forced me to drive to the beach. He threw me off a rocky ledge into these huge waves. He obviously left me to die, but I held on to a piece of driftwood and managed to make it to shore."

"Melissa, are you there? I can't hear you." Detectives Hall and Marino shared an eye roll. She was such an effortless liar. "I'm going to hang up and try to call you right back. Wherever you are, stay safe and stay put. I'll come get you."

Immediately after she disconnected, Brian Bloom's phone began to ring. They waited in silence. The ringing stopped and then started again. Then a third call also failed to connect.

"That's it," Melissa whispered, wishing her friend could hear her. "It's all falling apart now, isn't it?"

Bloom's phone lit up with a new message. *Call me ASAP. It's not done.*

She typed three questions marks as Brian Bloom's reply and hit Send.

The next message read, *She just called me. She's alive.* Melissa held the screen up for the detectives. "Is that enough?"

Hall flashed a thumbs-up, and Marino used his radio to give the order. "Wait until she's out of the vehicle," he commanded. "And remember, there's a child in the back seat. Take all precautions."

Melissa felt the crush of betrayal as the driver's side door of the white sedan opened and Katie stepped out.

It happened quickly. As Hall and Marino jumped from the rear exit of the van, two marked patrol cars that had been parked behind the motel pulled around on both sides of the building and flanked Katie as she was walking around the front end of her car toward the passenger side. She immediately raised both hands in the air. Melissa could not make out the words that the officers were yelling, but she saw Katie drop to her knees on the concrete and then lie flat on the ground with her hands behind her back. She swallowed as she watched the handcuffs snap closed.

The door to Room 106 swung open and then began to close immediately. Hall made it there in time to force her shoulder through the entryway, halting the swing of the door and pulling the room's occupant outside.

The detectives struggled to handcuff Rebecca Bloom as she tried to tear away from their grasp. Even at this distance, Melissa could make out the anguish in her face as she screamed toward the parking lot. *Riley!* She was yelling for her daughter.

Melissa reached for the van door, ignoring the officer in the front seat who ordered her to stay put. She jumped out and started running across the street toward the motel. She made it to the rear of the white rental car before one of the uniformed officers stepped in front of her. Over his shoulder, she caught a glimpse of Katie, her eyes narrowed into a heated glare, her lips pursed defiantly.

"How could you do this?" she cried out.

Even with an officer kneeling over her, Katie managed to turn her face away.

Beyond the parking lot, Rebecca Bloom was no longer resisting Hall and Marino. Melissa could tell that Rebecca was saying something to the detectives, who then stepped with her into Room 106 and closed the door. The shoulder-mounted radio of the officer next to her beeped, and then she heard Detective Marino's voice. "The mom doesn't want her kid to see her in cuffs. That's the girl's stepmother at the vehicle now. Let her take the child back to our van."

Melissa's hand trembled with anticipation as she reached for the back door. Riley's sleepy eyes gazed up at her. "Missa! Where's Katie?"

From Riley's vantage point, she had probably seen Katie stop with her hands in the air, but could not see her now on the ground in front of the car.

"She's helping the police do an important job, sweetie." She unbuckled Riley from the car seat and took a deep breath as Riley wrapped her arms around Melissa's neck to accept a lift. Her hair was warm and damp from the heat of the car and smelled like baby shampoo. Melissa shielded Riley's eyes with one hand as she carried her away from the chaos behind them. "Do you want to go see a secret police van? It's plain on the outside but filled with all kinds of cool stuff on the inside."

Riley's eyes lit up and a wide smile broke out across her face. She was such a curious child.

"And then afterward, guess who we can go see? Grand-Nan!"

"In her new house?" Riley asked.

"That's right. And I haven't seen you for two whole days. Where have you been?"

"With Mommy. We took the car on a boat, and I played turtle. There's a house way out in the woods. And then Katie came to babysit."

"You remember her, right?" Melissa asked. "My friend, Katie? You've met her a few times, plus she was at the wedding."

A haze of confusion crossed Riley's face. "Yeah. She made me a special cupcake. I didn't know Katie knew Mommy. I thought Katie was your friend."

Melissa bit her lip. "So did I. Now, are you ready to see the secret van?"

"I missed you, Missa." Riley held her pudgy hand to her mouth and blew a perfect kiss.

"I missed you, too, Riley."

50

Five months later

The fire licked hungrily at the thick logs. The smell of the warm hearth permeated Melissa's apartment and mingled with the scent of hot apple cider. What she had proposed as a simple Christmas Eve open house menu of spiral-cut ham, Parker House rolls, and a tossed green salad had grown into a full spread as her mother had continued to come up with additional dishes for the table.

By Melissa's count, Riley was on her sixth trip to an inviting bowl of crab dip. Melissa's mother joked that somehow the child was going to be a Cape Cod girl after all.

She watched as Mac quietly refilled her mother's teacup. He had withdrawn as Brian Bloom's attorney of record immediately after the arrest, on the grounds that his client had retained him under a false identity for the purpose of facilitating a crime. He was now her regular cohost on *The Justice Club,* which had quadrupled its audience since the summer. She was not certain the rest of the Eldredge family would ever fully forgive him, but she understood how much it had pained him to do what a lawyer had to do for his client.

Catching her eye, Mac waved her over to a quiet corner of the living room. "Did you hear anything more from the DA's office last week?"

"They think they're going to reach a cooperation deal with Rebecca."

So far, Rebecca Bloom was the only conspirator to speak with law enforcement. Melissa no longer thought of the siblings as Charlie and Rachel Miller. Those people had never really existed. She was having a harder time accepting the truth about Katie.

Rebecca told police she and her brother met Katie after they reached out to the district attorney's office during the trial of Jennifer Duncan and she was appointed as their contact person. Since the prosecution had no intention of calling them as witnesses, Melissa never met either of them. Katie, on the other hand, had what Rebecca described as "instantaneous chemistry" with her brother. Even as their relationship grew more intense, they kept it cloaked in secrecy because of Katie's work.

By the time Katie stopped practicing law, the two had a different reason for hiding their connection — the fight for Doug Hanover's estate. According to Rebecca, she witnessed a growing obsession in both her brother and Katie as Jennifer Duncan not only prevailed in her exoneration case, but also spun the story for wealth and celebrity status. She described Brian's disgust as being targeted primarily at Jennifer, while Katie was the one who seethed with resentment toward the lawyer at Jennifer's side.

"If Rebecca's going to testify against Brian and Katie," Mac said, "does that mean she'll finally admit she knew the plan all along?"

In her first statement to police, Rebecca claimed she had no idea that her brother and Katie were planning to kill Melissa until Charlie left their motel with a gun only hours before they were all arrested. She thought they were going to frame her for kidnapping and then force her to admit that Jennifer Duncan had supposedly planned the shooting of her husband.

"The prosecutors hope so," Melissa said. "In some ways, it doesn't matter. The phones they were using that night prove they were all involved in drafting my so-called suicide note, and that alone is enough to make her an accomplice to attempted murder. She says she was afraid Katie and her brother would turn on her next."

"Too bad for her that's not an actual defense," Mac said.

She felt a hand on her shoulder and turned to see her brother. "I hear law talk," he said. "This is ironic coming from me to you, but maybe now's a good time to choose to be happy. Clear those people from your mind and allow yourself a little Christmas cheer. I'm about to pop some wine open."

"Those are all excellent ideas," she said.

A tap on the apartment door was followed by the appearance of Amanda Keeney, her long blonde hair dripping wet. "Merry soaking Christmas Eve, everyone! Sorry I'm late. I hope Neil explained. The NYPD does not close for holidays — or rainstorms, apparently."

Riley wiped her dip-smeared fingers on a Santa Claus paper napkin and ran to Amanda for a hug. She was growing so fast, all the way up to hip height on Amanda already. Neil Keeney greeted his wife with a kiss and a mug of cider.

Melissa's brother moved to the kitchen and began opening a bottle of red wine. She was pleased that Mike no longer asked permission before touching anything in the kitchen. He had been visiting the city almost every month. At her suggestion, he was going to leave a few of his things in the guest room so he could come and go for short trips without even packing a bag, and he had reached a tentative deal to work as a boat captain in the Hamptons during the summer.

Once the bottle was open and on the dining room table, Patrick held an empty glass up in her direction, and she nodded her approval. He brushed her wrist gently with his thumb as she accepted the wine-filled glass from him, happy they had begun spending time together again once she understood why he had broken off their engagement. Unbeknownst to her, Katie had gone to Patrick, pretending that Melissa had confided in her that she did not want to have children, even though having a family was something Melissa and Patrick had discussed. Katie insisted that Melissa had only agreed to have children to give Patrick what he wanted. Katie's exact words were "Melissa thinks she can just choose to be happy even though she's forcing herself to go through with this. She will be miserable, and it will be your fault. If you really love her, you need to set her free." And Patrick did in fact love her — so much so that he had made the terrible mistake of ending their relationship.

It was possible Katie simply needed Melissa to be single and heartbroken to fall prey to Brian Bloom's attention, but Melissa suspected she had a secondary motive that was more personal. Though some of Truth-Teller's hateful comments had been posted by the Blooms, the police had traced nearly all of them to Katie's laptop. She had enjoyed watching Melissa in pain. Despite knowing as a lawyer that she should not speak to her directly, Melissa had even tried to visit Katie in jail to understand how she had come to despise her so deeply. Not surprisingly, Katie had refused to see her. The next time she'd be in the same room with her former best friend, it would be to testify against her.

Neil Keeney was on his feet, ready to make a toast. "I want to thank my old friends Melissa and Mike —"

"Watch it, Neil," Mike called out as he joined them from the kitchen. "You're older than either one of us."

"My *dear* friends, Melissa and Mike, and of course their mother, Nancy, for including us." She knew that Neil felt terrible guilt for helping Katie steer Melissa to a group

380

counselor where Brian Bloom was already pretending to be a client named Charlie Miller, but Melissa assured him that she knew he had only been trying to help. "I still remember my parents recalling warmly how grateful they were to be invited to the Eldredge home after another difficult time for your family, so it means the world to Amanda and me to be here with you today, celebrating your first Christmas with little Riley here to join us."

Riley squealed out a delightful "Cheers" along with the rest of them. She felt herself smiling as she watched Patrick help her to clink her juice cup against the other adults' glasses. When Riley was finished, she set down her cup and replaced it with the stuffed reindeer Patrick had brought for her. Only time would tell, but she suspected he had enough love in his heart to be there for both of them in the long run.

Riley was still clutching her new toy when she climbed onto Melissa's lap. To Melissa's surprise and delight, Rebecca had actually agreed to Melissa's appointment as Riley's legal guardian while she was incarcerated. Melissa's best guess was that Rebecca thought the move might help her legal defense, but the district attorney's office was confident that, even if Rebecca reached an agreement to testify against her brother and Katie, she would not be getting out of prison until Riley was at least eighteen.

Melissa's arms tightened around Riley as her body weight grew heavy from sleepiness. This child was not her daughter, nor even her stepdaughter. To each other, they were simply Riley and Missa. They would figure out the rest along the way. She had no idea whether Riley would continue to have contact with her mother in the coming years, or how much she would remember about her mother or her uncle Brian as she grew older, or what kinds of questions she might ask or when. Maybe she would be like Mike and have the courage to process the unvarnished truth. Or maybe, like Melissa, she would try to believe that the trauma of the past doesn't have to define us. The only certainty she knew, from the wellspring of her being, was that she would find a way for Riley to have a chance at true happiness, because this little girl had given that to Melissa.

She realized that the sleet was no longer pelting the windows, that the moaning sound of the wind had died. Riley stirred on her lap. Before slipping back into soft, even breathing, Riley murmured a single word. "Momma."

ACKNOWLEDGMENTS

This book is the result of a collaboration not only between two authors, but among an entire crew that supported the process from beginning to end. Thanks go to Jonathan Karp, Marysue Rucci, Sean Manning, Tzipora Baitch, Anne Tate Pearce, and Hana Park — all at Simon & Schuster — and to the friends and family members known in-house as "Team Clark."

Though no acknowledgment is complete without an expression of thanks to you — the reader — a special note is warranted here. Thank you for getting to know the Eldredge family once again, so many years after *Where Are the Children?* launched what would become a writing career that spanned six decades. Through you, the characters and their stories continue.

ABOUT THE AUTHORS

The #1 *New York Times* bestselling author **Mary Higgins Clark** wrote forty suspense novels, four collections of short stories, a historical novel, a memoir, and two children's books. With bestselling author Alafair Burke she wrote the Under Suspicion series including *The Cinderella Murder, All Dressed in White, The Sleeping Beauty Killer, Every Breath You Take,* and *You Don't Own Me.* With her daughter Carol Higgins Clark, she coauthored five more suspense novels. More than one hundred million copies of her books are in print in the United States alone. Her books are international bestsellers.

Alafair Burke is the Edgar-nominated, *New York Times* bestselling author of twelve novels, including *The Wife, The Ex, If You Were Here, Long Gone,* and the Ellie

Hatcher series. A former prosecutor, she is now a professor of criminal law and lives in Manhattan.

The employees of Thorndike Press hope you have enjoyed this Large Print book. All our Thorndike, Wheeler, and Kennebec Large Print titles are designed for easy reading, and all our books are made to last. Other Thorndike Press Large Print books are available at your library, through selected bookstores, or directly from us.

For information about titles, please call:
  (800) 223-1244

or visit our website at:
  gale.com/thorndike

To share your comments, please write:
  Publisher
  Thorndike Press
  10 Water St., Suite 310
  Waterville, ME 04901